Two Shades

Of Truth

To Kim,

Enjoy a taste of Scotland,

Best Wishes,

L Creswell

Lynette Creswell

Published in 2018 by FeedAread.com Publishing –
Arts Council funded
Copyright © Lynette Creswell

First Edition

Other Stories by Lynette E. Creswell

Romance:
Cracks In The Glass
The Witching Hour (Short Story)

Fantasy:
Sinners of Magic
Betrayers of Magic
Defenders of Magic
Clump A Changeling's Story

For my family, with gratitude and love

ACKNOWLEDGEMENTS

I would like to thank the following people for their help and encouragement during the writing of Two Kinds Of Truth:

My dear friend and fellow author, Joy Wood, for her inspiration and determination to ensure I wrote this book in the first place. Words fail me when I think of your unwavering support.

To Julie Best for enabling me to conjure a vivid image of a flower shop and for helping me shape the scenes within The Budding Florist.

To Fiona Graham, for her invaluable insight into daily life on a farm. Oh, and those puppies you hand reared are adorable!

I'm eternally grateful to Pauline Mountain for getting me in touch with Fiona. It's amazing how many lovely people you meet on Twitter.

To Madison Rose McDonald who gave me the inspiration for my protagonist, Maddie.

Cherisse Pymm who talks to me about my characters as though they're real people. You inspire me, frustrate me and give me a kick when I need it.

A huge thank you to Nikki Clark for her lightbulb moment and coming up with the Tarot Cards.

Carol Stevens, I promised you a mention in the acknowledgements. Thanks for guiding me to the ITU nurse.

Hannah Creswell, my daughter-in-law and brilliant nurse. Thank you for your guidance with Angina sufferers.

To Sandra Fraser for her in-depth knowledge of the Highlands of Scotland—well, who better than a wee friendly Scot from the town of Penicuik to check the local dialect. Thank you for your continual support. I'm grateful we've formed an eternal friendship.

Brittany Eckhardt, a talented New Yorker, who showed me how to make my story beautiful. I will be forever in your debt.

To Jacqui Barwell, proof-reader extraordinaire—remember: time is a great healer.

To Sallyann Cole for working hard behind the scenes to ensure you, the reader, received the finest print of this book.

Letitia Hasser, you're a truly talented lady. The book cover tells a story in itself and shows the world your unique gift to me.

Clive Johnson, aka my editor and miracle worker. None of this would have been possible without your magic touch.

You, the reader, thank you for picking up my book—I really hope you enjoy it.

CHAPTER ONE

Maddie

I grab the phone from its cradle and balance it against my ear.

"Hello…yes, you've reached The Budding Florist. How can I help?" I wave my hand in the air, trying to get Keira's attention. When I catch her eye, I gesture for a pen. "Yes, that's fine, and no, it's not a problem."

With the cheap Biro Keira offers, I scribble down the customer's details.

"Sure, we can do a mixed bouquet for that amount, and yes, delivery is included."

I swing around to stare at the calendar pinned on the wall behind me.

"Uh-huh. You said the twenty fifth of February? Yes, that gives us plenty of time. Thank you and you're most welcome."

I replace the handset onto the receiver.

"Is that yet another satisfied customer?" Keira asks.

I nod. "Yes, and that makes four bouquets in less than an hour."

"If we carry on like this, I'll have to take another trip to the wholesalers," Keira says.

I glance down at the pad and rip off the top sheet of paper. "I'll go and make a start on the flower arrangements. If I don't prep soon, we'll be here until midnight."

Clutching a reel of red ribbon in one hand, I grab a small handful of message cards with the other. As I visualise chopping one long-stemmed rose after another, the shop bell jangles and I turn around, a light smile on my face, a friendly greeting perched on the tip of my tongue. The customer approaches the counter, but I say nothing, letting my smile slide from my lips when I notice her large swollen belly.

The woman catches my stare and strokes her tummy with obvious affection.

"I've only got a few weeks left before he arrives," she explains with a grin. "Although, if he carries on kicking me as though I'm a football, I'll be glad to see him sooner rather than later," and she chuckles at her own joke, but her laughter dies away as I continue to stare.

"Is everything okay?" she asks, and a puzzled expression replaces her smile.

I lick my lips, but find I cannot form any words in response, then break eye contact and drop the red ribbon and message cards onto the counter. My fingers reach out for the cellophane wrapping instead, and I fiddle with the hinge, pretending the roll has come loose.

From somewhere behind me, Keira clears her throat.

"I'll help with this customer, Maddie. Why don't you go and sort out those arrangements?"

Keira pushes past me. "Is there anything specific you're looking for? Only we've got some beautiful orchids just in, and the yellow and purple Peruvian lilies are exceptional."

The woman's gaze falls onto Kiera, and although she hesitates, she follows her to where several aluminium buckets hold an assortment of fresh flowers.

"I'll just be out the back," I rasp, and without waiting for a reply, head straight for the toilet, slamming the door behind me and sliding the tiny silver bolt across the wooden frame. Standing in front of the pedestal sink, I look into the mirror. Tears burst from my eyes and the salty liquid streams down my cheeks, an explosive pain in my chest refusing to go away. Nestling my head in my hands, I allow my heart to break yet again as that nagging question continues to bounce around inside my head, over and over: Why me?

There's a gentle knock on the door, which stops me short.

"I'm going to put the kettle on, and then I'll help you with those arrangements," Keira whispers. I take a few deep breaths to steady my nerves, eventually managing to calm down, then I grab a handful of toilet roll and wipe the last stream of tears away.

I let myself out of the tiny cloakroom and make my way to the kitchenette, blinking away the last of my tears as I join Keira.

"I'm so sorry," I whisper, "I don't know what came over me. It's just…"

Keira rushes forward and puts her arms around me. "Shhhhh, there's nothing to be sorry for," she soothes. "After what you've been through it's hardly surprising you acted the way you did. It's only been a few weeks since the IVF failed again; what did you expect?"

Her embrace is warm and I feel safe and secure within her arms. With some reluctance, I pull away and wipe my nose with what's left of the sodden tissue.

"I know, but I thought I could handle it. But then, seeing that woman just now, made all the misery come flooding back."

"Come on, give yourself a break," Keira insists, and raises her hand to lift my chin gently towards her face. My sapphire-blue eyes lock onto Keira's brown-eyed stare. "You and Callum have suffered so much, and in such a short space of time."

I turn my face away and stare at the wall, concentrating on the ugly dark stain from last year's burst pipe, and shake my head in despair. It cost a fortune to fix and the wall could do with a lick of paint.

"Are you even listening to me?"

"Huh? Sorry…What?"

Keira heaves a sigh. "Maddie, I really do think it's too soon for you to come back to work. I know you insisted but look what's just happened."

3

I stuff my hands into my jeans pockets and give her my best attempt at a smile. "So, where's this tea, then?" and I glance towards the kettle.

Keira clutches my arm. "Maddie, please, listen to me. Why don't you let me run the shop for a while? Maybe you and Callum can get away somewhere? Somewhere nice. Give yourselves time to heal, both physically and mentally."

I shake my head. "No, thanks, you've been a rock already; I couldn't possibly."

"But I don't mind, and it isn't as though I've not done it before."

"Yes, I know, but things were different then."

"How?"

"Oh, I...I...don't know. It's Callum... he's been so distant lately, since...well, everything; and then there's his job. He works so hard and—"

"Then all the more reason to get away. Perhaps you both need some quality time together."

I lean against the edge of the sink as Keira finally reaches for the kettle. Absently, plucking a piece of white cotton lint from my jeans as I watch her pour boiling water into two mugs.

"I guess a few days away wouldn't hurt. The weather's mild for this time of year and a change of scenery might do us both good. I'm not sure where we'd go, though. The treatment's pretty much taken care of every penny we have."

Keira opens the fridge door and pulls out a carton of milk. "How about visiting Callum's grandfather? Doesn't he own a farm in the Highlands of Scotland somewhere?"

I nod, accepting the steaming mug Keira offers me.

"Yes, he does, just outside Inverness, a place called Camburgh. It's beautiful up there, and there's a stone built cottage at the back of the farmhouse where we stayed for our honeymoon."

"Sounds romantic," says Keira with a smirk. "Perhaps you can re-enact your wedding night there?"

4

I roll my eyes heavenwards. "Yeah, right; Those days are long gone."

Keira jolts back. "God, Maddie, I didn't n Oh, why can't I learn to engage my brain opening my big, fat mouth?"

I am not offended in the least, so I reach out and place a caring hand on her shoulder to demonstrate this.

"Relax; it's fine, honestly. The last thing I want is for you to feel you're always walking on eggshells whenever you're around me. Besides, you know all my secrets, good and bad."

Kiera shrugs. "That's not the point; that was just plain tactless."

"Ah, forget it. Just because Callum's the one with the problem downstairs, doesn't mean I don't want to talk about it. The truth is, if I didn't have you, I think I'd go insane."

Kiera covers my hand with her own and gives my fingers a tight squeeze.

"Anytime, chick. You only have to say the word, and I'll be there."

Keira places her untouched cup of tea onto the draining board, then gathers stem tape and floral wire needed to prep the rest of the bouquets. Keira's determination at her job and the devotion to our friendship moves and motivates me. I gulp a few mouthfuls of my own tea and then place the mug down inside the sink. Grabbing a pair of secateurs from off a shelf, I prune a bunch of baby pink roses that were lying waiting on a metal worktable in the centre of the room.

"Do you know, Keira, I think a break in Scotland's a great idea. We both need to get away, to recharge our flattened batteries. I'll talk to Callum tonight and see if I can convince him to go. You never know, he might actually agree with me for once."

***

Later that same evening, I sweep a white linen cloth over the polished mahogany table in preparation for supper. It's our best tablecloth, a gift from Callum's grandfather, and usually only sees the light of day on special occasions. I study the row of vibrant lilac thistles hand-embroidered around the edging and hope it will instil something of that same ambiance of our wedding day. I set down an uncorked bottle of Callum's favourite red wine, a fruity Merlot, which will compliment his much-loved dish of lamb stew with dumplings. Placing a small bowl of mint sauce atop the large flowerhead decoration I've set at the centre of the table, I go over in my mind how I'll broach the subject of visiting Scotland.

The mere thought of the Highlands gives me a moment of inner peace.

Once the table's set I make my way into the kitchen and empty the dishwasher whilst I wait for Callum to return from work. When I open the cutlery drawer to put away the clean utensils, I spot a dried-up sprig of white heather. My fingers curl around the silver paper holding the delicate flowers together, then I lift it to my face, close my eyes and try hard to relive the moment Callum picked it for me. Its scent is still present, and I inhale deeply almost smelling the sweet perfume of the fresh mountain air.

Sighing, I place the sprig back inside its resting place. It may have been a few years since we last visited his grandfather's farm, but the memory never fades. I was made to feel so welcome on our honeymoon. Callum's grandfather, Alasdair, fussed over me, nothing being too much trouble. He'd been interested in me as a person, and Callum's twin brother, Jamie, had treated me the same way, too. Jamie still lives with Alasdair on the farm. He lost his wife, Claire, just before I met Callum. I too understand loss, and Jamie is such a gentle and loving soul. He doesn't deserve to suffer such tragedy.

I light a candle and blow out the match, smiling to myself. Yes, to see him again, and Alasdair, too, that would be wonderful. Without doubt, the chance to be surrounded by close family is sorely needed right now.

My thoughts are interrupted by a key turning in the lock.

"I'm home," Callum calls out.

He's standing by the front door as I rush to greet him.

"Hi," I say, and give him a kiss on his cheek. "Had a good day?"

I wait for a response as he takes off his coat and hangs it over the bannister, a battered old briefcase in his hand, but he only brushes past me and heads down the narrow hallway.

"Hey, Cal, whatever's the matter?"

When he doesn't reply, I quickly follow him to the small reception room he uses as an office. He sits down at his desk and turns the chair around, so he can face me.

"Callum, talk to me. Is everything okay?"

He bites his lower lip. "If I'm honest, no, not really. I lost an important client today. Now my yearly bonus is out the window," and any hopes of visiting Scotland dissolve before my eyes.

"Seriously, that is bad news," I agree, and move closer and stand by his side. "What happened?"

Callum slams his briefcase down on the desktop and lets out a deep sigh.

"Bradley O'Conner's only gone and left us to go and work for Brookers."

Confused, I move even closer, resting one hip on the side of the desk.

"But that's not so bad, is it? Only last week you said he was shirking his responsibilities."

"Yeah, well, that was before I found out he'd been scheming behind my back. The tosser's screwed me over good and proper, and taken my best client with him in the process."

I shake my head in disbelief.

"Why, the conniving little runt," I say. "But don't worry, you'll get another client; you always do."

"Maddie, don't be so frigging naïve. Decent clients don't just wander in off the street. I've worked tirelessly for over five years to get Lord Fornhill's business. Now, everything I've done has been flushed down the fucking toilet."

There's no talking to him when he's upset, and to make matters worse, I can see the last chance of us having a holiday fade before my eyes. Inside, I shiver. The last time he lost an important client, he stormed out, got drunk and punched a shop window. Twelve stitches and a Police caution later, he finally came home.

I do my best to change the subject.

"Right, okay, in which case, I think I'd better go and see to dinner. It's your favourite: lamb stew." I wait for a response, but he only stares down at the floor. I turn away, and as I leave, I hear what I suspect is his briefcase hitting the wall.

Dashing straight for the kitchen, I open a cupboard door and grab an empty glass, filling it from a bottle of wine already open in the fridge. Taking a large swig, I try to ease my disappointment. I was hoping for a nice evening together, for us to reminisce about Scotland and Callum's family. Instead, I now realise I've been foolish enough to believe everything would simply fall into place.

A door closes. I spin around to see Callum enter the kitchen. His jaw is tense and there's a strange look in his eyes.

"I guess I'm the cause of yet another ruined evening," he snaps, but his tone doesn't hold one note of regret, and I shy away from him. Callum's nostrils flare, his lips drawing back in a terrible grimace, clearly trying his utmost to pick a fight. He's been the same ever since the first treatment failed. I close my eyes, determined to blot out the stark image that now flashes before me, but all I see is a river of red pouring from between my legs. I squeeze my eyes tighter shut when phantom labour pains slice across my abdomen. No. I'll be damned before I let him make me feel it's all my doing.

With some reluctance, I open my eyes.

He's staring right at me, and I've seen that look before. He's goading me, hoping I'll let rip, but I don't.

"Hey, why don't you join me?" I say, and snatch another glass from the shelf, pouring him a generous amount of alcohol. I give him what I hope is a peace offering, something that might quench the ominous fire burning behind those luscious green eyes of his.

Callum downs the sparkling white in three large gulps, but I can see the fire still burns.

There's only one way out of this situation, so I make my move.

"Callum, I understand you're upset about losing your client, but please, let's not fight."

He places the empty wine glass onto the kitchen counter.

I feel myself tense and I bite my lower lip, nervously. I know his tactic. He wants to antagonise me to the point where I'll explode and then he'll blame me for the aftermath.

But I'm playing it cool. I won't let him see that I'm seething inside.

Callum chooses his words carefully.

"Is that what you think? That I'm spoiling for a fight?"

"Well, aren't you?"

"No."

"What, then?"

He shrugs. "I don't know. Maybe I'm just angry with the world tonight."

"Or maybe you're just angry with me?"

He pushes his fingers through his head of thick curls.

"You changed us, Maddie. You did this to us."

"That's simply not true. We both agreed to go through with the treatment."

"You said it's what you wanted."

"And so, did you."

"None of this was ever about me. I feel like a constant failure."

"You're not a failure. The consultant said that catching mumps can always put a man at risk of infertility," and I rush towards him, trying to grab his arm, to pull him close, but he snatches it away. He holds his hand to his chest, as if my touch would fill him with a sickening disease.

"Just don't," he cries. "Just don't fucking touch me," and I take a step back.

"That's enough, Cal," I whisper and push past him to switch off the oven. I've now lost my appetite for lamb stew.

From behind me a clock chimes the hour, the silence which follows then deafening to my ears. Callum's shoulders tense and his eyes appear to mock mine. For a split-second, I fear he might reach out and grab me, but the moment doesn't come. I leave him standing there and dash upstairs, fresh tears behind my eyes which I then force back. This is not how it should be between us.

In the bathroom, I run myself a bath as a distraction, but then the front door slams and a car engine soon roars into life. My heart sinks, for I'm well aware that Callum will most likely go into town and drink himself into a stupor.

CHAPTER TWO

"Who's making such a racket?" Callum grumbles as he snuggles further under the bedcovers. A car backfires outside and I open one eye and glance at the clock, letting out a low moan. When I stir, Callum's leg brushes against mine. I never heard him come to bed last night.

Throwing back the duvet, I make my way towards the window, my feet silent as they press into the carpet. When I throw back the curtains, the glare of a streetlamp almost blinds me, and I shield my eyes with the back of my hand. I blink to see the next-door neighbour's white Beetle trundling off down the road. A trail of black smoke coils from its exhaust, like a pollutive snake escaping into the atmosphere.

"It's bloody Micky again," I say, and snap the curtains closed. "That's the third time this week we've suffered being woken up by that beaten-up piece of junk he calls a car." My gaze wanders over to where Callum lies, dozing. I'm soon back in bed, tugging the covers over me, expecting a response, only to frown when he simply pulls the duvet over his head instead.

"I think it's about time you said something to our noisy neighbour," I huff. "All this disturbed sleep isn't helping anyone. He knows I'm up early and that you work late."

Callum groans, rolls over onto his back and lets out a deep sigh. "Look, Maddie. You know full well that having words won't make a blind bit of difference. He's only just managing to keep the roof over his head, so it's not as though he'll be out buying a new car anytime soon." He punches his pillow and bounces back onto his own side.

I let out a deep breath, annoyingly aware that he's right. Still, I hate the thought that my neighbour will likely never be able to afford a new car.

Thinking about it, that's true for pretty much the whole neighbourhood. The entire town is full of people just like Mick, like us, struggling to make ends meet. I feel a moment of longing, wishing to get away from this place, to escape and live somewhere a little less—deprived.

My mind drifts back to Scotland, to rolling hills covered in a thick carpet of purple heather. I lick my lips as my thoughts turn to the ice-cold waters of the loch, and the river filled with trout that runs through his grandfather's property.

For us, the Highlands was the perfect honeymoon location. I love the great outdoors and I was happy to muck in around the farm. We walked along nature trails that led out into the glens, watched golden sunsets, and fished until dark. Later, by the fireside, we ate what we'd caught, cooked over the flames. I'd seen a different, more attentive side to Callum back then. He'd wished only to make me happy, not like now.

I press my lips together and squeeze my eyes tight as the reason why things turned sour creeps into my mind. I don't want to think about that now, or what happened between us last night. I want to start today anew.

I focus my attention on a time when we had both been so happy, in love and carefree. I treasure the memories of those few special days in Scotland and hold them deep within my heart, where nothing and no one else, not even Callum, can touch them.

The sound of deep breathing fills the air, and I open my eyes and stare at the top of my husband's head. I want to reach out with my fingers and stroke one of the auburn waves that taper into a soft curl at the nape of his neck, but instead, I wipe a tear from my eye. He's handsome, but that alone won't hold our marriage together. I love him so much and try to show him every day, but the gap between us is inexorably widening and I don't know how to stop it.

I do believe, in my heart of hearts, that Callum loves me still, but something isn't right; something's eating away at him, day by day. I can never put my finger on the exact moment things changed between us, but I'm certain about the root cause.

Snuggling close, trying not to wake him, I pull the duvet up to my chin and comfort myself with its manly smell of his skin. But knowing I'll never be able to have children with Callum haunts my every waking moment.

There's a continual buzz close by my ear, and I reach out, searching the top of the bedside table for my mobile. My fingers curl around the sliver of cool vibrating metal, and half asleep, I drag the iPhone to my ear.

"Hi," I mumble; "what's up?"

"Why aren't you at work yet?" Keira asks.

"What?" and I peel back an eyelid, trying to focus on the ornate clock on the bedroom wall.

I almost drop the phone as I tumble out of bed.

"Holy shit! Is that the right time? I must have dropped off."

"Relax," says Keira. "The shop's open for business as usual."

I rub the last of the sleep from my eyes.

"Sometimes, I don't know what I'd do without you. You're an absolute gem."

"Yeah, I know, so that's another pay rise you owe me, right?"

I smile down at the phone. "When we start making some serious money, I'll think about it."

Careful not to wake Callum, I drag my dressing gown from the bottom of the bed and swiftly push my arms through its sleeves.

"Oh, listen," I say, pulling the mobile closer to my mouth, "I completely forgot to tell you: there's a large shipment of red roses coming in this morning. Could you make sure you get a readable signature and that the delivery note matches items ordered on the invoice. I can't afford another cock up like we suffered at Christmas."

"Don't worry, that won't happen again. Besides, I've already had a text saying the shipment will be here within the hour."

Relieved, I make my way into the bathroom, my voice, which sounds a little more relaxed, rising an octave as I close the door behind me.

"Good, that's a relief. Still, I'll hurry and do my best to be there before the roses arrive. If you can start on the orders we prepped yesterday, we can get them ready for when Eddie comes with the van to pick them up at eleven."

"Chill. It's all in hand. I haven't forgotten we have five wreathes on order and nine bouquets for collection today," Keira assures me.

I squeeze a dollop of toothpaste onto my toothbrush.

"Mmm, that's right," I agree, scrubbing my teeth with Colgate. "They're all for Mrs Williams who passed away last week," I mumble through the foam. "She was a very popular lady, a staunch member of the community, so I don't want any hiccups, not like last time."

"You mean the humiliation we suffered when a certain local Mayor's flowers were delivered the day after his funeral?"

I grimace at the reminder.

"Yeah, like that one. Now beat it and let me get ready."

I hit the red button on my phone and try not to recall how I almost lost my entire business. Not that it was all my fault. The note the Mayor's wife had given me had been soggy from an unexpected downpour, the numbers having run into each other. Pushing that dreadful day to the back of my mind, I concentrate on getting ready for work. With no time to shower, I wash my face, brush my hair and tie up my natural blond tresses into a ponytail. Heading back to the bedroom, I hear Callum snoring. Without making a sound, I get dressed and go over and kiss the top of his head. Even as he sleeps, I cannot escape the emptiness of my life. But for better or worse, I made a vow and a promise. I still love him. No one told me married life would be easy, so I don't expect it to be. With a heavy heart, I hurry downstairs, grab my car keys and bag, stuff my arms through my coat sleeves, and within seconds I'm out of the door.

***

"After all that, you didn't mention having a holiday?" Keira asks.

I push the last of the wreaths into the back of the delivery van, close the set of double doors and try not to catch Keira's eye. "Seriously," she insists, "you didn't even broach the subject?"

I bang my fist on the side of the van and wave at the driver when I catch a glimpse of him through one of the side mirrors.

"Nope, I just couldn't seem to find the right moment," and I head back inside the shop.

"Hey, not so fast," Kiera yells, racing ahead and jumping in front of me. "So, what happened? You were up for it yesterday; what made you chicken out?"

"I didn't chicken out, well, not exactly."

Keira cocks one eye. "Really? Well, it sounds like you did from where I'm standing."

My shoulders droop as I gently push Kiera aside. "Look, K, how about we just let the matter drop?" I don't wait for a reply but push in through the main shop door. I proceed to unroll a scarf from around my neck and pull off a pair of motheaten mittens, which I then throw behind the counter.

Through a mirror on the shop wall, I watch Keira pulling off a fluffy blue and red beanie hat. "It's no use, I'm not going to quit asking questions until you explain why your bags aren't packed. Besides, you promised to bring me back a wee dram."

I turn towards her, deciding to tell her the truth.

"Well, the thing is…Callum came home last night in a vile temper. Some jerk at work stole his best client, and now he thinks he won't get his bonus this year. He's seriously pissed off, and you of all people know there's no talking to him when he's in such a bad mood. So...I decided to keep schtum about the mini break, for the time being at least; simply ride the wave and wait until the time becomes right."

Keira hangs up her coat and rubs her hands together for warmth. "That's such a shit thing to have happened to him, but I still don't see why you can't go to Scotland. His bonus shouldn't affect you going away on holiday. I don't mean to pry, but surely you only need to have a full tank of petrol to get you there."

I make my way over to the till, just as an elderly customer scurries into the shop.

"Have you any fresh carnations, dear?" she asks, warmly.

I point to a bucket near the shop window and the old lady waddles over. "I'll have a few of these," she says, pointing to a bunch of pink and white chrysanthemum's, instead. "Oh and add a couple of those lovely white lilies into the bunch, too, please."

I head over and pull the flowers from the water before taking them back to the counter and wrapping them in pretty patterned paper. The old woman thrusts a ten pound note into my hand.

"I'm off to the cemetery," she explains, opening her shopping bag and placing the flowers inside. "My husband passed away just over a year ago and I always try and visit him once a week."

I smile weakly as I give her, her change seeing the sorrow in her eyes, the way her mouth turns down ever so slightly.

"I'm so sorry to hear that," I murmur.

The woman's eyes glisten with unshed tears. "Do you know? he promised to take me to Paris, but we never made it. Time just seemed to fly by, and before I knew it, he was gone." She places the few coins I offer her back inside her purse, but then hesitates and leans a little closer. "Take my advice, lovey, don't leave everything too late. Enjoy your life whilst you still can. After all, you're only young once."

I nod and glance over my shoulder, to see Keira looking rather smug, then quickly return to watch the old lady as she leaves the shop, but that doesn't stop Keira from coming over.

"You see? Even the customers think you should go to Scotland," she laughs.

"Ha, ha; very funny," I splutter, trying to hide a grin. "That's not what she was saying at all."

"It is, too," Kiera insists. "She's telling you that life's too short."

I let out a loud sigh.

"Whatever she meant, it's not as though I'm going to die next week," I proclaim. "Well, at least I hope not. Seriously, don't you go worrying; I'll get to Scotland, one way or another. For some strange reason, visiting the Highlands has now become important to me. Don't ask me why, but I feel as though I'm spiritually being drawn back there. I want to... No, I *need* to see those glorious snowclad peaks again."

Kiera's face breaks into a glorious grin, but it just as quickly fades.

"So how will you convince Callum?" she asks.

I give her a wink. "Oh, that part's easy. I just need to think of a way of using reverse psychology, of making him believe a trip to Scotland is all *his* idea."

"Ah, I like your style, but do you have any idea how you're going to do it?"

"Oh, indeed I do, and as Baldrick would say: 'I have a very cunning plan'."

***

"Haven't you got any work to do?"

I glance up from the till, taken completely by surprise. "Hey, Callum, what are you doing here?"

"I thought I'd take you out to lunch," and he tugs playfully at the sleeve of my shirt. So, what do you say?"

"Listen, I'm sorry about last night."

"Forget last night. Let's start over. I thought maybe we could go somewhere nice, together."

I nod. "Sure; okay; so, where would you like to go?"

"Oh, I don't know. Anywhere. You choose. Besides, I want to make it up to you."

I catch Keira's eye as she arches a perfectly shaped brow.

"Well," I rush on to say, "I'm not one to turn down a free lunch," and I force a grin. "However, I am wondering whether you're coming down with a bug, or maybe even man flu?"

Callum chuckles, clearly trying to laugh off the dig, but I sense he isn't amused.

"No, I'm not ill. I just want to go out to lunch with my wife; is that really so unusual?"

"Well, then, if you're serious, we could go to Frankie and Benny's? I hear they do great specials on Thursday's."

"Fine with me," Callum acknowledges, then lifts my coat from its peg, and I'm soon zipped up, hat on my head, hands in my gloves.

"I'm ready," I announce cheerily and nod to Keira. "Thanks for holding the fort. I'll try not to be too long," and I grab my handbag.

Kiera waves her hand dismissively, then pushes open the shop door. "Don't worry. Take as long as you like," she insists. "We've survived this morning's mad rush, so go and enjoy yourself, for a change."

I relish the thought of escaping the shop for a while. It isn't often I get away and being with Callum makes this unexpected treat that much sweeter. I link my arm through my husband's and he pulls me even closer, crossing the street, laughing and joking as we go.

Callum swings open the restaurant door and I can't help but smirk as he acts the perfect gentleman. It's great seeing this side of him again. It's been far too long.

We hang about just inside the doorway for a few seconds, until an approaching waiter asks, "Table for two?"

I nod and he shows us to a vacant booth.

"This is nice," I say, pulling off my hat and gloves. "We should do this more often." I check out the restaurant as I unzip my coat, pleased to see the other customers are busy devouring their food. There's a nice atmosphere about this place. It's homely. A mixture of black and white photographs cover the walls, mostly of movie stars and famous people from the nineteen-fifties and sixties, a particularly striking one of Marilyn Munroe. She's so beautiful, I note, and she's placed next to Dean Martin, at whom I smile. They would certainly have made a dashing couple back then.

The smell of fresh garlic fills the air and I breathe in deeply, the delicious aroma making my stomach rumble. Soft music plays in the background, the dulcet tones of Frank Sinatra, and I relax further into the soft leather of my seat.

"It appears we've missed the rush," I say to the waiter as he hands me a menu. He nods as he wipes down the table, then heads off into the direction of the kitchen, but I frown, realising Callum isn't listening. He's too busy browsing the back page of the menu.

"Er… What did you say?" he asks, unable to tear his eyes from the list of alcoholic beverages.

I let out an exaggerated sigh and he looks over at me. "I think I'll have a beer; would you like a glass of wine?"

Inside, I want to scream. He knows full well I don't drink when I'm working.

"I'll just have a Diet Coke, thanks."

"Oh, for Christ sake, Maddie, live a little. Why can't you just let your hair down once in a while and have a drink with me?"

I'm shocked by his tone and feel my cheeks burn, but I don't wish to make things worse between us. I don't want to start a fight like last night. So, I keep it zipped and stay tight-lipped, studying the specials whilst watching Callum out of the corner of my eye, observing him tapping his hand over the table's laminated surface.

"Excuse me sir; are you ready to order?"

Callum's gaze shifts from the menu to the waiter.

"Actually, I can't decide. I either want the bacon double cheese burger or the turkey melt."

"Shall I give you a few minutes more?" the young man asks.

"Yes, if you wouldn't mind."

He nods and heads over to the bar, taking my gaze with him as far as the next booth, where a young couple are sitting together. They're laughing and joking, completely oblivious to the outside world, absorbed only in one another's company. The woman's cheeks dimple with a smile that moves fluidly across her face, her happiness clear to all who care to look, shining like a glorious beacon.

I let out a deep sigh and look away, staring down with unseeing eyes at my menu. I try to recapture a moment when Callum had looked at me in such a way, but I struggle. Perhaps it was the day he asked me to marry him.

Callum clicks his fingers just as the waiter walks by with somebody else's drinks.

"Hey, what are you doing?" I hiss in despair, sliding a little deeper into the booth. "How rude of you and can't you see people are staring?"

Callum shrugs. "I don't care. I'm ready to order, and we were here long before that couple."

"Well, you damn well should care. You can't go clicking your fingers at the staff, you'll get us thrown out."

"Is that right, little miss perfect," Callum huffs. "I was only trying to catch his attention."

The waiter hurries over. I can't look the man in the eye, and purposely fiddle with one of my gloves.

"Sorry about that," he says, "only I mixed up their beverages. I gave them sweetened tea instead of unsweetened. The lady's diabetic."

I lift my face and smile, but I still can't meet his gaze.

"Have you decided what you'd both like to drink?"

"Yes. My wife will have a Diet Coke and I'll have a Coors," Callum says. "We're also ready to place our lunch order."

"Absolutely," and the waiter lifts his notepad and pen. "What can I get you both?"

"I'll take the bacon double cheeseburger, and—"

"And I will have the baked lasagne," I say.

The waiter takes our menus and heads back through the double-doors to the kitchen.

"Callum, what's wrong with you?" I say firmly. "Lately, you've been acting like a Jekyll and Hyde, one minute you're nice and the next you're a monster."

Callum lets out an irritated sigh. "I'm sorry about…you know…earlier. I didn't mean to offend anyone."

I take a deep breath. "So, work's still busy, then?"

"No, not really. Since I lost Lord Fornhill's account, the business pretty much ticks along without me."

The waiter returns with our drinks, setting the Coors down next to Callum's hand and the Diet Coke right in front of me. "Thanks," I say.

"Your food should be out shortly. Is there anything else you need?"

"No. We're good," Callum nods.

I reach for my handbag and dig inside. Within seconds I find a copy of Cycling Weekly. It's a bit tatty at the corners and rather moth-eaten, but it's the only issue I have. Callum lifts an eyebrow and points the bottle of beer in my direction.

"What's with the mag?"

"Oh, it's just an old copy of an outdoor pursuits magazine I found at the back of the shop. It was mixed in with a couple of floral booklets. I've been thinking about getting myself a bike, you know, to try and keep fit."

Callum shakes his head and chuckles. "Are you serious? You've never been one for cycling."

"Well, that's just it: I think it's time I changed all that. A new bike wouldn't cost too much, and I think I'd enjoy it."

Callum snatches the rolled-up magazine from my fingers and uses the flat of his hand to smooth out its kinks, then he flips through the pages.

"Hey, look at these photographs," he says. "The location they've used for these shots reminds me a lot of the mountains around Camburgh." He pushes the magazine that bit closer to me. "Can you see? In fact, the more I look, the more I'm convinced it *is* Camburgh."

I do my best impression of being surprised, opening my eyes wide and saying, "Oh. Wow. I've never noticed that before."

I drag the pages to the centre of the table, so we can both see the colourful images, and point to a worn track, almost hidden behind a posing cyclist.

"Yes, I think you're right. The mountain range reminds me a lot of Loch Durrum and Inverness."

Callum sighs. "You remember."

I look up and smile.

"Yes, of course I do; how could I forget? It's where you gave me my first sprig of lucky heather."

Callum sits back and takes another swig of beer.

"We had a nice time back then, didn't we?"

I nod. "Yes, we did. Those few days away were magical."

Callum stares at me, and for a moment I'm worried he's seen right through my ruse.

"Maddie, I know I'm not one for being spontaneous, but I've a bit of time owed at work and I think the break would do us both good. How do you fancy a wee trip to Scotland?"

I try not to jump up and down, but inside I'm doing backflips. "Well, I'll have to speak to Keira, but if you're serious, I can't see it being a problem."

"Good. Then it's settled. I'll speak to my boss and ring my grandfather tonight and get it all arranged." He rubs his hands together and his mood lightens as the waiter brings over our meals. I want to jump up and tell the server how happy I am. I want to walk down the aisle between the booths in my husband's arms and kiss his face.

Instead, though, I take a mouthful of food and say, "The lasagne is wonderful. How's your burger?"

***

I watch Keira climb down a set of small stepladders, returning the twinkling set of fairy lights she's been trying to hang without success onto the floor. She swings the "Closed" sign over the door and pulls down the blind. I find it odd when she comes and sits beside me, behind the counter, where I frown, sensing by her expression that there's something she wants to get off her chest.

"Is everything okay?" I ask, trying not to panic, convinced she's changed her mind about running the shop in my absence. I lick my lips and wait for the blow.

Kiera pulls her wooden stool a little closer.

"Maddie, I don't want you to be angry or upset with me, but I've been meaning to give you a small gift."

My frown deepens, and I shake my head. "Don't be daft; why would you want to give me a present? It isn't my birthday or anything."

Kiera seems a little edgy.

"I know that, silly, but still, I have something here for you." She reaches inside the back pocket of her jeans and pulls out an envelope with my name on it. I can see it's full of money.

"Here, this is for you; I want you to have it," she says, pushing it against my fingertips, but I snatch my hand away.

"What? No way. There must be a couple of hundred pounds in there, possibly more. I know I'm stony broke, but I can't possibly take your hard-earned cash."

Keira shakes her head and her eyes narrow.

"Sure, you can. I want you to have it."

This time she thrust the envelope towards me, but I place my hands on my lap in protest, and Kiera lets out a sigh.

"But you're missing the point, the reason why I'm offering you this gift."

I fold my arms and draw my lips tight.

"It might help if you listen for a second and stop being stubborn," she says. "You see, I've been saving for months. You know, in preparation for your, for the arrival of..." and for the first-time, Keira appears lost for words. She falters, but before I can speak, she regains her composure.

"What I'm trying to say is that I was saving the money for when you and Callum had your baby."

I feel the bottom fall out of my world.

I eventually have to force the words out of my mouth, "But there is no baby, and there never will be."

"Then make the most of this golden opportunity."

I stare at her for the longest time, the ache in my breast spiralling slowly but surely into intense pain.

"Why are you always so kind to me?" I begin to cry. "I truly don't deserve it."

Kiera pulls me close, wraps her loving arms around me and hugs me tight.

"Because I love you like a sister," she breathes into my hair, "and I just want you to have enough money so you can make the most of this trip."

As Keira soothes me, I know I want a child of my own. Her hand strokes my face and she holds me tight, but it brings me little comfort.

I know I will never have children with Callum. I will be forever alone. And now, my marriage is a howling abyss.

CHAPTER THREE

Our car races through the old town square and I take a moment to drink in my surroundings. Camburgh is one of the most medieval places in Scotland. The town has served as a trading hub since twelve-fifty-four, and many of the beautiful buildings date way back to before the clansmen suffered atrocities at the brutal hands of the English.

An unexpected shiver snakes down my spine as we drive past the Scran and Sleekit.

"Didn't you once say the ringleaders organised the Jacobite rebellion of seventeen-forty-five in there," I ask, pointing out of the car window.

Callum flicks his gaze towards the local pub.

"Yes. Although historians claim there were many such buildings used in and around this area."

"And what of Bonnie Prince Charlie? What happened to him?"

"He disappeared after the battle of Culloden."

"He wasn't caught and put to death?"

"No. He hid in the heather and escaped."

"And he didn't raise another army?"

"He was finished; died an alcohol-sodden death in Florence in seventeen-eighty-eight."

I close my eyes and visualise what it must have been like back then. I see tall, strapping men dressed in kilts, a sharpened dagger clasped to the side of their hip while they collaborate and scheme to get Charles Edward Stuart onto the throne.

I'm aware it all ends in tears, but I adore the Scottish people and their history. The men honourable yet fearless, their women dangerous and loyal. Many of those who died fought for what they believed in, and it's that power, that stubborn determination to win, that sucks me in. The Scottish people have such passion in their blood, they are truly amazing, and I'm lucky enough to be married to a man with that same blood flowing through his veins.

We go over a sharp bump in the road and I'm brought back to reality, opening my eyes to see Callum smile. His perfect jaw is relaxed, not tight. Those frown lines, the one's which are etched so often onto his face these days, are nowhere to be seen. A contented sigh escapes me as Callum continues to smile, slight creases, tiny lines, forming around his eyes. They make my heart melt.

The bright red hatchback dashes out into open countryside and myriad snowy peaked mountains appear on the horizon. My own excitement grows. It's been far too long since we visited Callum's family, and now we're almost there, I feel an overpowering urge to hug them close, to feel part of a clan again.

The last time we visited, we were invited to the Highland games. It was such a wonderful day. Jamie competed in the caber toss, a traditional Scottish athletic event. It's a skilled game that sees all competitors show great strength. The competition's always fierce between the highlanders, and to our delight, Jamie won third prize.

That same day, Callum's grandfather bought me a classic tartan shawl. It was such a lovely gift and one I will cherish forever. His kindness, his generosity, has no bounds. His genuine openness gave me confidence whenever I was around him. I was never judged and soon became one of the family.

I open my window and enjoy the blast of fresh mountain air that takes my breath away. It's cold, almost freezing, but the sun is shining on my face, giving a false impression of warmth.

When I close the window, it's to hear the indicator clicking, and the car swerves gently to the right. We're going off road, and already the thought of being at the farm makes my stomach tingle.

Within ten minutes we reach our destination.

Balinriach Farm looks just as I remember. Built in the Victorian era, the stone building is surrounded by a pebble-chip driveway and pretty borders. There's a welcoming atmosphere to the place the minute one drives up to it. I felt it the first time I visited, and I feel it again today.

A warm smile appears on my lips when Alasdair and Jamie come out of the house to greet us. I'm always shocked at just how much Jamie looks like Callum, his twin brother. They're identical in every way: their strong jaw line, their faces chiselled and striking, and their shared thick and wavy reddish-brown hair.

Both are over six feet tall, broad shouldered and muscular, but for Jamie it's the hard life he leads on the farm, not the gym Callum attends twice a week that gives him such a powerful physique.

Callum gets out of the car and flings his arms around his grandfather. The old man hugs him tight and then slaps his grandson hard on the back.

"Och, ye took yir time coming home," he chides, good-naturedly.

"I know, granda. I'm sorry; I've no excuse other than work commitments."

Alasdair shrugs and shakes his head. "City life'll kill thee, lad, if ye let it, that is."

His grandfather turns his attention towards me, his arms already open once more, and I throw myself at him. Although he's in his late seventies, he's still powerful and strong, locking me in a solid embrace. I breathe in deeply. He smells of the farm, of loose tobacco and horses.

"Are ye willing to make an old man happy and stay in the main house?" he asks. I pull away and spot the spark of amusement that lights up his face.

"Well, er… I don't…" I splutter, but Jamie laughs out loud and interrupts his grandfather's game.

"Nah, granda, she'll be staying in the Garden House, just like last time." He gives me a wink and strolls over, hugging me tight in his strong embrace, pulling me so close to his chest I think I might suffocate.

"'Tis guid to see ye again, Maddie," he says with an endearing smile, the kind Callum hasn't used in quite a while.

The Garden House is a stone building with a pitched roof of slate. It's more of a cottage really, and I'm pleased we've been allowed to stay there again. It reminds me of a place Beatrix Potter might stay. There's watercolours hanging from the walls, homemade cushions, and crochet blankets covering the backs of the chairs. The furniture is rich in colour, polished mahogany and dark oak filling the rooms, and a wood burning stove stands in the middle of the hearth. It's simply perfect, and I love it here.

The house is clinging to the last remnants of a woman's touch, though. It's been years since Jamie and Claire lived here. Callum told me once that Claire's death affected Jamie so badly that even now, after all these years, he still can't bear to see pictures of her face without crumbling. I feel a pang of guilt at staying in what was once their home.

Callum comes dashing up the stairs with the suitcases. I push open the bedroom door a little wider, to allow him access. He throws the cases onto the bed.

"Do you want to unpack now or wait 'til later?" he asks, "Only granda has something he wants to show us."

I don't even have to think about it.

"Let's go," I say, loudly, "there's nothing I need right now," and I go to touch his hand, but the warmth I saw in his eyes earlier now disappears and he snatches his hand away.

"Aye, well, let's get going then."

I'm stung by his rebuff. It's as though he still doesn't want me to touch him, to get close, and a rush of despair sweeps through my gut. There's so much I want to say to him, but the words simply won't come.

Instead, I grab my coat and follow him downstairs.

We leave the cottage and Alasdair's waiting for us by the gate. He looks at me side-on, a glint in his eye, and I wonder what he's up to, what surprise he has in store for us.

"So, what's the big secret?" Callum asks, his voice light, carefree.

Alasdair taps the side of his nose and heads towards the stone barn, the one used for storing grain and the farm's machinery.

As we follow him, I hear birds singing in the surrounding trees, and a gentle yet cold breeze trills through the last of the leaves.

I realise we're heading for the stables, instantly forgetting Callum's rejection. The thought of spending time with the horses fills me with utter pleasure.

"I'd like to own my own horse, one day," I say to granda.

"If ye come and live here, ye can have whichever horse ye want." He slides back the bolt and I realise I'm holding my breath.

"I want to show ye a new addition to the family," he explains, and drags open the stable door. I'm already by his side, breathing in the woody smell that invades my nostrils. It's sweet, like new hay, and I see a flicker of a black ear from one of the stalls.

"You've bought a new horse!" I declare with glee, clearly stating the obvious, and Alasdair chuckles.

"Ye dinnae say, lass," he smirks, and his large hand takes mine and guides me closer to the magnificent beast.

"He's the most beautiful creature I've ever seen," I say, and he is.

Callum lets out a long whistle and the stallion throws its head and neighs.

"Whoa, steady, me beaut," Alasdair soothes, and he reaches out and strokes the animal's soft velvety nose.

"He's gorgeous," I have to admit, and turn to look at Cal. I'm surprised that he doesn't appear the least bit impressed. "Don't you think so, too?"

I raise my eyebrows and nudge him with my elbow, urging him to say something nice about the horse.

"If I'm honest, I think you've wasted your money, granda," Callum finally says.

My jaw drops at the insult, but Alasdair doesn't bat an eyelash. He simply continues to stroke the animal, and turns to me, instead.

"Would ye like to pat him?"

He stands aside and waits for me to approach. I'm a little apprehensive. The horse's black eyes watch me closely; they're like two large pieces of jet. I want the horse to like me, but I sense he's wary. When I take a step forward, the animal whinny's his mistrust.

"Oh, dinnae bother about him, lass," Alasdair insists. "He just thinks he's at the top of the peckin' order."

Behind me, Callum gives a deep sigh.

"Whatever's the matter?" I ask, turning my head towards him.

"This isn't floating my boat," he huffs and leans against the wooden doorframe.

My brows knit together as I turn my attention back to the horse. Slowly, I lift my hand and brush my fingers against the dark hairs on the stallion's jawline, soon tickling him under his chin, the skin silky soft beneath the stiffness of his whiskers.

I turn to Alasdair.

"What's his name?"

"I've called him Starsky."

I can't hold back the giggle that wells up inside my throat. "No, seriously, what's his name."

Alasdair stares at me. "I'm serious, hen; it's Starsky, after my favourite TV show."

I laugh, and Alasdair laughs with me, but Callum lets out another huff.

"I'm off to find Jamie, see if he needs a hand." He shoots out of the stable, back to the farmhouse, I assume, but when I stare at granda, he just chuckles.

"Dinnae mither about him, lass. He's ne'er had an interest in anything with more than two legs."

My laugh deepens. I find him incredibly funny. The last time I was here, he managed to tug out a more light-hearted side of me. I want to be like that again.

The light's fading as we stroll back to the main house, my arm linked with his, his hand patting mine as we talk nonstop about all things equestrian. A loud noise behind me makes me look around, seeing Jamie enter the yard, driving a tractor. He disappears around a corner, heading for one of the sheds.

"So much for Callum giving him a hand," Alasdair says.

We enter the farmhouse and it's just as I remember; old and musty, warm and welcoming. The panelled hallway leads to several reception rooms, but we both head for the kitchen, which turns out to be cosy and smelling of pie. A red tartan cloth is spread over the table and a large brown teapot dominates its centre.

"Have you been cooking in preparation of our arrival?"

Alasdair slips me a wink.

"I thought ye needed a bit of meat on ye bones the first time ye came here. I dinnae think much would've changed, and I was right. Ye still look as though ye could do with a decent meal inside ye."

I smile and love him that little bit more.

***

Once I've washed away the smell of horses from my hands, I help to set the table for supper. The house is alive with chatter as soon as Jamie and Callum enter the kitchen, both eager to rekindle their strong brotherly bond. If it wasn't for their clothes, I wouldn't be able to tell them apart. Both speak Scottish, but Callum can turn his accent off and on like a tap. Yet tonight, chatting with his brother, that sweet lilt to his voice is deliciously clear.

The table is set with an assortment of steaming blue dishes. Callum sits down and pours white wine into four glasses. I pull up a chair and sit beside him. A homemade venison pie has pride of place and is surrounded by hot mashed potato, buttered vegetables and two large gravy boats. The aroma is divine.

Granda offers me a piece of pie and Jamie passes the mash potato to his brother.

"So, what's yir plans for tomorrow?" he asks as he waits for the dish.

Callum ponders his question, busy spooning hot potato onto his plate.

"I'm not too sure. We haven't made any plans as such."

Jamie glances over at me and grins. "Surely, you'll take Maddie out to the loch? I understand it's a wee bit cold still, but there's a flock of goosanders on the water." His grin broadens and his enthusiasm grows. "It's a spectacular sight to see. Maybe ye could take a winter picnic and make a day of it?"

I wipe the corners of my mouth with a napkin. "Sounds terrific. Shall we go?" but Callum shakes his head.

"Nah, I'd rather take a rain check if you don't mind. I've never been keen on the feathered variety," and he averts his gaze, pouring a little gravy over his vegetables.

I hide my disappointment by taking a gulp of wine. The last thing I want is to turn this into a big deal. After all, it's just a flock of birds. However, it's clear Alasdair thinks it's a good idea and won't let the matter drop.

"Aye, lad, 'tis a sight to see all right, and not one to be missed." He points a knife in Callum's direction. "Go, take young Maddie up to the water. You can borrow the Land Rover if ye like?"

Callum frowns. "Are you ganging up on me?"

Alasdair chuckles. "Aye, lad; we are."

"And you won't take no for an answer?"

"Och, no. Maddie's our guest, and it'll not hurt ye to take her out."

Callum sighs. "Okay, if I must. But hunting's more my style."

Alasdair shakes his head and raises a white brow. "Buck season doesnae start 'til the first of April. You've a couple of months to wait yet, lad."

"Aye, more's the pity," Callum replies, stabbing a carrot with a fork and thrusting it into his mouth.

I shudder inside. Hunting is a big part of the McKinley's lifestyle, but it's still alien to me. Callum offered to take me hunting once, on our honeymoon, but the thought of killing one of those magnificent beasts seems unnatural. I can't even bring myself to hold a gun, let alone shoot another living creature. And if I ever saw a stag being pursued by hunters, I'd be horrified; his fear would become my own fear. I do understand it's all part of their conservation programme, to ensure they don't become overrun with wild deer, but I still find it hard to come to terms with this part of their way of life.

After supper, we move closer to the fire. Alasdair pulls out a pipe from his cardigan pocket. To my surprise, he doesn't fill it with loose tobacco like he usually does after a meal.

"I've given up smoking," he explains when he catches my eye. "Sucking on this old thing helps ease my cravings."

I nod in agreement. "If it helps your health, then that's all that matters," I say. "Although, I admit I'm a chocoholic, and there's no way I'm ever giving any of that up."

He laughs and pats me on my knee. "Aye, well, the doctor's advised me to stop. Says at my age I need all the help I can get."

Callum pulls out a small table, places it by my feet and then brings over a plate of cheese and biscuits. He takes a couple himself, then sits in the chair opposite. "So, what's been happening on the farm since we last visited?" he asks.

"We had to buy a new tractor," Jamie tells him, coming over to slide a cracker off the plate. He stuffs the whole biscuit into his mouth, chews it quickly, and then says, "Old Bertha coughed and spluttered her last breath just after the harvest."

"Aye, and the price of a new vehicle near killed me, I'll tell ye," Alasdair roars in exasperation. "Back in the day, I'd have bought twenty houses for the same price."

"You've had that tractor for as long as I can remember," Callum says.

"Aye, I bought if for less than a hundred pounds, second hand in the sixties."

Jamie chuckles and slides down his chair a little. "I thought granda was going to have a heart attack when the dealer told him how much it would cost for a replacement."

Alasdair noisily draws on his empty pipe. "Aye, and I'm sure I suffered a slight stroke when I was forced to part with my hard-earned cash."

Callum's laughter fills the room. His eyes are bright and his cheeks rosy from the fire.

"You've always been a tight-fisted old goat," he says.

"Och, well, it takes one to know one," Alasdair grins.

"Hey, less of the old, and stop casting aspersions on my good character," Callum teases.

As the evening draws to a close, both myself and Callum offer to do the dishes. There's no dishwasher in the house, no Wi-Fi or cable TV. The farmhouse is my retreat. The pressure of living in a digital society seems miles away when there's no electronic distractions.

I fill a bowl with hot soapy water and slide in a few dirty dishes. Callum comes over, a tea towel dangling from his fingertips.

"You okay?" I ask, "only you've hardly said a word to me all evening."

He nods. "Yeah, I'm just a little tired. It's been a hard drive and a long day."

He reaches for a plate covered in suds. The way he snatches hold of it tells me he's tetchy.

I stop washing up and turn towards my husband. "Callum…"

"Look, Maddie, I said I'm tired."

"I know, but I was just—"

"What? Making small talk? Let's just finish up here and then you can get yourself off to bed."

"So, that's it? I'm dismissed, like a child, on your say-so?"

"No, I'm not saying that."

"Then what *are* you saying?"

He shakes his head and lets out a deep sigh. "Look, forget it. Go and do whatever makes you happy, but I'm having a wee dram with the men before I retire to bed."

I turn back to the dishes and stare down at the bubbles, willing myself not to show any hurt, to hide it from him. I want to have a drink with the men, too. And doesn't he realise it's spending time with him and his family that makes me happy? I thought coming here, to Scotland, would rekindle the magic we once shared together, before our love life became focused on endless sperm counts and unsuccessful egg fertilisation. But now I think it's just about Cal seeing his brother and grandfather again.

I feel a surge of anguish and thrust my hands deeper into the hot water, determined to hold it together. There's no point getting upset. My energy would simply be lost on him.

We finish the washing up and I decide to call it a night.

"Goodnight. I'll see you all in the morning," I announce.

"Night," Callum replies, planting a kiss on my forehead. I study his face for a moment, trying to read his expression, but Alasdair interrupts my train of thought when his arms wrap around me.

"Sleep tight and dinnae let the bed bugs bite," he chuckles, giving me a tight squeeze.

"Aye, guid night, lassie," Jamie says, reaching inside a cupboard and pulling out three glass tumblers. "I guess it's been a long day for ye."

I stop at the door and watch the three of them as they prepare to enjoy a bottle of fine malt whisky. For the first time since I became a part of this family, I feel like I'm an English outsider—a Sassenach. I turn one last time, and Jamie catches my eye. His cheeks are pink and flushed. He gives me a wink, completely unaware of my torment and the sadness that plagues Callum and I. He doesn't know about the babies I cannot have. Without uttering a word, I return to the sanctuary of the Garden House.

***

The next morning, Callum wakes me with breakfast in bed, a tea tray in his hand. I smell the wonderful aroma of coffee and sit up.

My lip curls into a smile. "Hey, good morning. Is that for me? What a lovely surprise."

He has the decency to look a little sheepish.

"It's from granda. He thought you needed spoiling." I lift an eyebrow and my smile slips from my lips.

"Oh, and you don't, I suppose."

He offers me the tray and I take it, placing it on my lap. He doesn't say another word yet his eyes hold mine.

"Talk to me," I whisper. "Please, Callum, tell me what's wrong." He lets out a sigh and turns away, but I quickly grab his arm, forcing him to turn back to face me.

"I'm sorry; I can't take you to the loch today. Jamie's supposed to take granda into Inverness this morning, but the farm's prize bull has gashed its leg and it's badly hurt. Jamie's going to have to wait for the vet, as he's the only one who can control the beast, so, I've agreed to take granda, instead."

It's not what I expected him to say. Still, it doesn't matter.

"No problem. Give me five minutes and I'll go with you."

"I don't think so. Not this time, anyway."

I tilt my head in shocked surprise. "But—"

"I mean, thanks for the offer, but we're off to the farmer's market. Granda's eyesight isn't very good and Jamie and I don't want him driving all that way on his own. We're delivering livestock to sell and we'll be gone for the best part of the day. I'll also be helping him to unload the animals when we get there."

"But I can help, too," I pout.

"No, that's just it; you can't. Those heifers can be dangerous, and the market isn't safe for a greenhorn like yourself. The bottom line is that it's no place for a woman."

I throw back the covers, refusing to listen. He's implying I'm a liability and that's simply ridiculous. This is our holiday and I don't mind where we go…as long as we're together.

"Don't worry, I'll dress up as a bloke," I joke. "I'll put on a pair of jeans and borrow one of Alasdair's flat caps."

I put the tray aside and jump out of bed, but Callum uses his body to bar me from taking another step.

"Look, Maddie, I said no for a reason."

I shrug. "I hear you, but I'd like to come, anyway."

He stiffens, pushing his shoulders back, his eyes tightening in frustration, but I stand my ground.

He's so close now, our chests almost touching. I stare at his lips as I wait for him to say something— anything. I desperately want to go with him, but it's clear by his expression that he's not about to change his mind.

"It's simply not a good idea," he finally explains with a sigh. "Plus, the cattle pens stink to high heaven and the filth is ankle deep. The men are coarse and foul-mouthed, and I simply wouldn't want—"

"Your wife stopping you from having fun with the boys?"

Callum takes a step back. "No. What I was actually going to say was, my wife having to tolerate such disgusting conditions."

"But I don't mind."

"Aye, be that as it may, but I do. Besides, I've spoken to Jamie and he says that if the vet gets here by midday, he'll take you to see the ducks in my place."

I throw back my head and laugh for the first time, forcing the tension between us to ease.

"You make me sound like I'm a five-year-old," I snort, admitting to myself that I'm not going to get my own way this time.

He smiles back at me and the stiffness leaves his body. "Whatever you say, daffy," and a look of relief spreads across his face.

A car horn beeps, and I go to the window, sliding back the net curtain to see granda inside a Range Rover, behind which a livestock trailer's been hitched.

"I'll be back long before dark," Callum promises, and he gives me a peck on the cheek before dashing off, his boots thumping down the stairs.

I push open the window to see Callum climbing into the Range Rover and taking over at the wheel. I'm positive he'll sense me watching him and will him to look up at me. I find I'm holding my breath, hoping against hope that that special bond between us is still intact. It's silly of me to think like this, most likely building myself up for a fall, and sure enough, seconds pass, and to my dismay, his eyes not once search out mine.

Inside, I'm crushed, but I try to think rationally. After all, he's busy doing what any half decent grandson would do for his elderly relative. My attention is still on my husband when he thrusts the gearstick into first, hits the accelerator and drives away.

CHAPTER FOUR

The breakfast tray lies abandoned on the bed, the coffee stone cold. I can no longer stomach food or even the thought of it. With a heavy heart, I head for the shower, climb inside the cubicle and hit the power button. A stream of hot water hits my face and I close my eyes and breathe in deeply. I enjoy the sensation until my skin tingles with the heat, whereupon I open my eyes and get on with scrubbing myself clean. When I climb out, I wrap a thick purple towel around my body. The cold slabs of slate beneath my feet would normally seep through my soles, but I don't let them, walking on my tiptoes over to the basin. A layer of condensation clouds the mirror, and I wipe it clean with the flat of my hand, staring at my revealed reflection. A lonely figure stares back and I'm forced to turn my face away.

I get dressed and head over to the cattle shed, to see how Jamie's doing. The distinctive smell of the farm fills my nostrils, the stench of cattle dung and urine overpowering, so I pinch my nostrils together until I get used to it. I'm dressed in an old pair of jeans, a polo necked jumper and a waterproof coat I found behind the front door of the cottage. I'm also wearing a pair of wellington boots that I brought especially for the trip. They're bright pink with colourful blue and yellow daisies stencilled on them. It had been Kiera who'd helped me pick them out, and I smile, remembering her insisting I purchase them so they would remind me of her. And she was right, they do.

As soon as I enter the shed, I hear Jamie shout "Whoa, will ye stay still, ye stupid idiot. Ye cannae go out until you've been seen." He's in one of the metal pens, slurry splashed all over his bright yellow jacket, a layer of thick khaki-coloured manure. He's oblivious, though, his only concern is for the animal.

His strong hands stroke the back of a large golden-brown beast, its head secure in a cattle crush. I don't know much about cattle, but what I do know is that these Highland varieties are one of Britain's most distinctive breeds. With long, thick flowing coats and majestic, sweeping horns, these animals are truly exceptional. When I'm only a few feet away, it lets out a deep-bellied groan. The bull is clearly in pain and continues to bellow, its large bulbous eyes now staring right at me, a surge of hot breath shooting from its nostrils. It's cold inside the shed and the bull's vapours fill the air, reminding me of steam issuing from a boiling kettle.

As I draw nearer, I can see Jamie's doing his best to calm the animal. His devotion to the farm is clear, even to me, an outsider.

The last time I visited, I witnessed him saving a new-born calf. The latest addition had become entangled within its afterbirth, about to be trampled upon by the herd. Jamie had run between the cattle, shooing the mammoth beasts aside, as though they were overgrown flies. He'd reached the calf and cleared away the membrane from its body, and within seconds had the calf standing on all fours, clear to those who'd witnessed his courage that he'd saved the mite from certain death. For me, I'd seen at first-hand his dedication. He's simply a natural.

I move a little closer. There's splashes of red mingled within the hay and I notice splats of blood on the concrete floor. Realisation hits me as to just how injured the bull must be and I grow concerned for Jamie's welfare. If it gets violent, a kick from one of those powerful hind legs could be fatal. I edge my way to the barrier, which keeps me free from harm.

"Hey, Jamie, is everything okay?"

He turns and his brows are creased with concern. He moves to one side, revealing a thick bandage wrapped around the animal's foreleg. It's crimson with dried blood.

"Hi, Maddie. Nah, not really. As ye can see, he's lost a lot of blood and there's nae sign of the vet."

"Is there anything I can do to help?" I know it's a silly question, but I ask it anyway. What can I do in this kind of situation? Make tea?

"Aye, can ye just reach inside my overcoat pocket and get my mobile out."

He points to a dark green jacket lying on a bale of hay, just a few feet away.

I hurry over when I hear the urgency in his voice, fumble in the pockets and find his phone, quickly passing it to him. We're both taken by surprise when it rings.

He answers the call and the look of relief is instant.

"Aye, the gate's open," and he nods at me. "I'm waiting for ye. Come straight to the main cattle shed."

He ends the call and offers me the phone, which I dutifully place back in his pocket.

"Is he going to be okay?" I ask, and again, I know it's a stupid question, but what else can I say?

Jamie shakes his head.

"I cannae say hen, but let's hope so, eh?"

It's my turn to nod, and as I do so, a car door slams out in the yard.

"He's here," I declare, and dash off to greet the vet. I don't know why, but I'm expecting an elderly man with grey hair and brown breeches. So, I'm taken aback when I offer my hand to a thirty-something woman dressed in tight jeans, a waterproof anorak and a pair of green wellies. A baseball cap holds back long brown hair tied up into a ponytail. She's pretty and slim.

"Hi," I say. "Thanks for coming so quickly."

"No problem. I'm Ally," she replies in a curt tone. "And you are?"

"Oh, I'm Maddie. Callum's wife."

A look of astonishment crosses her face. "Wife? You mean, he brought *you* here?"

"Yes, that's right. We're on holiday."

Ally pulls her mouth into an unflattering line.

"Is there a problem, only you've turned rather pale?"

"No, I'm fine. Is the injured animal inside?"

I jump back and out of her way. "Oh, yes. Sorry, Jamie's waiting. Please hurry."

She dips her wellington boots into the disinfectant Jamie's left outside the shed door and then makes her way inside. I hesitate, as I'm out of my depth here, but I don't want just to walk off back to the farmhouse. I decide to follow her, in case they need an extra pair of hands. When I reach the pen, Ally's already assessing the damaged limb.

"Barbed wire?" she asks Jamie, and he nods.

"Aye, it'd come loose up on the glen, but 'tis fixed nah."

Ally heads back to her car and returns with an assortment of medical supplies, neatly organised inside a plastic tray. She places the tray on top of a bale of hay, so she can wash her hands in the stone sink in the corner of the shed. After snapping on a pair of latex gloves her fingers rummage through an assortment of drugs, sealed bandages and medicines. Finding what she's looking for, she turns her attention back to the injured animal. She cuts off the bloodstained cloth from around the leg, and washes down the wound with a hosepipe, then wipes away all traces of blood and dirt with saline and a sterile gauze.

"Don't worry, the laceration isn't as bad as you first thought. This bull won't be going for slaughter. Not today, anyway."

Jamie lets out a sigh of relief. "Och, that's guid news, and just what I wanted to hear. We cannae afford to lose him, not at this time of year." He places a small bucket of cattle cake in front of the crush, and the bull dips his head inside.

With the animal distracted, Ally bobs down onto her haunches and her fingers push the jagged pieces of skin back together.

"I can stitch up the leg," she says, "but you'll need to keep him away from the fold for a few days, at least." As she speaks, I notice for the first time that she doesn't have a Scottish accent. I try to place the soft intonation in her voice, but I can't quite pinpoint the dialect.

From a safe distance, I watch Jamie help the vet. They're a good team. Jamie appears to know her every move, and I stare, fascinated, as they work together. Jamie's right by her side and holds the bull steady whilst Ally prepares a large syringe and injects the wound with anaesthetic. The animal calms and the bellowing stops.

It takes well over an hour until the vet's done the best she can. Once the stitches are in place, she packs the medical equipment away and I hear her tell Jamie she'll be back in a few days. I walk back to the entrance of the shed and wait for her.

"Thanks for all your help," I say as she approaches.

She nods. "No problem," but her eyes don't meet mine and she carries on walking. I feel my brows loft in surprise. Head down, she goes straight to her car and drives away, leaving me staring after her taillights. I ponder what I might have said to cause her to be so dismissive towards me, coming up with nothing; a big fat zero.

"Maddie, where are ye?" Jamie calls, and I hurry back inside, convinced I must have been mistaken.

***

Fresh air, dark rolling hills and a backdrop of white misty mountains are enough of an incentive for me to help Jamie pack the winter picnic.

"Where are we going, exactly?" I ask as we head out into the farmyard. I'm dressed in warm boots and a thick woolly jumper, thankful there's no biting wind, but it's still cold. I pull a tartan scarf from my coat pocket and wrap it around my neck.

Jamie taps the side of his nose and heads over to the Land Rover. Throwing open the back door, he places the wicker basket onto the floor, alongside a red blanket.

"You've packed enough sandwiches to feed an entire army," I say, amused.

"I cannae have ye going hungry," he tells me.

"Hungry! Are you serious? Have you seen the size of those pieces of madeira cake? I swear, I'll be on a strict diet the second I'm home."

Jamie stops what he's doing to look me up and down.

"Och, I've seen more meat on a sparrow's kneecap."

"Oh, is that right?" and I raise my nose in the air. "I guess you must get up close and personal to a lot of birds, then."

I shove on a woollen hat with built in earmuffs that cover my ears and push my hair out of my eyes.

Jamie smirks, opens the passenger door and I jump inside. The Land Rover has no soft-padded seats or instant heat. It's what I'd call prehistoric and it's rather basic, but at least the engine's in good condition. He goes around to the other side and climbs in beside me, slamming the door hard so the metal groans in protest.

He turns to me and smiles.

"It's a heap of shite, I ken, but it'll get us to where we wannae be."

He playfully tugs at one of the tie-strings dangling from my ears, taken by surprise when my hat falls off. I'm quick to catch it and he laughs a huge belly laugh.

"Ye look silly wearing those earflaps," he chuckles. "All ye need is a pair of goggles and you'd have a canny resemblance to Biggles!"

I burst out laughing, and Jamie gives me a wink, a cheeky grin across his face. He starts the engine and I pop my hat back on. He thrusts the gearstick into first, and with a sharp jolt, off we go.

"It's one hell of a bumpy ride," I say, just a few minutes into the journey.

"Aye, I'm afraid the roads are little more than dirt tracks around here."

"I can tell. I think you've managed to hit every pot hole so far," I say with a smirk.

Jamie lets out a chuckle. "Sorry, I ken it isnae comfortable sitting in this tin can, but I promise ye the view will be worth it."

I stare out of the window. Although it's almost at the end of February we're still lucky with the weather. Little snow has fallen over the Highlands this year, although Alasdair says it's coming. I gaze wistfully at the white snow-topped mountains, but then Jamie points towards one of the peaks.

"There's snow all year round on them there bens," he tells me.

"Bens?" What do you mean?"

"Mountains. Ye ken, it doesnae matter how warm it gets, the snow ne'er melts."

I nod and smile. Sometimes, I just haven't a clue what he's talking about, but I like listening to him— a lot. We continue to chat about the passing countryside until we come to a fork in the road. There's no one else around, just Jamie and myself, and I can see for miles and miles. The Glen stretches out before me like a warm brown carpet and I can't wait to plant my feet onto its rich dark earth.

Jamie takes a left and the loch shimmers in welcome just a few miles away. The mountains roll up against a backdrop of dark green forest and its overarching pale-blue sky. I'm lucky enough to spot a wild hare dashing to its burrow and am thrilled when Jamie points out a red deer grazing in the distance.

He stops the Land Rover and we both clamber out. Jamie goes to the back of the vehicle and pulls out the picnic basket and the thick red blanket, passing them to me before fiddling about under one of the back seats. Out comes an old metal box, a pair of binoculars revealed when he lifts its lid. He places them around his neck and then closes the door, taking back the blanket and basket from my hands.

I amble behind as he edges closer to the water. The loch glistens as we 'approach. There's a tiny island in the middle filled with tall aspens and common alder. I stare way beyond the trees, though, to the majestically peaked mountains, their summits swathed in white fluffy clouds. If only Callum could see this.

I assume it must be hard for Jamie to bring me here to the loch and not his late wife. Callum says she was an Irish colleen, born in the county of Cork, with raven black hair and ocean green eyes. She must have been stunning. Callum once told me how a famous New York designer spotted her in a restaurant whilst visiting on holiday and practically begged her to become his fashion model.

"What was she like…Claire, your wife?"

Jamie turns to look at me, mid-stride, and I notice his brows knit together.

"Och, she was the most remarkable woman I ever met."

"I bet you miss her terribly," I say, treading carefully. "I mean…she must have been a big part of your life?"

He slows so he can walk beside me.

"Aye, I cannae deny that, and leaving me the way she did left a gaping hole in my chest where my heart should be. She was my everything," he whispers. "My sun and moon and stars all rolled into one. She had this crazy energy about her, so full of life, and when she died, a part of me died along with her."

I gulp and take a breath. I hadn't expected him to be quite so honest and open.

"How long were you married, before she became ill?"

"Just short of four wonderful years. I met her at the county fair, ye ken? She was visiting an old schoolfriend and they'd travelled down for the day. She was eating candy floss when I first clapped eyes on her, and I thought her the most beautiful creature I'd ever seen. Jet black hair right down to her waist, and those eyes...Wow. They were green, like ocean pools. She stared at me and her dazzling smile simply blew my breath away. It was love at first sight, for the both of us." He lowers his head and lets out a loud sigh. "A lifetime wouldnae have been long enough for that kind of love."

He drops to his knees.

"This'll do here," he says, and spreads the blanket over the ground. I hear water lapping over the tiny stones along the shore as the waves wash over them, and I sit down beside him, take off my gloves and help him unpack the lunch basket. I put two empty melamine plates onto the blanket and Jamie peels back tin foil to reveal ham and pickle sandwiches. He places them onto the plates and then fills two plastic cups with sweet white wine.

We eat and drink, side by side, in blissful silence.

I'm halfway through my second sandwich when Jamie jumps to his feet, startling me. I try not to choke, but my mouth's full of food and I swallow quickly. I want to ask him whatever's the matter, but before I get the chance, he picks up the binoculars. I'm busy brushing the crumbs from my fingers when he looks down at me, his eyes sparkling, a huge grin across his face.

"They're here," he cries, and offers me his hand.

"Who, the goosanders?" I ask, and strong fingers curl around mine.

"Aye, lassie; come see."

I jump to my feet and he offers me the binoculars, then points to the other side of the loch. My eyes and fingers take a few seconds to get the image in focus, and sure enough, he's right. The birds are there, right in front of me. I take a sharp intake of breath. There must be at least a hundred, maybe even two, floating on the top of the water. They're bobbing about, preening and washing themselves, oblivious to my prying eyes. I watch a few stragglers land, their wings beating against the water passing beneath them, creating a vortex of strong ripples across the surface of the loch.

"Wow, this is truly amazing," I say, turning my attention back to Jamie. I look down to find him lying on the blanket.

"See, I told ye," he says, cutting a scone in half and spreading lashings of strawberry jam on both sides. "And I wager ye dinnae ken that these birds nest in trees, either."

He's right, I didn't, and I raise my eyebrows in surprise.

"Honestly? Is that true, or did you just make it up?"

He laughs, and bites into the scone.

"Aye, they do," and he swallows. "They build their nests in holes in trees, or even tree stumps."

"But what if there aren't any trees? What then?"

"Och, if there's a problem, they'll nest on the ground, find a place where there's enough cover of vegetation."

I purse my lips together and nod. "So, the bottom line is that they're really not fussed where they build their nests?" I laugh, and Jamie laughs with me, and I feel there's a connection between us. I can't deny there's something about him that brings out the best in me. I'm sure it's because he's so laidback. Then again, perhaps it's because he's so approachable. Whatever it is, I like it.

I turn back to the goosanders to watch their escapades until my fingers grow numb with cold.

When I can't bear it any longer, I drag myself away to sit beside him. He's had the sense to bring a flask of piping hot coffee, and I'm grateful when he pours me a cup. I sip the sweet liquid and enjoy the sensation as it slides down my throat, but then I notice the sun's disappearing, that it's getting much colder.

"So, Sassenach, how long are ye planning on staying with us?"

I shrug. "Oh, I'm not sure, perhaps just a few more days. Why?"

"Och, it's just that the local pub's organising a quiz night on Wednesday if ye and Callum wannae come. It's nothing special, but it beats listening to Alasdair reminisce about his time serving in Sharjah."

I laugh. "Don't be so horrible," I protest, and throw a screwed-up piece of tin foil at him, accidently, hitting him right in the eye.

"Argh," he cries, covering part of his face and rolling around on the blanket. "That hurt." I giggle at his schoolboy antics. He's such an idiot.

"Oh, stop it," I say when my sides start to hurt from laughing. "You're being a drama queen."

He's still hiding his eye behind his hands and pretending to be in pain. I lunge forward, to try and pull his hands away, to end his silly game, but as soon as I touch him, he jerks back and I lose my balance and fall on top of him. His strong arms enfold me and I end up flat against his chest. I feel his warm breath upon my skin and gaze into a pair of dazzling green eyes, pushing myself closer as the desire to kiss him consumes me. I lick my lips in anticipation and close my eyes.

To my horror, he pushes me away, and I sit bolt upright, feeling my cheeks burn. "Jamie, I'm so sorry. I thought for a second you were Callum."

Jamie lifts himself onto one elbow and gives me a wide grin.

"Dinnae worry, Maddie. Nae harm done, eh?"

I try to smile, but the corners of my mouth just won't lift, and I realise there's this constant ache within my heart that's quietly killing me. There's so much I want to say, to explain, but before I get the chance, Jamie glances at his watch.

"Time's moving on. It's best we set off for home before it gets dark."

"Oh. Yes. Of course. Even the goosanders have fallen quiet."

"Aye, they'll be heading for their nests, just like we should."

I avert my gaze and pack away the picnic stuff, too aware that my courage has failed me.

***

As darkness descends, we drive back to the farm. It's only just after four but already the light's faded. Neither of us are quite so chatty this time around. I know it's all my fault. I'm consumed with guilt that I almost, *almost* kissed Jamie.

A shiver creeps down my spine. All I want is to get away from my brother-in-law as soon as possible. From the corner of my eye I see him peering at me. What if he tells Callum?

We enter the farm via the main gates and Jamie kills the engine as soon as we reach the farmhouse. The moment the vehicle stops, I fling open the passenger door and go to jump out, but then I hesitate and turn back towards him.

"Jamie, about earlier."

He shakes his head and I notice frown lines crease his forehead.

"Maddie, it's cool. Ye dinnea do anything wrong, so stop ye worrying."

I nod and slide out of my seat. A dark cloud's hanging over my head, but maybe after a goodnight's sleep it'll disappear. There's a bright orange glow from the downstairs windows, which makes the house seem warm and inviting, then a door opens, and the light spills out onto the path, the silhouette of a man blocking the doorway.

"Were you two planning on staying out all night?"

It's Callum, and there's an edge to his voice.

"Hi, it's good to see you, too," I say lightly, and hurry over to plant a kiss on his lips. There's warmth in my kiss, but he doesn't return it. Instead, he stares down at me and I can see his eyes are wide with frustration.

"Whatever's the matter?"

Callum lets out a huff. "I thought you'd be back hours ago."

"Really? But you knew we'd be late leaving because of the injured bull."

"Aye, well, I didn't expect you to be gone for over four hours. You only went to see a few wild birds. I returned from the market earlier than expected and thought you'd be home."

I'm exasperated. "Well, I didn't realise I had a curfew; you should have said."

Footsteps approach from behind me and Callum glances over my shoulder. His demeanour changes instantly.

"You two had a good time?" he asks his brother.

"Aye, we did," Jamie replies, "but I think we're both ready for a wee dram. It's biting cold out near the water and I cannae feel my toes."

Both men laugh and Callum stands aside to let me pass.

I go inside while Callum waits for his brother.

"While we were out, Hetty visited and left us some goodies today," I hear Callum say. "She's even baked a clootie dumpling."

"How is she?" I interrupt. "Is she still doing the cleaning and keeping you all up to speed with all the local gossip?"

Jamie takes off his coat and flings it over a hook.

"Aye, that she does, week in, week out, without fail, just like clockwork."

I hear a squeaky floorboard and then the door leading to the kitchen is flung open and Alasdair comes bundling through.

"Maddie, did ye get the chance to see the goosanders?" he asks, excitedly.

I nod, "Yes, I did, and it was an amazing experience, thank you."

"Excellent news, then let's talk more about it over dinner tonight. Shall we say six o'clock?"

"Sure, why not. That gives me plenty of time to have a hot shower and change my clothes."

"That's settled, then, but come inside and have a cup of tea by the fire before ye go."

I smile at him. "Oh, I'd love one. My fingers think they're falling off with frost bite."

"'Tis a wee bit cold for the English," he cries and tips me a wink. "You're lucky it isnae snowing, though."

I take off my coat, hat and gloves and leave my boots by the kitchen door.

"I hear Hetty's been to see you today," I say, going over to the table and lifting the lid on the teapot to check it's brewed.

"Aye, and a godsend she is, too. She brings us our supplies and gives the place a quick spruce at the same time. What she cannae do with a mop isnae worth knowing."

I laugh as I gather four china mugs from the cupboard.

After going to the fridge for the milk, I return to find Jamie and Callum already at the table, Alasdair standing by the fire. I pour the tea and offer a drink to each man in turn. Jamie puts his hand in his pocket and pulls out a small silver hip flask.

"A wee dram to warm the cockles of yir heart," he says to me.

I shake my head, but Alasdair and Callum are quick to offer him their cup. He pours a good measure into each.

I turn my attention back to Alasdair.

"So, did Hetty bring you any news from the outside world?" I ask as I sit down and take a sip of hot tea.

"Aye, lass, that she did. Told me young Ally, the vet, is back. She caught sight of her up at Mary McEwan's farm last week when she visited."

To my surprise, Callum chokes on his drink.

"Are you okay?" I ask, concerned.

He looks startled. "What? Oh, yeah, I'm fine. It went down the wrong hole."

My gaze shifts to Jamie. "Ally? She's the woman I met this morning, right?" and although I've directed the question straight at Jamie, it's Alasdair who replies.

"Aye. Nice looking lassie, clever too. She left a few years ago; sudden it was. I thought she'd met a nice wee man but Hetty says she just couldnae settle."

I turn towards Callum and notice he's avoiding my gaze. Minutes later, I finish my tea.

"Okay, boys, I'm off for that hot shower I promised myself."

I take my empty cup over to the sink, wash it and put it away. All the while, the silence that surrounds me is deafening.

"So, dinners at six o'clock sharp," I reiterate to granda. He nods. "Okay, see you all then."

CHAPTER FIVE

*J*amie

I watch Maddie leave the kitchen. I don't know all the ins-and-outs of what's going on between her and Callum, but I sense it's bad. As his brother, I want to help, to reach out to them both, but he's closed that door between us, made it clear I have no right to interfere between husband and wife. He's always been a stubborn bastard, the one who slaps the hand of friendship away. If he wasn't my kin, we would have parted ways many years ago.

I let out a deep sigh, for all I can see is a man drowning in his own misery.

"Is there any more whisky?" Callum asks, breaking my train of thought.

I reach straight into my pocket and pull out the flask. The metal feels cool around my fingers and I quickly unscrew the cap and pour a stream of golden liquid into his cup.

"Will that do for ye?" I say with a forced smile, but Callum's expression stays sombre. He takes a large mouthful and then hesitates before downing the rest. I watch him swallow.

"So, ye dinnae know Ally was thinking of coming back, then?" I ask.

He shakes his head then slams the empty cup onto the table.

"No, and why should I? What she does with her life is none of my business."

I nod and replace the flask back into my pocket.

"Och, I was just asking."

"Well, I'd prefer it if you didn't."

My gaze doesn't waver, staying direct. "So, maybe you're the reason why she left in the first place?" at which he balls his hands into fists.

"I have no idea; I was never her keeper. It's her life and she can do what she likes with it." He glances down at his watch. "No offence, but I think I'll skip dinner tonight, maybe take the Range Rover into town."

"You mean go to the pub?"

"Yeah, why not. It beats sitting around here all evening."

Alasdair comes and sits beside him.

"What's eating ye up, boy? What's wrong? Somehow, you've changed."

I switch my gaze to Alasdair, then back to my brother. I want to urge him to answer, but push him too hard and he'll do the complete opposite. I can see he's struggling with his emotions, but he's tenacious and holds everything inside, just like always.

I'm taken by surprise when he jumps to his feet.

"Nothing's wrong, granda," he declares, defensively. "Why can't you just leave it alone, eh?"

I rise to my feet. "Hey, take it easy and calm down. There's no need to lose yir temper. If ye so desperate to get out of here, I'll drive ye myself."

His glower is one that would have suggested guilt had I not known him all my life. As I watch him closely, his glare slides without effort into a sulk. He turns towards me. "Come on, then, drink up and let's go."

"But what about Maddie? You're not going to go without telling her, are ye?"

Callum doesn't reply; he's already halfway out of the door.

"Cal, wait," I cry, and hurry on after him.

By the time I catch up, he's standing by the Range Rover. I have the car keys in my hand and the doors are unlocked.

"Are ye sure ye don't wannae tell Maddie where you're going?" I ask, glancing towards the cottage.

He shrugs. "No, granda can have that privilege," and he opens the passenger door and climbs inside. I feel like shit taking him to the pub without Maddie's knowledge, but I'm aware that if I don't, he'll drive himself, anyway. I've seen my brother fall into a drunken rage on many an occasion. Although he's been a different man since he met Maddie, I sense the demon is pushing its way back to the surface once again. I've no wish to witness that side of him, so I'll do everything in my power to avert the violent monster from showing its face.

I make my way to the driver's side, and even before I turn on the engine, Callum's urging me to put my foot down.

"What's making ye so edgy tonight?" I ask.

"Nothing; I just need a change of scenery."

"We don't have to go to Camburgh for that. We could easily go for a walk if that's all you're after."

"Just drive," Callum snaps, "or I will."

I push the Range Rover on down the narrow country lanes, not slowing until we reach the outskirts of Camburgh. In the distance, a floodlit medieval church appears on the horizon. The sight of it still fills me with awe, even at this distance. The gothic style building is a sanctuary to many who use it, its two stone turrets rising either side of a magnificent stained-glass window in its eastern front. There's also a cross chiselled from a single piece of stone that stands between the two turrets. The whole edifice looks formidable, a beacon of hope for many perhaps, yet inside my head I simply pray there'll be no trouble this night.

I watch my brother out of the corner of my eye. His face is tense and his jaw twitches. I try to think of something funny to say that might bring him out of his dark mood.

"Do ye remember the time when we were coming back from town and McDougal's prize cow chased us up this hill? We both near pissed our pants."

My ploy fails. Callum doesn't crack a smile.

"Save it for the old man," he says, glancing over. "I'm not in the mood for reliving the good old days."

I shake my head, exasperated. Sometimes, there's just no talking to the stubborn wee fool.

I park up in the market square and Callum is halfway across the road by the time I step out of the car. The old church bell chimes the hour and I think of Maddie coming down to dinner only to learn her husband has left her for a night of binge drinking. I hurry to catch up with my brother, even though I know where he's heading; there's only one pub in town and it's busy there every night of the week.

Callum opens the door to the Scran and Sleekit and I'm right at his heels. High-pitched laughter and the smell of stale beer hits my senses the second I'm inside, where I follow Callum straight to the bar.

The pub is made from local stone, the dark wooden beams above my head having been in place for centuries. It has a rustic feel and lots of charm. The soft furnishings are dressed in tartan and tweed, and a pair of antlers hang on the wall. I spot a half-dozen watercolours of Bonnie Prince Charlie with the Jacobite rebels, fighting the English. Their red and black uniforms are a vivid contrast to the wishy-washy pale-cream walls.

There isn't a single person here who doesn't know me and my brother. It's a small community and identical twins are a rarity. I nod and smile at the many familiar faces, some of whom I went to school with, whilst others are farmers, enjoying a quiet drink with their wives.

The barman comes over and shakes Callum's hand.

"What are ye doing here, Callum; I haven't seen ye for ages?"

It's clear Callum hasn't come here for pleasantries; a quick hello and he's ordering a beer for himself and a pint of Coke for me.

There's an empty table in the far corner, close by a wood burning stove, which, considering it's a damn cold evening, is a boon. Callum hands me my drink and I nod for him to follow. We make our way over and I take off my coat, hanging it on the back of a chair. Callum sits on a stool beside me, soon closing his eyes and taking several long swigs of his pint.

"Ah, that tastes good," he says, and before I can reply, he's off to the bar for another.

He returns with two whisky chasers.

"Hey, slow down," I hiss, "the bar doesnae close 'til eleven."

Callum grins for the first time since we arrived.

"Chill out. I'm just catching up on lost time. I'll not be downing these so quickly, so stop your haverings."

He slips a whisky into his drink and my earlier worry about him comes rushing back. I needn't have worried, though, and much to my surprise, Callum behaves himself. After he's downed both chasers, he chills out and begins to socialise, mingling with the locals and greeting his old pals from school with genuine warmth, quickly becoming the Callum everyone remembers.

Eventually, he comes back to the table, where I'm still sipping my Coke, now swaying, his mood clearly having turned melancholic. He stumbles as he sits beside me, spilling his beer all over the table.

"Easy, Cal," I say, mopping up the mess with a couple of beer mats.

He laughs and slides what's left of the spilt beer into his glass with the side of his hand.

"Not to worry, I'm not about to waste a single drop," he chuckles into his glass.

"I think you've had enough for one night. God knows what Maddie's going to say."

The mere mention of Maddie's name wipes the smile off his face, the expression that replaces it shocks me. There's a wretchedness to him now that I've never seen before.

I reach out my hand and squeeze his wrist.

"What is it?" I ask, and when he doesn't speak, I add: "For Christ's sake, Callum, and for once in your life, talk to me."

He lifts his head and turns towards me, his eyes shining like glass, filled with unshed tears, and my heart lunges in my chest. Whatever it is, it's tearing him apart.

"Please, let me try to help," I beg. "If only ye would confide in me."

Callum takes a deep breath and I find I'm holding my own. Then he looks me straight in the eye, and I know he's going to tell me the crux of his despair.

"The truth is," he says, so quietly I find myself moving closer to hear him, "I can't give her what she wants," and he looks down at his beer.

"What do ye mean?"

"A baby; I can't give Maddie a baby."

I struggle to find the right words. Callum said they were having problems conceiving, but so do many couples.

"Everyone knows it takes time," I say, trying to sound supportive. "Sometimes it takes years. Ye just have to keep on trying."

He looks back at me, a single tear trickling down his cheek.

"You don't understand. I've had tests. They say I'm infertile."

I'm stunned. Words fail me and I catch my breath, trying to think of something positive to say, but I can't. I never knew. None of us did.

"I'm so sorry, Cal." My mind scrambles for something else to say, the words having spilled from my mouth before I had time to think, but Callum gives a bitter laugh.

"I don't want your sympathy; I just want to get my wife pregnant."

I try to think on my feet.

"What about...adoption? Surely that's another option?"

Callum shakes his head. "Maddie tried to persuade me. Said if we were able to adopt a baby then we could bring it up as our own." He places his elbows on the table and inches closer. He reminds me of a spy who's about to divulge top-secret information.

"But it wouldn't be mine. Every moment of every day, I'd be reminded that I couldn't father a child with her."

"But ye cannae think like that," I burst out. "If ye do, it'll ruin yir life."

Callum lets out a forced laugh and I realise it's too late, he's already destroyed inside.

"Wise words," he states, flatly. "However, the bottom line is that I don't want a kid that's not mine."

"What, not even a sperm donor? I hear they're very successful. I dinnae know all the facts, but don't they try to get the best match they can. Use someone who has yir hair and eye colour, even yir build?"

He lifts the pint glass to his lips but stops halfway. "What, like a twin?"

"Ach, away with ye," and I attempt a smile. "Now, I dinnae say that."

A shudder sweeps down my spine and alarm bells ring inside my head. I'm aware it's just the beer talking, but I'm wary all the same. I glance up and Callum's eyes are suddenly clear. The tears have all gone and his expression has completely changed.

"You could be the one, Jamie. Me and you: we're the same person, split from the same egg. If you got Maddie pregnant, technically it would be the same as if I'd fathered the child."

"Stop talking out of yir arse," I object. "Whatever you're thinking, it stops right nah. I cannae sleep with yir wife. Are ye mad? And besides, I wouldnae do something like that. It's wrong and I couldnae live with myself afterwards."

But Callum isn't listening.

"Please, Jamie, do this one thing for me, for Maddie. All she wants is a child of her own. If it was you who got her pregnant, it would be as if I had done it. Can't you see the gift you would give us both."

I want to help, but what he's asking is beyond my own ethics, beyond my comprehension.

"Och, maybe ye should talk to Maddie first; see what she thinks."

Callum shakes his head vigorously.

"No, we can't tell her. She'd go ballistic. Even if she wanted to go through with it, she'd deny herself because she wouldn't wish to betray me. She's an old-fashioned girl with old-fashioned values. Even if she had the chance she wouldn't take it, because of me."

I sigh with relief.

"So, she would ne'er agree?"

Callum brings his hand close to his head and clicks his fingers.

"Wait; I have an idea. Didn't I hear something earlier about a quiz night here on Wednesday night?"

"Aye, ye did."

"Perfect. Then we'll bring Maddie along."

I feel my eyebrows knit together. "I've already invited her, but what does that have to do with anything?"

"It's simple. She wouldn't sleep with you knowingly, but...if we get her drunk enough, she wouldn't know the difference and we could swap places for the night."

I jump to my feet. I've heard enough.

"I'll nae be part of no such thing, do ye hear?" I hiss at my brother. "I'm sorry ye cannae have any kin of yir own, but this is wrong on so many levels."

I grab my coat from the back of the chair and storm out of the pub. All I can see is a haze of red around my eyes. How could Callum ask me to do such a despicable thing to the woman he loves?

"Jamie, wait," Callum shouts after me as I head for the car, but I ignore him. I'm angry and hurt that he'd ask me to do something so appalling, so unforgivable, but then heavy footsteps come up behind me and strong hands grip my shoulders.

I spin around and glare at my drunken brother.

63

"Enough," I cry. "You've crossed the line and dinnae ken what you're saying."

I march back to the car and fling open the driver's door and jump inside. Callum chases after me.

"Jamie, please. Just hear me out."

I start the engine and thrust it into first gear, but then turn and face him.

"Either ye shut up about me getting Maddie pregnant or ye can find another way to get home." He hesitates, but then climbs inside.

I drive like a madman, unable to think of anything except what my brother has had the audacity to ask of me, until I take a bend a little too sharply and almost lose control.

"For Christ's sake, take it easy," Callum cries, but I can't. I glare at him and press the pedal even harder as I look back at the road, barely focused on what's in front of me, miles away inside my own head. Inwardly, I curse my brother over and over as my anger simmers within me. I'm barely in control and I've a real fight on my hands.

By some miracle, we make it home in one piece. I drive through the gates, break sharply and kill the engine. Without a backward glance, I head straight for the farmhouse. Alasdair has left the downstairs lights on, but he's nowhere to be seen. I look down at my watch: it's eleven-fifteen. I guess he's in bed, and Maddie, too.

I make my way towards the study, where there's a full decanter of whisky, for I now badly need a drink. I open the door and switch on the light. The room smells musty, of old books and cigars, and I head straight over to the oval bar server and pour myself a stiff drink, knocking back the golden liquid in one shot. It burns my throat, but I quickly pour another.

The door creaks and I spin around to see Callum standing there. He's no longer defiant. Now he stands before me, his shoulders hunched over and

64

his eyes pleading. I turn away from him and pour myself yet another shot of whisky.

"Ye need to go to bed," I state, placing the stopper back into the decanter.

I'm surrounded by silence, so I assume Callum's taken my good advice, and I let out a sigh and turn around. He's still standing there.

"Dinnae ye hear me?" I snap. "Time for talking's over." I go over to a high-backed chair that faces a fire that's no longer lit, and there I sit down, swirling the drink around the crystal tumbler.

To my dismay, Callum comes and sits beside me. He coughs, clears his throat and I look up to see the image of a broken man, one now wringing his hands. He's clearly desperate for help, but I'm not the one he should turn to.

"Jamie," he says in a small, defeated voice, "I want you to know our marriage was perfect in every way until she wanted a child. Not being able to give her the one thing she desires most in the world haunts me and has left the deepest furrows of pain in my heart. Up until that moment I'd provided her with everything she ever wanted. It was me who put up the capital for the flower shop when it was a goal she thought she'd never reach. I supported her through her training, watched her determination to succeed grow, like the flowers in her shop. I've always loved Maddie because of her unreasonable wildness. Every day with her is a challenge, but I wouldn't change her for the world. She's been so strong these past months, much stronger than I ever could be, and I feel myself growing weak."

"Cal, I hear what you're saying, but what you're asking…"

"Do you not think it kills me to beg my own brother to do what I should be man enough to do myself? And the fact is…I'm ashamed. Ashamed I've dropped so deep into my pit of despair that I'm asking my own flesh and blood to do something that goes against everything we've ever believed in. But there's simply no other way, not for me…not for Maddie."

I shake my head. The booze is starting to hit me, but I'm still in control.

"Ye have nae right," I declare, "to ask me to do such a thing, to ask…anyone."

"Do you think I don't know that? But I implore you to reconsider and think this through. I know what I'm asking goes beyond brotherly love, but I'm a drowning man begging you to throw me some rope."

"I cannae do it, Callum; I just cannae," and I watch my brother push his fingers through his hair, slowly inching his chair a little closer. His voice becomes low, conspiratorial, just like back in the pub.

"All I'm asking is for you to think about it. The quiz night is two days away. It's just one night with her, Jamie, one night that could change everything."

"Och, so let's say for argument's sake, I agree to go along with this crazy idea of yours. What if I sleep with her and she doesnae fall pregnant. Let's face it, the stakes are stacked against us. What then?"

"Then at least I know we tried, and gave it our best shot."

Before I can say anything, Callum pulls himself from his seat and pats me with affection on the shoulder.

"Two days, Jamie. Please think about it. That's all I ask," and I remain noncommittal as I watch him take himself off to bed.

CHAPTER SIX

*M*addie

I open the kitchen door to find Alasdair sitting alone by the fireside.

My gaze sweeps around the room.

"Hey," I say lightly, "where's Tweedle-dee and Tweedledum?" but he doesn't crack a smile, and so I hurry over to him.

"Alasdair, what's wrong? Has something happened to one of the farm animals. Is that why neither Jamie or Callum are here?"

He shakes his head then turns to stare into the flames. He lets out a deep sigh and points to the chair opposite.

"Sit down, lass. I've somethin' I need to tell ye."

"Why? What is it? What's happened?"

He lets out another long sigh, turns to me and pats my hand gently. I look down. His knuckles are gnarled with age and his weathered skin feels as tough as old shoe leather. I curl my fingers around the palm of his hand and hold his fingers tight.

"'Tis Callum," he says. "He's gone out…drinkin'."

"Sorry, he's what?"

He points a thumb towards the door. "Aye, him and Jamie have gone into town."

"But I never heard them leave." I pull my hand away and turn to stare at the door, as if by doing so he'll walk through and prove the old man wrong. I wait, but when he doesn't materialise, I realise that what Alasdair has said is true. My cheeks burn with humiliation. "You mean he just up and left without a word?"

Alasdair nods. "He said he needed a drink and not one he could find in the house. I dinnae know what came over him. One minute he was fine and the next…"

"He turned into Mr Hyde?"

Alasdair looks alarmed then nods. "Aye, that's about it, lassie."

I dig into my jeans pocket for my phone, dial Callum's number and clutch the mobile to my ear. I wait urgently through four rings, but get his voicemail and hang up.

I want to scream out loud what an inconsiderate arsehole he is for abandoning me—like this, without a thought. I then try ringing Jamie, but when it connects, I hear a familiar ringtone sounding out in the room, from where his mobile sits on the windowsill.

Defeated, I shove my phone back into my pocket, hardly noticing Alasdair get up from his chair. Nor do I register the two pieces of Salmon he takes out of the oven.

"Maddie, are you all right, lass?"

I stand up and stare vacantly in his direction. He places the baking tray he's holding down onto the side, making his way over to me and steers me over to the table.

"Come on, sit down," he insists.

"Is dinner ready?" I say, absently.

A memory flashes through my mind: I'm nine years old again and in the foyer of one of the many foster homes I'd had to endure. The Smyth children were simply immature psychopath's, the spotty teenager of whom, no older than fourteen, blocks my way. He prods a stubby finger into my chest. It hurts, but I don't cry.

"Oh, look, it's little orphan Annie," he teases. "If it isn't the miserable kid that nobody wants."

He laughs, and his younger brother, standing next to him, pinches my arm. I yelp and he too laughs out loud. "You stink like dog poo," he cries and holds his nose as he runs down the corridor to tell all his friends.

An involuntary shiver escapes me.

I push the terrible ordeal to the furthest corner of my mind. All I want is a man to love me. I want

Callum to protect and respect the person I am. But I'm afraid of our future: the emptiness waiting for me is like a physical punch in the chest.

I sit, eating my meal as though I haven't a care in the world, but the fish tastes bland and small pieces get stuck in the back of my throat. The wine is sour and tastes like vinegar in my mouth, yet I do my best to swallow it down.

"I think I'd best have an early night," I say and press my fingers to my forehead.

"Do ye have a headache?" Alasdair asks.

I nod and stand up from the table. "Yes. I think it's the start of a migraine. I'd best go and lie down."

Alasdair shakes his head. "Aye, lass. Sounds like the right thing to do. Off ye go. I'll clear up here."

"Are you sure you don't mind?"

"'Tis no trouble, and I'll see ye in the mornin'."

I give him a hug and he pecks me on the cheek before I pull away and make my way to the door.

"I'm sorry," Alasdair says. "About Callum."

I turn to face him. "It's isn't your fault. You're not his keeper."

Alasdair nods and pulls out his pipe from his cardigan pocket. He places the end in his mouth and sucks in fresh air. "That maybe so, but I want ye to know: I dinnae agree with his behaviour tonight."

I force a smile. "Goodnight, Alasdair. I'll see you in the morning." I turn away and leave him standing by the fireside, then head for the seclusion of the Garden House.

As soon as I close the door behind me, I burst into tears. I feel such a fool. I can't believe he went into town without saying a word. I try to figure out why he would do such a thing, feeling humiliated, abandoned, angry, and upset. And I'm also afraid. Perhaps he doesn't want to be with me anymore, or even need me any longer. I cover my face with my hands, allowing hot tears to pour down my cheeks, the day he asked me to marry him springs into my mind. I can see him as clearly as if he were standing right in front of me.

We were out on a lake in a rowing boat. It was a hot summer's day. The local park was filled with young lovers enjoying a lazy Sunday. The lake was surrounded by a multitude of weeping willows and a family of swans adorned the water. It was simply idyllic.

The day out was all Callum's idea. He'd brought a small picnic and a fishing rod, which he insisted only he should carry. We bobbed about on the water for at least an hour, eating our sandwiches and enjoying the sun on our backs. He'd appeared a little fidgety that day, and out of the blue, he sat poker straight and proclaimed his fishing line had a bite. I hadn't seen it tug, but Callum insisted he'd caught something big and started reeling in the line. I sniggered when he told me the fish was going to be huge, and I played along and laughed even louder when he faked losing his balance and almost fell into the water. He was having a whale of a time acting juvenile and I didn't want to spoil his fun.

To my surprise, the line suddenly shot out of the water, and I'm sure my mouth gaped wide open when I realised it wasn't a fish at the end of the line, not of any size, but a small black box hooked onto the float. Callum reeled it in and then sat down, the box in the palm of his hand.

I inched closer. "How did that get there?" I asked, somewhat puzzled. When he looked up at me, I swear his eyes glistened, then he took my hand in his own.

"I love you," he whispered and opened the box. Inside, sat a sparkling solitaire diamond ring. I pressed my lips together. I hadn't suspected a thing. Callum pulled the ring from the box and held it up towards me. "Make me the happiest man alive. Say you'll be my wife."

I now twist the two gold rings on my wedding finger, one of which has adorned it since that very day, but then I drop my hand and let out a sigh.

Opening my eyes, I wipe away the last of my tears and head for the stairs and my bedroom.

I undress, then get into bed. I lie awake, waiting for Callum to come home, surprised sometime later when I hear a car door slam. I glance at the clock. It isn't even midnight. I listen for the downstairs door to open, but hear male voices heading towards the farmhouse, instead. And so I lie in wait as another hour passes before Callum finally makes an appearance.

I turn to watch him enter the room.

"Where the hell have you been?" I ask.

Callum lets out a deep sigh and sits on the edge of the bed. He kicks off his shoes and throws them into the corner of the room. The first thing that strikes me is that Callum isn't drunk; not what I expected at all. Although I can smell alcohol on his breath, he appears relatively sober.

"Callum, I think I deserve some kind of explanation at least."

He gets up off the bed and takes off his shirt and trousers.

"I'm going to take a shower," he says and heads towards the bathroom.

"Callum?"

I'm infuriated by the way he dismisses me so easily, but try to keep a lid on my frustration. I'm struggling, though. The shower comes on and a loud screech announces that the cubicle door has closed. I listen to every sound he makes until I hear him switch off the water, then he walks back into the bedroom, a bath towel wrapped around his waist.

"So, are you going to explain what happened tonight?" I ask.

"What can I say? I needed fresh air."

"And you had to go all the way to Camburgh to find some."

"I guess. It can get pretty stifling around here at times."

"And you're not going to at least apologise for your behaviour?"

"You think I should?"

"Are you serious?"

He shrugs. "So, I felt like a night out with my brother. Is that really such a big deal?"

"Actually, yes. It is. How could you do that to me? Just piss off out without a word?"

He peels back the covers, pulls off the towel and throws it on a nearby chair. He gets into bed and turns off the bedside light.

"Callum," I fume, "at least have the decency to answer me."

He throws himself over onto his side. "What, exactly, do you want me to say?"

I reach over and switch on the light. "How about saying you're sorry for leaving me in the lurch. Or better still, explaining why you felt the need to go into town with Jamie."

"Okay, I'm sorry," he grunts. "I've no excuse other than I wanted to share some quality time with my bro."

"But all you had to do was say. I wouldn't have stopped you."

"Yeah, well, that thought never crossed my mind. I simply acted on impulse. I'm sorry, okay? And I promise it won't happen again." He punches his pillow and snuggles himself under the covers. "Am I forgiven? And if so, can we go to sleep now?" and he soon falls asleep.

I simply can't speak, flabbergasted by his nonchalant attitude towards me. I lie there, in bed, wrapped in the luxury of the duvet, but feel no comfort from its warmth. The truth is chipping away at me, like a sculptor working tirelessly with his chisel. Bit by bit. Chip, chip, chip. And he's revealed something I don't wish to see, but I'm starting to face reality.

My husband is falling out of love with me.

My heart contracts as I stifle a cry. It's as though my soul is twisted in barbed wire, caught and pierced until every last drop of blood flows out. Another soft whimper escapes and I stiffen, terrified he'll awaken, but he turns in his sleep and mumbles something incoherent. Amongst it all, though, he says one word I do catch, a name, and my confusion deepens—"Ally."

I catch my breath, unable to unhear what I just heard. Isn't she the woman who visited the farm today? The vet? Callum has never mentioned that he knew her. I suffer a moment of uncertainty. She's turning into an itch I can't quite reach to scratch, and I picture her in my mind; long dark hair, luscious red lips, legs of a Goddess. There's something about her that's getting under my skin, and so I toss and turn all night, only falling asleep just as the farm's cockerel proclaims the start of a brand-new day.

I rise early and leave Callum asleep. I get dressed and head over to the farmhouse, where I'm relieved to find there's a warm welcome waiting for me.

Alasdair's standing by the stove, cooking bacon and eggs.

"Mornin', Maddie," and he stops what he's doing to come over and plant a kiss on my cheek. "Has yir headache gone?"

I nod and he hugs me before heading back to the cooker. I go over to the kitchen cupboard, pull out two mugs and make us both tea.

"How's Callum?" he asks, his face sombre. "Suffering with a bad head, no doubt?"

I shrug. "More than likely."

"Jamie'll be back soon; do ye want some breakfast making, hen?" but I shake my head. It's far too early for me. "No, I'm fine, thanks, granda. Have you eaten?"

Alasdair nods. "Aye, I've had a bowl of porridge. Fill's ye up for the day, so it does. Anyway, I was wonderin' what ye going to do with yourself today?"

I shake my head. "I haven't the foggiest idea," I admit. "Perhaps I'll go for a walk, or hang around the stables."

"Och, ye could maybe go down to the burn? It's a wee bit bleak this time o'year, but there's a wee stone erected by the locals to commemorate the Battle of Culloden, which ye might find interestin'."

I place both cups onto the table before pouring the tea.

"The Battle of Culloden is pretty big in these parts, yeah?"

"Aye, of course, it's big. 'Tis the place where the clans were almost wiped out by the English. Approximately seven hundred Jacobite warriors were killed within minutes of the battle commencin'."

I pull a grimace. "That's terrible. All those poor people, how they must have suffered."

"Aye, that they did. And over twelve hundred clansmen either lost their lives or were wounded that fateful day. It were a terrible time for Scotland, and one that will ne'er be forgotten."

The front door bangs, and seconds later, Jamie comes hurtling into the kitchen.

"Mornin', granda," he says, but he's not so enthusiastic when he spots me sitting at the table. He nods, curtly, then looks away. He heads over to Alasdair. "I could eat a scabby horse, I'm so damn hungry," and he grabs a buttered bap and takes a large bite.

"Ne'er mind ye stomach, lad; are the cattle fed and watered?"

Jamie nods, swallows, and then stuffs the last of the bread straight down his gullet. I can't help but chuckle: he really has been around the animals for far too long.

"What's so funny?" he asks.

"You; your silly antics remind me you're just a big kid at heart." He comes over and tousles my hair.

"Hey, keep your hands to yourself," I cry. His fingers entwine with mine as I try to force his hands away, but he's strong and I have to squirm to get out of the way.

"Who's the kid now?" he laughs, letting go.

I smile. The truth is I'm not mad at Jamie for what happened last night. I understand he drove Callum to the bar, but it's better he went with someone who'd watch over him than go into town alone. It frightens me when my husband drinks too much. He's another person when he does. Callum admitted himself that after binge drinking he's like a timebomb waiting to go off. I don't wish to see that part of him, ever again. Having the Police bring him home once is once too many.

I sip my tea and watch Jamie out of the corner of my eye, when he comes and sits beside me. Granda places a greasy fry up in front of him and Jamie reaches for the salt and pepper. On his plate there's eggs, bacon and traditional potato scones. There's also three slabs of black pudding. They remind me of the Leaning Tower of Pisa, but then I look away: they're made with pig's blood, which I find totally disgusting.

"What's wrong, Sassenach, don't ye want to eat something that'll put hairs on yir chest?"

I turn back towards him and slap his shoulder, playfully with the back of my hand.

"No, thanks. You can keep that revolting stuff to yourself." He sniggers, picks up a fork and starts eating his breakfast as though he hasn't had a decent meal in days.

I pull my lips into a frown. The smell of fried food so early in the morning turns my stomach queasy.

"I think it's best I get going before that grease clogs up your arteries and I have to administer CPR." I grin to myself, convinced neither of these two have ever heard of high cholesterol or heart disease.

I go through the ritual of going over to the sink and washing up my cup, then push it back into line with all the others in the cupboard.

"Where ye off to?" Jamie asks, shovelling the black pudding down his throat.

"Oh, just down to the burn. I'd like to go and see the memorial stone granda was telling me about earlier."

"Aye, it's a sight to see, all right. Do ye want any company?"

I give him a broad smile. "Thanks for the offer, but no. I'd like to go there on my own if that's okay?"

Jamie shakes his head. He doesn't appear offended.

"Och, very well, but watch yir step on the brae."

I cock my head to one side. "Sorry…the what?"

"The slope. It's a wee bit slippery this time of year. Stay on the path if ye can."

"Thanks for the sound advice," and I leave him to finish what's left of his breakfast and head off in the direction of the hallway. I can smell the beeswax of its oak panelling as soon as I enter. There's several large coat hooks on the far wall behind the front door. They're filled with a variety of outdoor gear. I delve between the layers of Barbour jackets to find a couple of waterproofs, trying each one in turn until I find one that fits. When I choose a matching scarf, I realise it probably belonged to Claire. For a second, I have the urge to retrace my steps and invite Jamie to come along, but I let the idea fall away as I get ready to experience my next adventure. I stuff my hat over my ears, zip up the jacket, push my feet into a pair of hiking boots—brought especially for the trip—and I'm ready to roll. When I open the front door, I'm embraced by a burst of fresh air.

As I leave the cottage behind me, I glance back, seeing nothing of Callum, so I head over to the lane that runs parallel with the farm. It's certainly colder today than yesterday, but it's one of those mornings that's sure to blow those lingering cobwebs away.

Scurrying grey clouds scud across a wintry sun, then I catch sight of a single lapwing. Its little black and white body dives closer, heading for a low branch of an oak tree. My gaze follows its descent, mesmerising me, and I'm sure I glimpse an orange vent under its tail. It's certainly beats the common sparrows I'm accustomed to at home. There's a real sense of nature here, of beauty and seclusion. The lapwing flies away and I close my eyes and pretend I'm flying by its side. Oh, how I wish I could live here, surrounded by such serenity.

My mobile goes off in my pocket and I open my eyes, shoving my hand inside to retrieve it. It's a new text message, and it's from Keira: "*How's it going? Ring me when you can xxx*".

I stuff my phone back into my pocket and make my way onto the lane. I know Keira will be disappointed that this mini break hasn't repaired any of the damage, as we'd both hoped it would, but then Rome wasn't built in a day. An image of the famous colosseum crumbles behind my eyes. Callum is the one destroying us. Pain, raw and frightening, claws at my heart. But I'm not giving in so easily. I will never leave him. I love him. Why should I walk away when I've done nothing wrong? It isn't my fault we can't have children, yet I believe he somehow blames me. Tears prick the back of my eyes, but I force them away. Now isn't the time to wallow in self-pity. There'll be time enough later, if I find I cannot salvage what's left of our marriage.

I take a deep breath and fill my lungs with fresh mountain air. You just can't beat it, I tell myself. It's like sweet nectar and I'm invigorated. I shove my hands inside my pockets and set off at a brisk pace.

"Hey, Maddie, hold yir horses," and I turn around to see Jamie jogging towards me. I frown. Whatever's the matter? But then I realise he's carrying something in his hand.

"Here, lass; ye cannae go out in the wilds without taking provisions."

I look down at a small black rucksack. "I don't need that," I protest, rolling my eyes. "I'm only going for a walk."

"Aye, ye do," Jamie insists. "There's nae much inside, just a bottle of water, a first aid kit and a map of the area. Take the backpack, ye ken? Just in case ye get lost, or worse, injured. Ye cannae be too careful. Oh, and the Mountain Search and Rescues mobile number's written inside the front flap."

I let out an exaggerated groan. "I'm only going a few miles. It isn't as though I'm off climbing Ben Nevis."

"It doesnae matter," Jamie says, his voice now firm. "Ye can ne'er tell when the weather will turn for the worse."

With some reluctance, I accept the rucksack and push my arms through the nylon straps.

"Okay; if it'll make you happy, I'll take it," I huff. "Anything to keep the peace."

"Aye, I'd feel better," Jamie nods, and I set out on my journey without a backward glance.

I head down a footpath and follow a sign to the stone. To the north, there's gently rolling hills carved up by lazy stone walls. In the distant sky, far away, there's a dark band of cloud rolling in from the sea. A chill in the air makes me shiver and the few leaves left on the surrounding trees flicker in the wind.

I veer onto a narrow bridle path and I strain my eyes across the glen, in the hope of seeing the odd stag or doe scrambling through the bracken. All I see is open farmland covered in a sea of yellow gorse. It's in bloom and the profusion of pretty yellow flowers stand out like the dappled light of sunshine seen beneath a woodland's high canopy.

In the distance, something else catches my eye. It's flying straight towards me and I squint, unable to make it out at first. I'm not one-hundred-percent certain, but I'm convinced I'm staring at a golden eagle, its wings flapping effortlessly against the strength of the higher blowing wind. I stop dead in my tracks and curse myself for not bringing the binoculars. It's ginormous wingspan dips and sweeps across the sky, and just for one second, I wish Jamie was here to share this breath-taking moment with me.

I rummage in my pocket, pull out my phone and quickly take a picture. He may not be here, but I'll show him what he's missed later. The phone flashes and the bird changes course and flies off towards the mountains. I'm about to put my phone away when I remember Kiera's text message and decide to ring her.

"Maddie?" and her squeal is infectious. "I thought you'd never call."

"Hey, how are you doing? I've no excuses," I confess, "I've just been really busy."

"So, you're both having a great time. Right?"

I heave a heavy sigh.

"Maddie?"

I look across at the mountains, as though they'll help me with my inner struggle. "Well, so far the trip hasn't quite gone to plan."

"What do you mean?"

I pause. "Things still aren't right between us. Callum's acting like a Jekyll and Hyde, and I don't know what to do."

"How? In what way?"

"Well, for instance: only last night he just took off. I came down to dinner to find he'd left for town. I tried to ring him, but he'd switched off his phone. I was left fuming all night. Then, when he came home, he was so flippant about it. It was as though he didn't care that his actions had hurt me, as if I didn't mean anything to him. I'm losing him Keira. I swear, I can feel it."

"I'm sorry, hunny, but I don't know what to say."

"What is there to say? And then of course, there's Jamie."

"Jamie? What's he got to do with anything?"

I look down at the ground, see a small stone and give it a kick.

"Maddie, spill. Right now, you hear?"

I heave another huge sigh. "I almost kissed him."

"You did what?"

"I know. It just…happened."

"How the hell could it 'just happen'. And where was Callum while all this was going on?"

"It's a long story, but to cut to the chase: he was at the farmer's market with granda and Jamie took me to the loch in his place. We were just enjoying a picnic and messing around, and…and I lost control."

"Did he try to kiss you back?"

"No. He acted the perfect gentlemen and I played the fool. I apologised, and he said to forget it. He said he wouldn't tell."

"And has he been true to his word?"

"One hundred percent."

"And nothing's happened since?"

"No, of course not. Like I said: he's a real gent."

"Do you want it to?" she asks, lowering her voice.

I press my lips together and shove my fingers through my hair.

"Maddie? Maddie, are you still there?"

"Hmm, yes, I'm here."

"Look, I've got to be honest: I think you're playing with fire."

I hear the concern in her voice and try to reassure her. "It was just a silly mistake, and it was all over in a millisecond."

"And you've learned your lesson? After all, you've a lot to lose."

"Yes, and I do love Callum. I just need to get things back to how they were before we lost our way."

Tears are now stinging the backs of my eyes. "Look, I have to go. I'll call you later…tonight."

"Okay, but promise me you'll not be foolish again."

"Oh…I think I'm losing the signal. I've got to go. Bye."

As I wander over the grassland, I go over our brief conversation. Keira will understand my torment, and I do feel better for having told someone about Jamie. Now I've come clean, even if it's just to myself, I can finally put the whole episode behind me.

I catch sight of a stream running past to one side, an old stone bridge up ahead. I leave the path and make my way over, soon spotting a strange-looking stone sticking out of the earth on the far side of the stream. I assume it's the one Alasdair told me about earlier this morning.

As I cross over the bridge, I see the stone stands by the water's edge, and Jamie was right: it is wet and muddy. But I'll have to go down the bank if I want to read the inscription, which I can't quite make out from where I'm standing.

I go to plant a firm foot on the damp grass, but no sooner does my boot come down than my foot slips and I practically do a somersault into the air. It happens too quickly to save myself, and my legs fly from beneath me, my arms flailing above my head. It's over in seconds as I bang the back of my head and land on my backside, all at the same time. I've hit my coccyx and boy does it throb. The ground is littered with sharp stones and large tufts of grass, which feel like knives pressed into my back. I close my eyes and take several deep breaths, angry and upset that I've managed to hurt myself. I wait until the pain subsides before I try to sit up. When I do, I rub the back of my head to discover a painful lump.

"Hey, are you all right?"

I let out a low groan, feeling mortified: someone just saw me make a complete spectacle of myself. I wish they'd disappear and leave me alone, but the stranger calls out to me again and then she rushes over. A young woman bobs down in front of me and wags a finger in my face.

"How many do you see?"

I shake my head. "Really, I'm okay. I'm not concussed. The only thing I'm suffering from is a dent in my dignity."

She stares at me for a second longer, as though I've said something nuts, and then realisation must dawn on her, because she smiles. At thirtyish, she's perhaps a year or two older than me, but I can't quite tell because she's wrapped up in layers of winter woollies from top to toe.

"What are you doing out here alone?" she asks as her brows knit together.

I glance around. There's no one else here except the two of us.

"I could ask you the exact same thing," I say, and she laughs.

"Yes, good point. Although I'm guessing you're not from around these parts?"

"You mean the fact I've slipped down the bank? I simply wasn't looking where I was going."

"No, the fact you didn't use the path that leads down to the water."

I gaze to where she's pointing and my cheeks burn once again.

"Oh, I guess you're right. I didn't notice that track before."

The stranger shakes her head. "Never mind. Let's get you up and make sure you're okay."

She looks as though she's going to try and help me, so I rise to my feet unaided, to prove I'm quite capable and still in one piece.

"So, no bones broken, then?" she asks, and I'm touched by her concern.

"Honestly, I'm fine. I'm just a little shaken, that's all."

"Do you need a drink or anything?"

I shake my head. "No, thanks. I have water in my rucksack if I need it."

Jamie pops into my head, his words of warning bouncing against my brain: *Take the rucksack, ye ken? Just in case ye get lost, or worse, injured.* I despise that he clearly has more sense than I do, not that I'm about to admit it.

The woman takes a step back and I try to brush the dirt from the back of my clothes.

"By the way, I'm Maddie," I say, in way of an introduction.

"Hi, I'm Bridget." She gives me a cute little wave. We both laugh and I don't feel quite so uncomfortable in her presence anymore.

"Do you live locally?" I ask.

Bridget shakes her head. "No, I'm on holiday. I'm staying in a remote cottage a couple of miles from here."

"What? Alone?" I can't keep the surprise out of my voice.

"Yes. I try to visit here three or four times a year. I write, so it's a perfect location."

I nod. If I was a writer, this would be exactly where I'd want to be, too.

Bridget points to the stone. "Did you come here today to see the memorial?"

I nod again. "Yeah, I wanted to see what all the fuss was about."

She stands aside to let me pass. "Go ahead. It's certainly worth the trek."

I hesitate, fearful I might slip again, but Bridget powers full steam ahead and makes her way to the edge of the stream. I'm not so sure-footed and walk behind, treading with care in her footsteps.

The stone is little more than two metres high by a metre wide, but there's something haunting about it. I brush my fingers against its solid rock. It's ice cold to the touch and I'm quick to pull my hand away.

Bridget stands beside me and explains the history of the memorial.

"This rock is a symbolic reminder of the clansmen who died fighting in a most harrowing battle in April seventeen-forty-six. This monument was erected to face north, towards the battlefield of Culloden. Those who come here pay their respects to their ancestors whose souls will forever wander along the moor."

My gaze sweeps across the chiselled words cut deep into the stone. They're written in Gaelic, though, a dialect centuries old and one I cannot understand.

"I have no idea what the words mean?" I sigh, and turn to Bridget.

"It's the same inscription that's written on a wall at Culloden," she explains. "Translated, it says: 'Our blood is still our father…And ours the valour of the hearts…'.' "

She speaks softly, her lips rounding as she says each word with careful precision. A cold breeze appears from nowhere, perhaps blowing in from off the distant sea. In my mind's eye, I see those fateful clansmen fighting for their lives, for Scotland. A river of red lies before them, the ground soaked in their own blood. I shiver.

"Wow, I have to say: the way you conveyed those words just now sent a chill down my spine."

Bridget shakes her head. "I just think, if you're going to remember the dead, then you do it from the heart."

I nod. "Yes, and you caught the mood perfectly."

"Thanks. I appreciate you saying so."

I glance at my watch. "Sorry, I've got to go. I didn't realise the time, and I'd better get back before my husband sends out a search party."

She gives me a wide grin. "No problem. It's been great meeting you."

"Likewise, and at least my fall wasn't counterproductive."

"Oh, in what way?"

I grin. "I met you."

CHAPTER SEVEN

When I reach the farm gate, I see Jamie sitting on a low wall next to one of the many raised flowerbeds. His rich curly hair has fallen into his eyes and I have a sudden urge to go over and brush it aside. He looks up and waves. I lift my hand and automatically wave back, then push open the gate and make my way along the path towards him, the gravel crunching noisily beneath my feet.

He's playing with one of the farm dogs, a cute black fluffy Collie with a white patch splashing one ear. Its inquisitive eyes flick towards me, then he barks and jumps up onto his hind legs, keen to make my acquaintance. A long, narrow nose twitches as he takes on board my scent. Jamie holds his collar and the dog wags its tail. I hold my hand out and it's diligently sniffed before the tips of the fingers are licked. I chuckle, the dog's tongue is like sandpaper, and it tickles.

"What happened to ye," Jamie asks, pointing to my filthy jeans. I look down and see streaks of dried mud running past my thigh, right down to just below my knee.

I shrug. "Nothing much. I just had a fight with a tuft of grass."

He chuckles, and I'm about to confess all about my good Samaritan when Callum calls my name and I see him heading from the cottage towards us.

"Hey, you're back," he says. "Did you enjoy yourself?"

I nod. "Yes, very much, and to be honest, it was quite an eyeopener." He pecks me on the cheek then turns to his brother. "Have you finished up for the day?"

"Aye, I have, and I'm making the most of it." He throws a tennis ball down the yard for the dog, who shoots off like a bullet out of a gun. I laugh, and so does Jamie.

"He's fast," I say.

Jamie grins. "That he is, and he's intelligent, too."

The dog comes back with the ball in its mouth and drops it at my feet.

"Och, he likes ye," Jamie teases, and I roll my eyes and grin. I crouch down to pick up the ball, but Callum kicks it out of my reach.

"Hey, what did you do that for?" I moan. "I wanted to play."

"Never mind the damn dog, we've got to decide what we're going to do with the rest of our holiday." The words have no sooner left his mouth when his phone rings. He reaches into the back pocket of his jeans and removes it, peering at the screen.

"I've got to take this," he says and pushes a button, placing the phone to his ear.

"Hello. Yes, this is Callum McKinley speaking." His voice, his tone, is now sweet, like honey. He can be such a charmer and I move closer, curious to learn who's on the line, but he walks away from me, although I can still hear his every word.

"Uh-huh, are you sure? So, when did this happen? Yes, of course. Leave it with me and I'll get back to you as soon as I can."

He swivels around, his face a picture of pure joy, his elation so infectious that I smile back at him.

"Who was that?" I ask, "on the phone."

"It was Lord Fornhill's solicitor. By all accounts, his lordship has sacked Bradley. The solicitor says the millionaire wishes to come back to the firm."

He scratches his head, clearly unable to digest the unexpected conversation he's just had, then he looks back at me.

"Apparently, he's seen Bradley for the conniving scumbag he is and requested that I run his account."

He beams at me and I'm genuinely pleased for him.

"That's fantastic news, honestly; I'm so thrilled it's all worked out in the end." My smile fades. "But does this mean we'll be leaving straightaway?"

He shakes his head. "No, of course not, but I'll have to set off early Thursday morning."

He does a sideways glance at Jamie, who then jumps to his feet.

"Right. I'll…er…leave ye to discuss yir plan of action," Jamie says, and strolls off, the dog close at his heels.

"But tomorrow's Wednesday," I huff at Callum. "It doesn't give us much time." A wave of sadness washes over my entire body, and I guess it shows in my face, because he comes closer.

"Don't worry. I won't be gone forever. Why don't you stay here and I'll come back once everything's sorted?"

I force my lips into a pout. "And how long will that take?"

"Not long. Just a few days. I'll be back after the weekend. Stay here and unwind. Keira won't mind running the shop for a few more days, surely? She loves it."

I seriously don't know what to say. Part of me wants to stay, but the other wants to return with my husband.

"But, Cal, there's no point me being here on my own. This trip was supposed to help us reconnect. It isn't right me being here without you."

He shakes his head. "Maddie, I insist. There's no point in us both being dragged back to work. Enjoy your time away and get to grips with the great outdoors. We've got the rest of our lives together, so a few days apart won't hurt. And besides, this place is good for you. Already you're far more relaxed than I've seen you in ages."

"Okay," I whisper, without an ounce of enthusiasm. "If that's what you want."

He nods, "It is. And this way, everyone's a winner," and his cheeks dimple into a smile. "Come on, let's go inside and tell granda the good news."

***

"I'm telling you, you could have knocked me over with a feather."

Granda lets out a chuckle. "Well, it dinnae take Bradley long to show his true colours. And what a bonus. Fancy Lord Fornhill askin' for ye personally."

It's after supper, and I'm sitting in one of the red Chesterfield sofas, listening to Callum talk tirelessly about his return to favour. I snuggle down. The leather is soft against my skin and the room warm and cosy. A fire roars in the hearth. The orange and red flames dance wildly and the heat has turned everyone's cheeks pink.

The room reminds me of something out of Country Life magazine. It's quaint with its large picture windows and classy antique furniture. The floor is highly polished, covered in thick colourful rugs, and the pristine curtains are made of raw silk. I'm aware it's down to Hetty keeping everything spick and span. I've yet to meet her. She's like a ghost, invisible, and I swear she only comes out at night. Yet, when I went into the kitchen earlier, I found a mountain of goodies she'd brought up from the village.

On the wall, there's a large coat of arms. The McKinley crest is red, emblazoned with two stags, both standing tall on their hind legs. I'm reminded of Callum's heritage, of a family tree which originated on the rocky Hebridean islands. Their name is said to go as far back as the tenth century.

I know little of my own. My parents were killed in a car accident when I was just nine years old. Their death left me with no family. I'd been in the car with them when it happened, but I have no recollection of the accident. My only memory is of being in hospital and of the kind nurse who tended to the severe cuts and bruises I suffered. I clung to her as though she was a lifeline, but it was no use. Within days she'd been sent to another ward and I was left to fend for myself.

A strange man with narrow eyes and large black glasses came to visit me whilst I was still in hospital. He carried a shiny black briefcase with a gold-plated combination lock. He opened the case to reveal a thick wad of official paperwork. He explained to me, in words which I was too young to understand at the time, that I was deemed far too old for adoption and therefore fell under the care of Social Services. He checked my details, my date of birth and my last known address, before taking my hand in his and guiding me to his car, a sleek racing green Jaguar, as I recall. I sat on the cold back seat, fearful of where I was heading—terrified of being left alone. The fear, and the abandonment I felt that day, has never truly left me.

I stand up and go over to the mantelpiece, from where I pick up a photograph of Callum's mum and dad, both living in America now. I glance over at Callum. He's discussing with Jamie the undoubted demise of Bradley O'Conner. I glance back at the photograph, staring down at a woman who barely finds the time to speak to her sons twice a year.

I brush my fingertips across the glass, over her face, as though this gesture will enable me to touch her physically.

"Can ye see a resemblance?" Alasdair asks, close to my ear.

I replace the picture and turn towards him.

"Yes, I can; it's the curly auburn hair."

"Aye, and the shape of the eyes. Dougal ne'er got a look in."

I glance at their father. He's a thin weedy man with a long neck and jet-black hair.

Alasdair's right: the twins look nothing like their father.

"Have you heard from your son or daughter-in-law lately?" I ask.

Alasdair shakes his head and sighs. "Are ye kidding me! They're both too busy dinin' with the president of the United States to think about the likes of us."

I too let out a sigh. "I understand what you mean. They didn't even make it to our wedding. She wrote us a letter, explaining that, with his dad being in the oil business, they couldn't possibly get away at such short notice. Strange, considering we gave them eight months. More than enough time, I would have thought, to make any crucial arrangements so they could attend their own son's wedding."

Alasdair pats me gently on the hand. "It pains me to admit it, but they've grown a wee bit big for their breeches. However, their loss is my gain."

I cup his hand in mine. He's been a wonderful father figure to both Callum and Jamie. It must have been hard for the boys, though, to live at boarding school for most of their young lives and then to come home to just one grandparent. He raised them to work hard and be independent young men, and although he doesn't have much money, Callum would never ask his parents for a penny.

I let go of Alasdair's hand and he heads over to the drinks cabinet. To my surprise, he pulls out a bottle of Bollinger.

"I think we should toast Lord Fornhill for coming to his senses," he declares, unscrewing the small metal cage that protects the cork. He throws it onto the counter before forcing the champagne cork out with his thumbs. "May he come to realise that a McKinley is always the right man for the job." The cork flies into the air and hits the ceiling with a pop.

I clap my hands in celebration and stare over at my husband. He's beaming from ear to ear, and I can honestly say I've never seen him look so proud.

Alasdair pours the bubbly into four crystal flutes, coming over and placing one in my hand. He gives me a wink.

"I always have a bottle handy. Ye ken? Just in case."

I don't catch his meaning, not at first, but then, to my horror, he gently pats my tummy. My heart skips a beat as I realise what he's been trying to say. I suddenly feel like my life has no purpose without the child Alasdair's expecting to appear at some point in my married life.

He turns away, unaware of the pain he's caused, and offers a glass of champagne to Callum. "Ye see, boy, ye just needed a little patience. If this here Lord Fornhill has his wits about him, he'll be thanking ye for taking him on."

Alasdair thrusts a glass into Jamie's hand and we all move to the centre of the room, so we can toast Callum's success.

I refuse to let Alasdair's innocent comment ruin the entire evening. It's tough, but I'll have to learn to live with unexpected remarks like his for the rest of my life.

"To Lord Fornhill," Alasdair cries.

"To Lord Fornhill," we echo and raise our glasses into the air.

I sip my drink and the bubbles go up my nose. I laugh out loud, rubbing my nostrils to relieve the tickle.

"You're supposed to drink it, not snort it," Jamie chuckles, and I suffer a fit of the giggles.

"Oh, now you tell me," I say, and my attention flicks over to Callum.

I don't know why, but I expect him to be watching me, but he's too busy talking to granda, thanking him for the champagne.

Jamie offers me a tissue, which I readily accept. His gaze jumps from me to Callum and then back to me again.

"Mark my words, he'll be head of the company by the end of the year."

I nod. I don't doubt it for a second.

"So, are we still on for tomorrow night?" I ask.

To my surprise, Jamie chokes on his champagne, but he's quick to regain his composure.

"Er, sorry, what do ye mean?"

My brows knit together. "The quiz night at the Scran and Sleekit."

The tension in his face dissolves and he lets out a light sigh.

"Och, aye, that's still on the cards if ye wannae go?"

"Yes, of course I do. I've been looking forward to socialising with the locals."

"Aye, they're a friendly bunch," he declares, "and it's guid you're keen to mingle. Tell me, though, how did ye get on at the memorial stone today? Ye ne'er did say how ye ended up covered in mud."

Heat flushes my cheeks, only this time it isn't from the fire. I laugh again, take a gulp of champagne and give a dismissive flick of my hand. "Oh, it was nothing. I just wasn't looking where I was going and ended up in a heap."

Jamie's forehead creases with concern. "Ye sure ye dinnea hurt yourself?"

I rub the back of my head to find the lump is still there. "I'm fine, if not a tad embarrassed," I admit and quickly change the subject. "Besides, I saw a golden eagle on the way and took a photo to prove it."

I search for my mobile, but I've left it in the cottage and let out a sigh. "Oh, never mind. I'll show you tomorrow."

"And what of the stone? Was it as ye imagined?

"Oh, no. The memorial wasn't what I expected at all."

"And what did you expect?"

I shrug. "I can't quite put my finger on it, but the words…they…well, they struck a chord. All those brave clansmen and women who lost their lives."

"Aye, and all we have left are ghost stories to scare the wee bairns. Many say they can feel the clansmen's presence. Did ye?"

"I'm not sure," I confess. "Although, it was as though the dead knew I was there remembering them. To be honest, I found the place a little eerie. And, I met this…"

Jamie interrupts my flow with a nudge from his elbow. "Talking of eerie, did ye ken it's a new moon this Saturday? There's a festival this weekend, and the local witches are holding a pagan ritual down by the water at dusk."

My eyes grow wide. "No, you never said."

He grins. "Aye, well, 'twas Claire who got me interested in paganism. She liked having flowers in her hair and nothing on her feet. She said it made her feel closer to nature."

"Oh, I have to agree. I visited a pagan festival once. I was still at college and got invited by a friend. It was held near Stonehenge, and I confess, the music stole my heart. Such haunting melodies. The drums they used were soulful, and the guitars… Everyone was swaying to the beat and dancing. Some wore homemade sandals, whilst others went barefoot. It was uplifting to see young and old mixed together in perfect harmony. And when I left, I felt so at peace with the world."

"Aye, it can have that kind of an effect on ye."

"Will there be a priestess performing the ritual?"

Jamie's voice turns into a whisper. "Och, aye. Usually, she makes an altar close to the stone, then welcomes in the new moon. Most of the local women dress in long flowing robes and chant a few wee spells. It's a great evening if it doesnae rain. Then they have a cake and ale ceremony; that's my favourite part."

I'm intrigued. "I've never seen practicing witches before, or witnessed a cake and ale ceremony. Would you take me, please?"

Jamie nods and sips his champagne. "Sure, if ye can handle such excitement, and all in one night."

***

It's late by the time I ring Keira again. "Hey, it's me. Sorry, did I wake you?"

"No, of course not. I've been sitting here waiting for your call."

"I'm sorry…about this afternoon. I shouldn't have burdened you with my mess-of-a-life."

Keira's tone changes in an instant. "Seriously, if you hadn't and I'd ended up hearing it from somebody else, I'd physically kill you."

I chuckle because I know she would.

"So, how was tonight?" she asks.

"Much better. But that's mainly due to Callum receiving a phone call offering him the Fornhill account."

"Wow, that's great news. Does this mean you're coming home?"

"Well, Cal says he's leaving for work first thing Thursday morning, but wants me to stay on until after the weekend. I said I'd come home, but he insisted. I'm just concerned he might be delayed and you're left—"

"I seriously hope you're not worrying about the shop?"

"No, but I wouldn't want you thinking I'm taking advantage of you, that's all."

Keira lets out a sigh. "As if."

"I'm serious. I wanted to check with you first, to make sure you're happy to continue running the florist in my absence."

She clicks her tongue in the roof of her mouth— an annoying habit she picked up after hitting puberty.

"Like you need to ask. Of course, it's fine. I've told you before: stay as long as it takes to get you two back on track. Besides, the shop's thriving and I haven't run off with the takings…yet."

"I'd hunt you down and stab you with a prickly rose if you did," I tell her, and Keira lets out a chuckle.

"Ah, just the thought is enough to keep me on the straight and narrow," but then she hesitates. "And what about Jamie? Have you given him a wide berth?"

"I told you, he was a mistake."

"Good. I'm just checking. I don't want any more revelations that could cause me sleepless nights."

I play with a strand of hair and curl my feet under a cushion on the sofa. I enjoy hearing her voice. She cares what happens to me and it soothes me. By the time we finish catching up, the clock on the wall chimes midnight.

I'm far more relaxed when I end the call and head to the bathroom, to clean my teeth and undress. The bottom of my spine still hurts, though. I turn on the tap, fill a glass with cold water and take two painkillers, then swill my mouth and replace the glass.

My bare feet fall silent as I come out of the bathroom and into the bedroom. I adore this room, decorated with its blue and white chintz. The bed frame's white, the mattress thick and luxurious. I switch on a bedside lamp and smooth my hand over the duvet before flicking over the corner, then climb into bed, easing my aching limbs onto the cold sheet. Once I've punched my pillows into shape and made myself comfortable, I pick up a book from off the bedside table and open it at its bookmark. I want to try and wait up for Callum, to talk to him. So far today, we've hardly had the chance to say two words to each other.

I've only read a few pages before my eyelids grow heavy, unaware when the book slips from my fingers and onto the floor. I don't hear Callum come to bed an hour or so later, or feel the gentle kiss he plants on my forehead. Nor am I aware that he picks up the book and places it onto the bedside table, or that he strokes my face as he switches off the light.

CHAPTER EIGHT

Jamie

I enter the kitchen and sit at the table, reaching for the morning paper. My stomach tightens as I glance at today's date: Wednesday, 23rd of February.

I feel a draught against my cheek as the kitchen door swings open.

"Hey, bro, looks to be the start of a mighty fine day."

I tear my eyes from the newspaper. "Speak of the devil and he's sure to appear," I say, turning over the page.

Maddie enters the room. She comes and stands beside me.

"Morning, Jamie," she says lightly, "any tea in the pot?"

I nod, glare at Callum and then focus my eyes back towards the headlines. Brexit is still hitting the news and I try to digest the words, but I swear to God I can feel Callum's eyes burning right through the back of my skull. I throw the newspaper down onto the kitchen table and the chair scrapes against the stone floor as I rise.

"Going somewhere?" Callum asks, cocking his head to one side.

"Aye, I'm off to clean out the stables."

Maddie takes a sharp intake of breath.

"Oh, would you like help with that?"

I stop and turn towards her. I want to say no, to ask her to stay away from me, but I can't. She's standing there, her eyes keen, and I clench my jaw, unwilling to give in. But she bounces from one foot to the other, like a little school kid.

"Come on Jamie, let me."

I lean against the doorframe. "Aye, all right, if ye wannae come, that's fine with me."

She gives me the widest grin I've ever seen as she dashes past, then I hear her scrabbling about in the hallway, searching for her boots.

I turn to leave, but Callum rushes over and grabs me by the arm.

"Tell me you'll go through with it," he hisses, close to my ear. My muscles tense and I yank my arm free, then turn towards him, our faces just millimetres away from one another. We're so close, our noses almost touch.

"Nae. I'll do no such thing," I say through gritted teeth. "Not now, not ever."

His eyes search mine as though he's looking deep inside my soul, his expression unfathomable, until he lets out a defeated sigh. I turn away, leaving him standing there, alone.

"Are you all right?" Maddie asks when I slam the kitchen door behind me. I thrust my fingers through my hair and put on a painted smile.

"Aye, I'm grand, lassie. I just need to get a move on."

"Wait for me," I hear her cry as I make for the outer door, but I don't. I keep on going, out into the yard. I'm angry and afraid, afraid of what I might say to her. I can't do what my brother asks of me, yet I'm filled with guilt. I'm not to blame for the predicament they find themselves in, and I curse my brother for ever having told me the truth. However, no matter how much he begs, I could never fulfil this wildest desire of his.

I lift the latch and pull open the door to one of the large sheds. Inside, I fish out a wheelbarrow and a couple of pitchforks and a shovel. I throw them into the barrow and use it to push the doors wide as I make my way out.

"Out the way, Maddie," I cry; "I dinnae want to run ye over."

She laughs and grabs hold of one of the pitchforks.

"You just try it and you'll feel the sharp end of a prong up your arse," and she pretends to stab my backside with the fork.

A smile reaches my lips. "Och, I'd better watch out, then."

She giggles. "Yes, you'd better, or you'll not be able to sit down for a week."

I push the barrow through the yard and she follows. I really don't want her around me, but although I'm loath to admit it…my dark mood is lifting, if just a little. Perhaps having Maddie around isn't so bad after all.

We head straight for the stable block. Starsky has his black head out of the stable door. As we approach, he shakes his mane and lets out a snort. It's his way of saying hello. Maddie lets out a squeal of pure delight.

"He's such a character," she says, "and gorgeous with it."

My heart lurches in my chest. In a different life, a different time…I could say the same about Maddie. I put down the wheelbarrow and head over to the tack room, where I grab a headcollar and lead rope.

"Let's start with the stallion," I say when I get back, and I offer the collar to Maddie. She takes it and strokes the horse's forehead before pushing the straps up over his nose and towards his ears. She makes sure it's snug and secure before clipping the lead rope onto a ring on his headcollar, now at the side of his mouth.

She nods to say she's ready and I unbolt the stable door.

"Why don't ye take him down to the lower field?" I suggest. She stares at me as though I've gone stark raving mad, but then her expression changes to one of pleasant surprise.

"Are you sure it's okay?" she asks, leading the stallion out into the yard. "Only, I've never handled any of the horses before."

"Och, you'll be fine. Keep him on a short leash and you'll have nae bother."

She grins and I can see her excitement grow. I'm amazed how such a small gesture has made her day. I keep a watchful eye on her as she guides the horse away from the stable block and onto the track that leads to the field. She's a natural with horses, that's plain to see, for Starsky's now become putty in her hands. I can hear her talking to him, passing the time of day as if he were human, to which he snorts and grunts in reply. Yes, Maddie certainly has a way with horses.

I concentrate on mucking out the stable, soon filling the wheelbarrow with a mixture of manure, and damp hay and straw. I'm almost done by the time she gets back. Maddie helps me cover the floor, laying a fresh straw bed which quickly drowns out the musky odour of urine with its own dry and dusty smell.

"Maddie, can I ask ye something…something personal?"

She stops what she's doing and leans on the pitchfork.

"Yeah, sure; what is it?"

I stare at her, not sure where to begin, then clear my throat. "The thing is… Callum told me something the other night when I took him into town."

"Oh, yeah. Like what?"

I lick my lips. "Och, Maddie, I dinnae wish to pry, but he said that ye couldnae have a bairn. I've been cut up about it ever since he told me. Is there nothing anyone can do to help ye?"

She drops the pitchfork, lets out a deep sigh and then goes and sits on a small bale of hay.

I swallow. I've clearly upset her.

"Maddie, are ye all right, lass?"

She puts her head in her hands. "What? Oh, your question… Yes, it's all true; we can't have children, and no, no one can help us."

"I'm sorry, Maddie, I had nae right to ask."

She lifts her head and glares at me. "Then why did you?"

I sense her anger, her bitterness, and shrug. "I dunno. I think I just dinnea believe it, ye ken? 'Tis a lot to take in."

She turns her head away, but not before teardrops drip from her lashes. I'm then by her side, down on bended knees.

"Maddie, I dinnae mean to make ye cry." I frantically search for a hanky, pulling one out from inside my pocket, and go to wipe her face. I expect a rebuff, or for her to slap my hand away, but she doesn't. She allows me gently to wipe the tears away, but more continue to fall.

She finally looks back at me. "We've tried everything," she whispers. "Even three sessions of IVF." Those same teardrops catch the light and now sparkle like diamonds. They may be beautiful, but they only enhance her look of sorrow.

"Did Callum tell you why we can't have children?"

I heave a sigh. "Aye, he did. Said he's infertile."

She nods. "Yes, that's right. The last time they managed to find one living sperm and placed it with my egg. I knew then it was our last hope, so when it failed…"

"I'm sorry, Maddie, for yir loss; and for asking."

She dries her eyes with the palms of her hands and rises to her feet. "It's fine. You're my brother-in-law. You should know what we're going through. It's been horrible having to suffer without the support of close family."

"Och, you'll always have mine," I tell her, and rise to squeeze her shoulders gently.

She stares deep into my eyes. "Do you know what the worst thing is?"

I shake my head; I can't even begin to imagine.

"It's the baby hunger. I'm tormented, every minute of every day, no matter where I go. If I visit the park, all I see are mummies and daddies pushing their prams, swinging toddlers and buying their kids ice cream. Or…or…I'll log onto Facebook to find my newsfeed full of ultrasound scan pictures, their threads filled with expressions of congratulations to the happy couple."

Again, I shrug. "It must be hard for ye both."

She turns on me then and bares her teeth, like a wounded animal.

"Hard? Christ, that doesn't even come close. What pain do you think comes after all that? Well, I'll tell you: it's their birth, their first steps, first words, their first birthday. It's listening to other women moaning about being a mother while I'm dying to be one," and she thumps her chest with her hands, over and over.

"Maddie, it's okay; I understand," I soothe, but she isn't listening. She's consumed with grief, then her voice rises as she pulls away.

"Being unable to have a baby sours friendships and destroys marriages," she cries, just inches from my face. "For Christ sake, Jamie, look at mine."

She bursts into tears and I pull her towards me, taking her in my arms. I hold her close, rock her two and fro as she sobs unconsolably against my chest.

"I'm such a dick," I chastise myself. "I've hurt ye and I ne'er meant to. I just wanted to hear yir side of the story, to get to grips with what's happened from yir perspective."

She sobs for what seems like an age, until the cries turn to whimpers. She's calmer now, just light sniffles, and then she pulls away. Her shoulders are hunched over, her eyes red and swollen. She glances up and offers me a weak smile.

"I've…er…got to go," she says, and before I can stop her, she dashes from the stable. I chase after her, but to my despair I see Alasdair walking towards us. I stop dead in my tracks as Maddie runs towards him and he opens his arms, embracing her. I can see his lips moving, but the wind catches his words, sweeping them away. Although I can't hear what he says, when he looks across at me, I can read the expression on his face. Oh, yeah; I really am a complete prick.

***

When I open the main door to the farmhouse and take a deep breath, I inhale a spicy aroma: beef curry, my favourite dish. My mouth waters at the thought of eating some tender chunks of sirloin covered in a rich madras sauce. Then Maddie's laughter comes to my ears and a niggle of uncertainly crawls down my spine, unsure what kind of a response I'll receive when I open the kitchen door.

I hang up my jacket, take off my boots and reluctantly head for the warmest room in the house. Tonight, though, I expect a chill in its air.

I push the door wide open.

"Oh, there you are," says Callum, cheerily. "I thought you were never coming home." He's standing at the cooker, stirring the curry sauce whilst Maddie lays the table for supper. I try not to make eye contact, but I've already clocked that she's wearing a pretty red blouse and a tight black pencil skirt. The top is flattering and shows off her neckline, revealing milky white skin. Her skirt clings to her thighs and I force myself to avert my gaze.

I clear my throat. "We don't usually have curry on a Wednesday," I say to Alasdair, who's busy serving up rice.

"Aye, ye right; 'twas Callum's idea. He thought ye deserved a treat." He turns towards me, his eyes narrowed: his way of telling me that he doesn't agree. My gut churns. Let him believe what he likes; after all, he isn't aware of what's really happening here.

"What time does the quiz start?" Callum asks, pouring the madras over the rice.

I have to think for a second. "Er, about seven o'clock." I head over to the sink and give my hands a thorough scrub, ready for supper.

"I'm not too fussed what time we get there," Callum explains, "but Maddie says she'd like to enter."

I turn towards her, my hands covered in soap. She's been busy folding napkins and placing them inside the wine glasses, but looks up on hearing her name.

"Isn't that right?" Callum says.

She nods and gives a warm smile. "Yes, why not. After all, there's no point going if we can't take part."

Callum's eye catches mine and we exchange glances. I'm no fool, and I don't have to be his twin to know what he's really thinking. Irritated, I turn away.

I rinse my hands under the hot tap and dry them on a hand towel. I can't explain it, but my nerves are jangling like alarm bells and my stomach's churning into knots. I try to shake off the feeling of trepidation, but it won't budge. I'm dreading tonight. Callum appears to be living in hope that I'll sleep with Maddie. How many times do I have to say no before he gets it into his thick skull that it's never going to happen?

I head over to the kitchen table. As I approach, Maddie sits down, and I take a seat at the opposite side of the table.

Alasdair and Callum bring over the food and the smell makes my mouth water yet again. As the plate is placed in front of me, I take a deep breath and inhale the spicy aroma of Turmeric, Cumin and Ground Coriander, licking my lips in anticipation. Although my stomach's in knots, I'm still ravenous.

As I pick up my fork, Maddie flicks her napkin and folds it neatly across her lap.

"Alasdair, why don't you come along tonight?" she asks.

He shakes his head and chuckles. "Nae, lass, it's not my idea of a guid night out. I'd have more fun chewing a brick."

She laughs, "Oh, don't be such a spoilsport. We're going to need all the help we can get."

"Aye, maybe so, but if it's brains you're after, you've come to the wrong place."

I watch Maddie out of the corner of my eye. She's thoughtful and loving, and right now, at this very moment in time, I believe Callum doesn't deserve her. The light shimmers across her face and I notice the long silver earrings she's wearing. They elongate her neck and her dark red lipstick emphasises her cupid-bow lips. I don't mean to catch her attention but I do, and she blinks those liquid blue eyes at me.

"What about you, Jamie? Are you a walking encyclopaedia?"

"Nah, I take after granda. I'm more brawn than brains. Get me to wrestle a pig or a sheep and ye might be onto a winner."

Her gaze flits towards Callum. He's now sitting at the kitchen table, an amused expression on his face. Her gaze returns to me. "I'll have to remember that the next time I need some muscle."

"Och, you dinnea need mine, not when you've got Callum."

She shrugs. "Really. Now that would be a first."

***

After dinner, Callum grabs a set of car keys from off the table.

"I'll drive," he says, waving them above his head. "And before you protest, I'll not hear any arguments."

I hesitate. I thought he'd want to enjoy a few pints at least, tonight.

"Don't look so surprised," he says, reading my expression. "Contrary to belief, I don't actually drink—all of the time."

I shake my head. "Och, it's fine. It's yir holiday. I'll drive so ye can make the most of yir last evening together."

I lean forward, to grab the keys, but Callum clutches them tightly to his chest.

"No, not tonight. Like I said: my treat."

Maddie puts on her coat and reaches for her handbag. "Come on, let's go. I'm feeling lucky," she says. I follow them out of the house, but I'm aware I'm dragging my feet.

I open the car door and climb into the back. Maddie goes around the front and sits beside her husband.

"Brrr, it's freezing," she says with a shiver. She isn't dressed for the weather, in a thin padded jacket with a belt that nips in at the waist. On her feet, there's a pair of red high heels and her legs are clad in black nylon. It's not what women wear around here. It's all wellington boots and waterproof jackets. It's no wonder she's freezing, and tonight, dressed like that, she'll have every man in the room drooling over her.

Callum starts the engine and I catch his gaze in the rear-view mirror, his eyes relaying a message I don't wish to read. They're telling me tonight's the night he hopes I'll sleep with his wife. I glance out of the window, but it's dark and there's nothing to see except my own reflection. A lonely man stares back at me. I close my eyes and rub my thumb and forefinger across my temple. Inside my mind, I try to conjure Claire's face, but it's Maddie's that floats behind my eyes. I blink, and the vision vanishes. I switch my attention towards my brother, his eyes still fixed on mine.

"What are ye looking at?"

"Nothing," he chuckles, averting his gaze. "Besides, I can think of better things to stare at than you." He glances over at Maddie, tips her a wink and then sets off. I can't shake the sense he's still watching me, but every time I flick my gaze at him, his own is fixed elsewhere.

A flicker of light from a nearby farm catches my attention. Its golden glow, its warmth, reminds me why I adore my homeland, although there have been times when I've been tempted to leave this place, this country. Losing Claire destroyed my life, but whenever I think it's time to move on, I look at granda struggling on the farm, and I lose heart.

Callum hits a bump in the road and I avert my gaze from the window.

"Perhaps it's best if I drive," I say as he swerves to miss the curb.

He laughs out loud. "Now, don't be a party pooper. After all, where's the fun in that?"

We arrive at the market square with half an hour to spare. I quickly push open the car door and clamber out, hit by a biting wind which sends a chill straight through to my bones. I watch Maddie pull her jacket that bit closer and Callum puts his arm around her shoulders. It's odd: apart from a kiss, it's the first time during their visit that I've seen him physically touch her.

I look up at the dark sky, catching a glimpse of the crescent moon as it's swallowed whole by thickening cloud. The cold night air has left the streets deserted. Only the light from several street lamps illuminates our way to the Scran and Sleekit. I hold the pub door open for Maddie and Callum, the warmth from the wood burner hitting my cheeks as I follow them in. I'm thankful to be indoors. Maddie points to a vacant table in the far corner of the dining section, and we make our way over, passing a crowd of young revellers enjoying shots at the bar.

"How about I get a round of drinks in?" I say.

"Sounds great. But they're on me," Callum tells me. "Maddie, what will you have?"

She smiles up at him. "A Gin and Tonic, please. And easy on the ice."

"Jamie? What about you?"

I shrug. "I'll come with ye and have a look what's on offer."

106

Maddie sits down at the table and I point to the pub menu. "Why don't ye have a look for next time ye visit. They cook great food here, and I promise ye, the Rosemary and Minted Lamb is to die for."

"All right," she says, and places her handbag down onto the chair next to her before picking up the laminated menu.

"We'll be right back," I say, and Callum and I head towards the pub's entrance and make our way to the front of the bar. The bartender is stacking glasses, and Callum waves a hand in the air to catch his attention. The man puts down an empty crate and hurries over.

"Hey, Stuart, how's it going?" Callum asks.

"Not too bad, thanks. I'm just covering for a lassie who's sick tonight." He greets us both with a firm handshake. "Okay, lads, what can I get ye?"

"I'll have a pint of Stella," I say. "Callum? What will ye have?"

He moves closer to the bar, pondering the choices, leaving me free to steal a quick glance over at Maddie. She's still studying the menu, but she looks lost sitting there, all on her own. There's other customers milling around her yet it's as though she's the only person in the room.

"Isn't that right, Jamie?"

"Eh? Sorry, what was that?" I say as I snap my head back towards Callum.

"Stuart, here, reckons his team's going to win tonight, but I've told him we've got a secret weapon in Maddie."

I laugh and grab my beer. "Yeah, sure; whatever ye say, bro."

"Here," and he thrusts his wife's drink into my hand. "Can you take it to her. I'll be over in a minute."

I nod and head back towards the table. I notice a look of relief sweeps across Maddie's face as I approach.

"Sorry about that," I say. "Callum's busy telling anyone who'll listen that we're going to win tonight. The bartender's an old mate from university."

"Oh, it's fine with me," she says and takes a sip of her Gin and Tonic. "It isn't often he gets the chance to see any of his old friends."

"'Tis true; he's rarely home these days and is a sight for sore eyes to some."

Maddie nods and takes another sip of her drink.

"So, what's yir first impressions?" I ask, pointing to a black and white picture of a famous sculpture of two horse's heads known as *The Kelpies*. "I think they've done a great job giving the old pub a modern twist."

"Yes, it works," she says. "It's certainly pleasant enough, and it seems popular with the locals."

I lean a little closer. "Maddie, about earlier, in the stable. I really am sorry."

She looks down at her drink and wipes condensation off the side of the glass with her index finger.

There's a noise beside us and a door flies open. I glance up to see the landlord make an entrance. He shakes my hand as he passes. "It's guid to see ye here tonight," he says and gives Maddie a welcoming nod. I've known Malcolm since I was a child; played rugby for the county with two of his sons.

He dashes off and goes to stand beside a table that's been prepared especially for tonight's quiz.

"Guid evening, folks," he says, picking up and blowing down a microphone. "I'll be round shortly with pens and paper whilst Susie," he points towards a barmaid, "will be taking yir money."

The pub is much busier now. Most of the tables are occupied and there's a buzz of excitement in the air. There's a commotion, and I turn in my chair to see the regular customers, sitting at the other tables, start to clap their hands and cheer. I glance at Maddie, but her eyes are on them, too. I strain my neck to try and see what's created such an uproar and spot a young couple making their way through the crowd at the bar. The man is all smiles and waving, and the woman, who I recognise as the landlord's daughter, clutches something small to her chest.

My jaw drops when I realise she's carrying a new-born baby, all wrapped in a white knitted shawl.

I turn back to stare at Maddie and watch as her face turns to stone. She doesn't move a muscle, her eyes fixed solely on the child.

Once again, the landlord picks up the mic. "Come here, ye two," he says, gesturing for the couple to make their way over. When they reach him, he puts his arm around his daughter and pulls her close.

"Ladies and Gentlemen. I'm sure ye all recognise young Rhona and her husband, Gordon. And I'm most proud to announce the safe arrival of our first grandson, Findley Fraser McGregor." The whole place erupts with loud cheers and whistles.

I reach out and squeeze Maddie's hand.

"Are ye all right," I ask, but she's quick to snatch her hand away, then jumps to her feet.

"Er, sorry, I have to go to the toilet," and she grabs her bag and hurries through the applauding crowd, into which I watch her disappear. I imagine the sorrow she must feel looking at the child in its mother's arms: to be physically able to bear children and yet not conceive, for the sake of her husband. Maddie's determination to live a life under such constraints reminds me of Claire. All we wanted was to be a family, to have children of our own, but that and our every desire was snatched away in an instant.

I head over to the bar where Callum is still chatting to his old Uni pal. I nudge him and gesture for him to come and talk in private.

"Whatever's the matter?" he asks, his brow creased.

"It's Maddie; did ye see her reaction when she saw the bairn?"

Callum sighs. "Yes, of course I did. But there's nothing I can do."

I shake my head. "It kills me to see her like this. It must be pure torture for her."

Callum places a hand on my shoulder. "She suffers in silence every day. However, as you well know, only you have the power to change all that."

I continue to shake my head. "I cannae do it, Cal. I just cannae."

He drops his hand. "What you need is a stiff drink," he says, and goes to turn towards the bar.

I stop him and give him a half-hearted shrug. "Nah, thanks. I'm not in a drinking mood right now."

"I understand," Callum nods. "Maybe later?"

"Aye, maybe."

Callum turns his attention back to Stuart, and I head towards the table and take a seat. In a little while, Maddie steps out from the ladies' toilets. She's wearing a stiff upper lip, and as she approaches, I notice her eyes scan the crowd to see if anyone is looking at her; judging her from afar, I guess.

"Is everything okay?" I ask when she sits down.

"Yes, I'm fine," and she gives me a weak smile before finishing the last sips of her Gin and Tonic. Her eyes have become bold, her insecurities gone now she's reapplied red lipstick.

"Would ye like another?" I ask, and she nods and offers me her empty glass.

"Sure, why not?"

I stand up from my seat and turn to face the bar. Malcolm, the landlord, is walking towards me, carrying the baby in his arms.

"Ye can tell this wee 'un's made of McGregor stock," he chuckles. "He's got a grip that's as strong as an ox." I look down at the little cherub, at its blue eyes and light tuft of red hair.

110

"Can I hold him please?" and we both turn our heads to see Maddie standing next to us.

"Sure ye can, lassie," says Malcolm with a broad grin. "Go on, sit thee down and I'll pass him over to ye."

Her expression changes to one of excitement as she hurries back to her chair. There's a spark in her eyes that I've never seen before. Malcolm places the child inside her arms and she gasps then giggles.

"He's as light as a feather," she declares. "Somehow, I thought he'd be heavier." The baby starts to cry and she pulls him closer to her breast.

"Shhhh, there now. Everything's going to be all right." She rocks the mite gently, all the while keeping her voice low and soothing. She brushes her lips against his tiny cheek and the baby murmurs then falls silent.

"You're guid with bairns, I see," says Malcolm, clearly impressed. "His mammy says he usually screams his head off for a feed about now."

Maddie turns towards me, her smile triumphant, then she stares down at the child and her expression yields to a look of grateful satisfaction. There's a complete transformation in her body language. She's kind and gentle, and I find this makes her deeply womanly. I'm drawn towards her muliebrity; it's like a hormonal magnet.

She glances up, catches my eye, and smiles. It's soft and tender and I go weak at the knees. Just as quickly, she breaks eye contact when the bairn grabs hold of her little finger.

"You're right, he is strong," she giggles, and her long lashes flicker as she looks up to hold my gaze once more. "I bet if you ever have a boy, Jamie, he'd be a strapping wee man, too," she says, and it's then, right at that moment, that I come face to face with what I must do.

***

Susie the barmaid comes and taps Malcolm on the shoulder.

"It's time for the quiz," she says.

"Och, aye, you're right," he acknowledges. "Sorry, lassie, I've got to go." He bends down and takes Findlay from Maddie's arms. I notice the light in her eyes goes out. Malcolm turns, just as Rhona, Findlay's mum, appears.

"Here ye go, darlin', back to yir mammy," he says, pride still in his voice, and Rhona takes the child into her arms, but then she turns to Maddie.

"Hi," she says, "are ye Callum's wife?"

Maddie nods and jumps to her feet. "Yes. That's right. I am."

"'Tis nice to meet ye. I'm Rhona, and I see you've taken a shine to young Findlay. If ye ever want to pop in and see him, you're more than welcome."

Maddie gives the biggest grin ever. "Can I? That would be lovely," she says.

Rhona flicks a finger towards me. "Jamie, here, knows where I live. He can bring ye next time you're in town."

I nod. "Aye, I can do that."

Rhona waves goodbye. "I'm off to take the wean home," she says and makes a beeline to her waiting husband, standing at the door.

We both sit down, just as Callum returns from the bar. "I've got the pens and paper and I've paid the entry fee," he says, and places the items onto the table. "We just need to think of a team name, and quickly."

"Any ideas?" I ask.

Callum sniggers. "How about Norfolk and Chance?"

Maddie rolls her eyes and sighs. "Do you have to be so uncouth?" she chastises.

Callum looks down at her. "Can you think of something better?"

She nods. "Yeah. I thought we could call ourselves Les Quizerables."

I take a swig of beer and chuckle into my glass. "I like it," I say. "It sounds classy."

"Yup, something you'll never be," Callum jokes.

"Ye, neither, arsehole," I comment, and we both laugh out loud.

Callum jumps up and heads over to register our team.

"'Tis a great name," I say, and Maddie swipes a lose curl away from her cheek.

"Thanks. I stole it from the internet."

Callum rushes back and sits down. "The quiz is set to start," he explains, and a hush sweeps across the entire pub.

"Right, folks, if I can have yir attention," says Malcolm over the mic. "We'll begin with question one: Which James Bond theme song, which starts with the words *Meeting you*, was the only double-O-seven theme song to reach the US charts?"

I can feel a blank expression crossing my face. I flick my gaze towards Callum, who has the exact same look on his face, too.

Maddie picks up a pencil and taps it lightly against the end of the table. "Off the top of your head," she says, "give me some pop artists who were famous for singing on the James Bond movies."

"Shirley Bassey," I say.

"No way," Callum replies, pulling a grimace. "She's way too old."

"How about Sheena Easton; she went to America."

"Hmm. Think of the clue: *Meeting you*," Maddie says and starts humming. "Wait, I think I've got it. Meeting you…with a view to a kill."

"Aye, that's it," I say, and lower my voice to make sure the other teams can't overhear. "Wasn't that a hit for Duran Duran?"

Maddie nods enthusiastically and writes the answer on the piece of paper. "Yes! That's it. Well done, Jamie."

I grin smugly at Callum who glowers at me.

"Beginners luck," he says.

"Ye either have it or ye dinnea," I reply, and Maddie and I mark our victory with a high five.

CHAPTER NINE

It's almost midnight by the time we arrive back at the farm. It's been an entertaining evening, and although we didn't win the quiz, we certainly gave the other contestants a run for their money.

"I've had a fab night," Maddie says, kicking off her shoes. She stands on each leg in turn, so she can massage the balls of her feet. She bends a little too far and loses her balance, grabbing the arm of a nearby chair to stop herself from falling. "Oops, I think I've had one too many," she giggles, then plonks herself down into the chair and tucks her feet underneath her.

"I enjoyed tonight," she adds. "The locals made me very welcome and they're such lovely people." She sits back and closes her eyes. "Oh no, everything's spinning. I think I'm going to suffer a cracking hangover in the morning."

"Away with ye. One more for the road won't kill ye," I say and pour three shots of Whisky. We're in the study and I walk over and nudge her knee with mine. She forces her eyes open and I offer her the nightcap.

She tries to stifle a loud yawn as she takes the tumbler. "Thanks. But after this, I'm off to bed."

I pass a glass to Callum. He's sitting in one of the fireside chairs. "Slàinte mhath," I say and we tip our glasses simultaneously, knocking back the golden liquid in one large gulp.

I go back to the bar server and refill both glasses.

"What does that mean?" Maddie asks, thoughtfully.

"Good health," Callum explains, and he raises his glass towards his wife.

Maddie tries to pronounce the words in Gaelic. "Slanj-uh-va," she says with a hiccup, then she giggles again. "Was that even close?"

Callum grins. "Not bad for a Sassenach."

"Aye, we'll make a Scot out of ye yet," I joke.

"I doubt it," Maddie replies, rolling her eyes. "I didn't even know until tonight that the Loch Ness monster inhabits the second largest lake in Scotland."

"Ah—that maybe so, but remember the loch has the freshest water. 'Tis also the deepest in the whole of Scotland, and why it's able to hide monsters."

Callum chuckles. "Oh, wee Nessie. The folklore never ceases to amaze me. Every time I come home, there's been at least one more sighting."

I lean against a large mahogany desk that sits in the centre of the room.

"And don't forget there's supposed to be more than one monster in the loch, ye ken?" I tease.

Maddie's eyes grow wide. "You mean Nessie's had babies?"

"Aye, so they say, but no one's ever seen them. It's pure speculation."

Maddie turns towards her husband. "Oh, Cal, that reminds me: did you see the new-born baby tonight at the quiz? Wasn't he adorable. Rhona, his mum, says I can pop by and see him anytime I wish."

Callum's grin slides from his face and he takes a large gulp of Whisky.

"That's nice," he presently says, "but don't go getting emotionally attached."

"What do you mean by that?"

"I mean: perhaps it isn't such a good idea."

"Why not?"

"You know why. Don't make me spell it out."

She heaves a sigh and pulls her lips into a tight frown, then stands to place her empty glass on a nearby table.

"I think it's time I went to bed," she says, then makes her way over and kisses me on my cheek. "Goodnight, Jamie, and thanks for a great evening."

She goes to Callum's side but hesitates before her lips rest against his. "Night, Cal."

"I'll come with you," he says, and starts to rise from his chair. His movements are slow, half-hearted.

Maddie put's a hand against his chest. She shakes her head and smiles, but her smile doesn't reach her eyes. "No, you stay. Finish your drink. You can join me later." She shoves her shoes back on and heads for the door, and without a backward glance, closes it behind her.

"I can't carry on like this for much longer," Callum whispers into his glass. "I feel so guilty that I'm unable to give her what she wants. I know she pretends everything's okay, but without a child of her own, it's as though she's on self-destruct."

I throw back my head, downing the last of my Whisky. "Are ye sure you're not willing to adopt?"

Callum shakes his head. "No, as selfish as it sounds, I just can't. It wouldn't be Maddie's baby or mine. I couldn't bond with someone who wasn't ours from the start. The thought makes me shiver inside. I'd always be…detached."

"And you'll nae reconsider?"

"Never. It's our blood or nothing."

I clear my throat nervously.

"Okay. Against my better judgement, I'll do it."

Callum shoots me a confused stare. "You'll do what?"

"I'll sleep with Maddie, if ye still want me to."

Callum bolts upright. His jaw drops, his eyes now wide in disbelief.

"Are you serious?" he asks. "I mean: you're not fucking with me, are you?"

I slam my empty tumbler down onto the desk. "Christ, Cal, like I'd ever joke about sleeping with yir wife."

Callum jumps to his feet and grabs hold of me, pulling me close. His eyes search mine, as though if he stares long enough he'll find the answer there.

"What changed your mind?" he asks.

I let out a sigh, shrug him off and go and sit in one of the fireside chairs. Callum follows and sits directly opposite.

I look down at my hands. They're shaking. "If I'm honest, Maddie did."

"But how? When?"

"I spoke to Maddie at the stables. I asked her, when we were mucking out the horses, what it was like not being able to have children."

"And what did she say?"

"More than I deserve. I shouldn't have gone prodding and poking about in her personal life like that. I simply had nae right."

"Just tell me what she said that changed your mind?"

I jump to my feet. "I cannae pinpoint one exact moment," I confess.

Callum lets out a frustrated sigh. "But something must have triggered this change of heart?"

"Aye, tonight at the quiz. When I spoke to her, it was as though something just clicked inside my head. It was as though I understood her pain. I came to realise just how much she desperately wants...no, *needs* a child of her own. It's as though without a bairn she's empty inside, and my asking her those questions earlier must have ripped her heart out."

"Sit down," Callum insists. "I need to get my head around all this."

I stumble into one of the chairs and Callum presses a hand to my shoulder.

"Don't be so hard on yourself," he tells me. "You just wanted to learn the truth from both sides."

"Aye, maybe you're right. But tonight, at the pub, I saw her face when she held that bairn in her arms. I've never seen her look so radiant. She was a different person. She came alive and she was happy. I cannnae turn my back on her now, and I cannae deny her a chance to become a mother, either."

I watch Callum go back to the bar server, where he pours two more Whiskies, soon placing one in my hand. "Here, drink this, then we'll change clothes."

I stare up at my brother. "Do you understand the implications of what I'm about to do?" I whisper. "They'll be no turning back once I leave this room."

Callum drops his voice an octave. "I understand and take full responsibility."

"And if I do this, it must remain our secret forever."

Callum nods. "I'll take it to the grave if I have to."

"Then let's pray we don't ever live to regret what we've now agreed to do."

***

I open the front door and let myself into the cottage. Large black shapes, silhouetted by the darkness, rise and fall before me like ghostly giants as I make my way through the living room and head for the doorway to the stairs.

The only sound is my own breathing, which does nothing to help calm my taut nerves. When I reach the bottom of the stairs, I look up towards the landing, a part of me expecting Claire to be standing there, waiting for me to come to bed. We had such hopes, such dreams together.

I curl my fingers around the bannister, the wood cool against my skin, then lift my foot and take the first step, climbing each in turn. My heart beats loudly in my chest and I'm fearful of waking Maddie. It's as though my own body will betray me.

I'm dressed head to foot in Callum's clothes. Our tastes are not so different; jeans and a long-sleeved shirt. We've changed everything, right down to our socks, shoes and underwear. I pull the neck of his shirt away from my throat, smelling his aftershave on its collar. It's clean and fresh and citrusy. When I reach the top of the stairs, I stand there in the darkness for what seems like an age. There's a slit of light shining down the hallway from the master bedroom, the door slightly ajar.

Slowly, I make my way towards it, inching closer to the bedroom with each step I take. I'm filled with nervous energy, my hands shaking when I lift them into the light of the moon coming in through a window, then it seems I'm there, pushing the door wide open.

I don't want to disturb Maddie. She's fast asleep, her tousled blond hair fanned out across her pillow. It reminds me of yellow corn, and I can't deny she looks beautiful lying there. Her cupid-bow lips are alluring and seductive and her long dark lashes flicker, like butterfly wings, in her sleep.

As I draw nearer, I slowly unbutton my shirt and gaze at her beauty, her skin creamy white, like porcelain. A deep sigh escapes me, for her lips are so tantalisingly plump and moist. They make me want to kiss her, to taste her.

As though in a dream, I gently brush my lips against hers and she stirs and I take a step back, afraid she'll awaken and realise I'm an imposter. I convince myself there's no way she could tell the difference between Callum and me. Even Alasdair has difficulty telling us apart at times.

Taking a deep breath, I chide myself for overreacting and close my eyes and calm my beating heart.

When I blink my eyes open, it's to let out a sigh of relief at seeing Maddie still sleeping.

I brush my hand across the counterpane of the bed; it feels familiar, the quilt soft beneath my fingers, and a vision of Claire materialises inside my head. I see us both naked, wrapped in each other's arms, making love on this very bed. Even when I squeeze my eyes tight shut, to obliterate the memory, it doesn't fade. I sit on the edge of the bed and untie my laces, then take off my shoes.

"Callum?" Maddie murmurs without opening her eyes.

I freeze for a moment, then whisper, "Go back to sleep," and she turns onto her side and mumbles something incoherent.

I wait for her to settle and listen to her breathing, watching her chest rise and fall. When I think it's safe, I gently pull back the covers.

"I love you," she mutters and flings herself onto her back.

I unclasp my belt and unfasten my trousers, letting them slide past my hips and down onto the floor.

***

Maddie

"Callum, don't leave," I say.

"Maddie, I have to," he replies, picks up his bags from the driveway and flings them onto the backseat of the Peugeot. I take a step closer and pull at the sleeve of his jumper.

"Please. Stay here with me," I plead.

"I wish I could, but I can't." He's clearly controlling his face, trying not to grin—again. He's been laughing and joking all morning. I guess it's down to the amazing sex we had last night, and I hide a shy smile behind the back of my hand. He woke me up at some ungodly hour to make love to me, just like in the old days.

He gives me that stare, the one which makes his eyes smoulder. I know what he's doing. He's trying to make me blush, to relive the passion we both shared together in bed.

I feel like we've only just met, shy and giggly and not wanting us to part ever again.

He kisses me on the lips and gently slides his tongue into my mouth. It's warm and seductive, and my body responds, but he lets go.

"There'll be more of that when I get back," he says, huskily, then opens the driver-side door and eases down into the leather seat. Clicking on his seatbelt, he closes the door and winds down the window.

"See you next week."

"Ring me when you get home," I say and wave goodbye as he drives away, my hand halting a mid-farewell gesture as an emptiness engulfs me. I look towards the rolling hills and hate that I need Callum to be happy.

Back in the kitchen, I make myself a pot of tea. In the background, an old battered transistor radio is playing famous songs from the seventies. I glance at the clock; it's almost eight. Alasdair should be back soon. I grab yesterday's newspaper and go and sit by the fire. It's a frosty morning and I enjoy warming my toes over the glowing embers.

I'm glancing at the lonely-hearts page when I hear a car approach outside and sit bolt upright. I wonder if it's Callum, whether he's forgotten something important, and listen for the front door opening. When it doesn't, I fold up the newspaper and place it onto the chair, leaving my cup on the kitchen table before hurrying through the hallway, to peer out of the front window. I push back the net curtain and see the back of a woman's figure, someone who looks oddly familiar. But then I recognise the long dark hair and her slimness: it's Ally, the vet. She's dressed in tight blue jeans that make her legs look deliciously long as she stands beside a white 4 x 4. She slams the car door and kicks one of the silver wheel hubs. Then she lets out an infuriated scream. She's pissed off about something, and so I press my nose closer to the glass to see whether she's suffered a flat tyre, but doesn't seem to have, not as far as I can tell. I'm about to pull on a pair of boots and go outside and investigate when I see Jamie hurrying towards her. As soon as he's within earshot, Ally raises her voice and shouts: "I need to see him, now."

I crane my neck a little closer to the glass and see Jamie's face turn deep crimson. He throws his arms into the air, and in return, Ally points an accusing finger close to his chest.

"Don't come here causing trouble," he says, and they engage in a full-blown argument. My eyebrows knit together with concern, so I dash into the hallway and pull on those boots and grab a coat.

Just as I'm opening the front door I hear Jamie shout "Get back in yir car and get off our land".

"Hey, what's going on here?" I ask, hurrying towards them. I'm just a few feet away when Ally spins on her heels, her mouth twisting into an expression of disgust. Her green eyes now bulge wide as she looks at me as though I'm something she's found stuck to the bottom of her shoe.

"Oh, look who we have here. If it isn't the temptress herself."

"What do you mean by that?" I say.

"I thought he would have chosen someone a little more…educated, but then again, he always had a weakness for a pretty face."

"I don't think there's any need for you to talk to me like that," and I jut out my chin in disdain.

Jamie clears his throat. "I'll not tell ye again, Ally. I said get yir arse off my land!"

She spins around and glares at him. "Fine. If that's the way you want to play it. But just make sure Callum knows I need to talk to him," at which she grabs the door handle and climbs into the front seat of her car, starts the engine and slams the door shut. There's a crunch of gears and the back tyres spin before she releases the hand-break and leaves the farm in a cloud of smoke.

"What's got her all riled up?" I say.

Jamie shakes his head and takes a deep breath.

"God only knows, but she's mad about something."

"Why, what did she say?"

"Och, she was upset. Kept repeating over and over that she needs to speak to Callum."

"About what?"

"I couldnae say."

"Was it animal stuff?"

"Nah; I dinnae think so."

"What then?"

Jamie takes in a deep breath, letting it out slowly before he turns away from me, as though trying to find a means of escape.

"Jamie, tell me; what is it?"

He rubs the back of his head with his fingers, then thrusts his hands inside his pockets and takes a steadying breath. "I hate to be the one to tell ye, but she's Callum's ex."

"Oh?" I gulp. "He never said."

"Aye, and I'm sorry to be the one to break it to ye. However, she dinnae leave me much choice."

I pull my coat a little closer. "No, I guess not. But I just don't get it. I mean, why now? What's the meaning of her turning up here, unannounced, and shouting the odds?"

"I dinnae know for sure. I thought she was coming to check up on the bull, but as soon as she got out of the car, she demanded to see Callum. I explained he'd returned home and she just flew off the handle."

My eyes search out his. "But why the sudden urgency to speak to Cal? Did she give you any clues at all?"

"Nah, she talked in riddles. Said she wasnae willing to keep secrets any longer."

I suffer a shiver of unease. "Secrets; what secrets? What the hell is she talking about, Jamie?"

He shrugs. "You'll have to speak to Callum, I guess."

I bite my lip. "Don't worry, I will."

Jamie shoves his hands deeper inside his coat pockets and takes a step closer.

"Are yir all right, lass?" he asks, "because ye look a wee bit upset."

"I'm fine," and I give him a wide smile to prove it.

"Do ye want to do something today?"

"Like what?"

"Perhaps take a drive into Camburgh to do a bit of shopping?"

I shake my head. "Thanks, but I don't think so. Maybe another time."

"If ye like, we can always call in to see Findley on the way back?"

My head snaps towards him and he laughs out loud.

"Aye, I thought I'd catch yir attention if I mentioned the wee bairn. Do ye want to go and visit him?"

"Yes, that would be great."

"Then I'll see ye once I've finished workin' in the barn," at which he strides off across the farmyard. I hesitate, just a tad, and then head back to the sanctuary of the farmhouse.

***

I'm inside a quaint little shop that sells an array of Scottish souvenirs. There are shimmering glass cabinets filled with silver brooches and bright shiny pins, jewelled daggers and highly polished whisky flasks. It's eye catching, but not enough for me to want to buy.

"Let's go and grab a coffee," I suggest to Jamie.

He heaves a sigh. "I thought you'd ne'er ask," and he turns and grabs the door handle.

A small bell jangles overhead as we step outside.

"Huh, where did the rain come from?" I huff and pull up the collar on my coat.

"The sky maybe," Jamie suggests with a snigger as he quickly zips up his jacket.

"Oh, very funny, but I didn't bring a brolly with me and I'll get soaked."

"There's a café in the department store over the road," he tells me, and points to a black and white building. "It isnae grand, but it's close enough so ye dinnae get yir hair wet."

We make a dash for it, crossing the road and pushing our way through a set of revolving doors.

It's how I find myself sitting in a somewhat mundane café on the third floor of House of Fraser. It's all beige walls and plastic chairs, but I have to admit, the coffee's pretty good.

The shop's heaving with a multitude of daily shoppers. Damp coats from the unexpected downpour cover the chairs, and sodden pushchairs filled with baby bottles and towelling bibs block the aisles. Young children share muffins and kick each other under the tables, whilst grandparents give each other warning glances as they sip their Frappuccinos, looking frazzled.

Jamie's oblivious, enjoying a large Mocha with a convoy of marshmallows floating on the top, which reminds me of white fluffy pillows. Considering I wasn't in the mood to shop, he's surrounded by several large shopping bags. Inside one of these is a new transistor radio for Alasdair.

Jamie lets out a contented sigh. I've pretty much dragged him halfway around Camburgh today and yet he's never grumbled once. I thought he'd be miserable or even moody after the explosive argument with Ally earlier, yet it doesn't appear to have dampened his spirits one iota.

Jamie drains his cup of the last marshmallow and I help gather up all the shopping bags. We head towards the escalator, which will take us back towards the perfume counter. I've still to find the perfect gift for Keira.

I don't know how, but we haven't come back the way we came in, taking us past a brightly coloured decorated section filled with miniature tutus, bright buttoned onesies and a selection of *I love my mum* bibs. My heart sinks as I spot the baby clothes, and no matter how hard I try, I can't stop myself from pawing at the soft material of a little boy's sailor suit. It has a tiny beret, edged with blue ribbon, and there's matching booties, too. Miniature dolphins jump over wiggly blue waves, too much for me not to resist lifting the outfit off the hanger and letting out a sigh.

"It's cute," Jamie says, and I nod in response. I've developed a lump in my throat as I visualise the little boy, my little boy, who should be here to wear it.

"Yes," I rasp, reluctantly putting it back. "I guess we should be going."

"Why not buy it for Findley?" he suggests.

Surprised at his thoughtfulness, I turn and face him. I can read his expression, though, the sorrow he feels for me, and my spine stiffens.

"No, it's okay," I say and turn to walk away.

"Och, don't be like that. 'Tis a lovely gift, and I'm sure Rhona would appreciate the gesture."

I reach out to take the suit and his fingers brush against mine. Just for a second Jamie's eyes meet mine and there's a moment of shared understanding. We both jerk back, though, as if we've each touched a live wire.

"Sorry," we both say simultaneously, and then we laugh at our awkwardness.

"Best take this wee suit to the cashier's desk," Jamie says, and I nod and open my handbag, lifting out my purse.

"Put yir money away," Jamie insists. "I'll get this for the bairn."

"But—"

"Nah, no buts. It can be a gift from the two of us."

I follow Jamie to the counter and watch the assistant place the sailor suit inside a pretty yellow and white cardboard box, which she then ties up with white ribbon. Jamie pays the assistant and then presses the package into my hand, as though the gift is for me.

"Here, take it," he says, and my fingers cling to the bow as though I'm carrying something precious inside.

"I'm positive Rhona will love it," I say, and we make our way to the escalator.

We head over to the perfume counter and I pick out a beautiful boxset of perfume with matching body lotion. "Keira will adore these," I tell Jamie. "She loves anything that smells of flowers or the orient."

"Have ye been friends for long?"

"Yes. Since school."

"Ye seem to rub along well together."

I laugh. "That's one way of putting it."

"Is she married?"

I give him a sideways glance. "Why, are you interested?"

He chuckles, opens the door to the department store and stands aside to let me pass as he shakes his head. "Nah, I'm just curious, that's all."

I'm pleased to see the rain has stopped, but it's left an assortment of grey puddles, shimmering like silver mirrors along the road. We dash along the pavement, careful not to get our feet wet, and cross the street to where Jamie's parked the car.

"She's divorced, actually," I say as I wait for him to open the back, so we can pile in the shopping bags.

"Is that why she's always happy to help run yir shop?"

"One of the reasons, I guess," I say and walk around to the passenger door. "We both have a passion for nature, especially flowers. But she's extremely creative and makes the best bouquets and arrangements. Keira's even taken top prize at The Hampton Court Palace Show and came runner up in Interflora's Florist of the Future Award."

"Really; she sounds very talented. So, what about ye?"

"Me?"

"Aye, haven't ye won any awards?"

"Yes, of course I have, but we were talking about Keira."

"So, tell me about yir accomplishments."

"What would you like to know?"

"Everything."

"Oh, well, let me see. I've been crowned Interflora's florist of the year—twice."

"Wow, I'm impressed."

"And I was runner up in the British Florist Association, last year. That competition was fierce, and my Brazilian headdress was pipped at the post by a woman from Woking."

"Aye, well, truth is, ye cannae win them all. Come on, jump in. I want to show ye something."

"Show me what?"

"Well, if ye don't get in, you'll never ken, will ye?"

I'm intrigued by the sudden air of mystery in his voice. I'm keen to find out where he's taking me, so I quickly strap myself into my seat as Jamie starts the engine. He clicks on the indicator and turns, leaving the centre of town behind. The buildings soon fall away, and open roads stretch before us. I wonder if we're going to Inverness, but when he doesn't turn off at the exit, my excitement grows. My gaze notes the road signs, and then, after another sixteen miles or so, he steers the Range Rover off the main road. That's the moment I realise we're driving past a deep inlet of the North Sea.

I suck in my breath as my eyes devour the passing scenery, staring out of the car window as Jamie concentrates on the road ahead. We follow a straight road until we reach a quaint fishing village with row upon row of whitewashed houses. Out to sea, there's a harbour wall, and the water sparkles like diamonds as we pass by. The tide is out and the water is still, the surface of the sea shimmering despite it being as smooth as glass. I glance towards the shore, seeing ripples in the sand and barnacle shaped rocks protruding out of the ground.

"Where exactly are we going?" I probe.

"Wait and see," Jamie says, clearly refusing to give anything away. His foot eases off the accelerator as we come into the village, then we're out the other side, soon surrounded by open countryside again. He slows even more, though, when he sees horses on the road ahead, but then he indicates left and pulls up just inside a small carpark. Killing the ignition, he gets out of the car.

"And here we are," he says as I climb out of the passenger side, to stare at a beautiful church standing in front of me.

"Is this what you wanted to show me?"

Jamie grins. "Nah, not exactly, but it's breath-taking nonetheless."

There's a sign to one side of the church which says: "Welcome to Ochmore Gallery". I let out a deep sigh. I've seen a few old churches turned into living accommodation, but never an art gallery before.

"Let's go inside. There's something I want to show ye," Jamie says.

He hurries ahead and I follow him in through a set of double doors, whereupon I'm left speechless by what now lies in front of me.

Rising over two floors and with multi gallery spaces below it, a large church window anoints an array of unique paintings, crafts and silverware, the room shimmering with golden rays of sunlight. The entire gallery is bright and airy, and there's sleek white boxes on which the glass art, sculptures and ceramics are shown off. I'm in awe of this place in seconds, and it makes my creative juices flow. I'm like a river that's swiftly transforming into white water rapids.

I follow him to where a painting rests on a large wooden easel. The wood has been sanded down to look distressed and it's very affective in drawing one's eye to the painting, but before I'm even up close, I'm in love with it. The image is of a potted plant, a fuchsia, but it's like nothing I've ever seen before. Its dark green leaves are vibrant and bold, and the tiny dancing ballerina flowers, with their purple and pink skirts, are plump and heavy with colour. The backdrop is a vivid blue, the whole painting alive and vivacious.

"It's stunning," I say, tentatively stroking the canvas with the tips of my fingers. "The colours:

they pulsate with life, and the picture lights up the entire room."

Jamie nods, "Aye, I thought it might be to yir taste."

"I have to buy it for Keira," I insist. "My God, but this painting will make her year."

I flick over the small white tag and catch my breath at the price. It's over one hundred pounds and will take most of the money I have left, but I don't care; I must buy it for her. I'm quick to grab the sales assistant and point out the painting.

She smiles then nods. "Yes, it is rather beautiful," she says in a posh British accent.

"Will ye take eighty for it?" Jamie asks. I swing round in surprise and he tips me a wink.

I turn back to notice the young assistant's cheeks are now flushed pink. She flutters her eyelashes, as though she's got something in her eye.

"Well, I'll have to speak to the manager," she tells him and hurries off to the office.

"Ye have to barter," Jamie says with a shrug. "Ye ne'er willingly pay the full asking price."

I hear tip-tapping of high-heels on the floor as the assistant makes her way back.

"Yes, we'll accept eighty pounds," she says and goes over to the painting and takes it off the stand. Her nimble fingers are soon busy wrapping it up, as though it's a priceless piece of art—which it is to me. And I just know how Keira will react the moment she claps eyes on it.

"Jamie, I simply can't thank you enough for bringing me to this wonderful place," I say as we walk back to the car. "The picture: it's simply perfection."

"I'm glad ye like it. The gallery is one of my favourite places," he says.

"I can see why. I've never seen so much talent under one roof."

"Aye. I'm proud to say the local artists around here are second to none."

"I'd have never put you down as the arty type."

"Haven't ye seen the paintings in the Garden House?"

"Yes. The watercolours…they're magnificent."

"Aye, and they're all originals, too."

"You bought them? You've surprised me," I admit.

Jamie shrugs. "Quite often, there's more to a man than first meets the eye."

We get back into the Range and travel the rest of the way listening to the radio. It's a farming programme and they're discussing which fertiliser to use on this year's crops. I glance out of the window as the car weaves around tight bends and pushes its way over lush green hills. We hit the crest of one, and as we descend, the road dips and I catch a last glimpse of the sea. It sparkles and I let out a sigh. Outside it may be bracing, the sun often dull and the breeze cold, but there's something special about this place, this haven.

We arrive back at Camburgh just as the radio presenter announces it's time for Woman's Hour. Jamie fiddles with the dials and *Mr Blue Sky* blares out. I clap my hands with glee.

"I love this song," I say.

Jamie grins. "Och, so do I," and we both sing along to it. As the orchestra reaches a crescendo, I put on my best interpretation of an operatic voice.

Jamie puts a hand over his ear and winces. "Guid God, woman, ye sound like you're being strangled," and we both burst out laughing. We head straight through the town centre, and Jamie pulls up outside a quaint little cottage.

"This is Rhona's house," he explains, and switches off the engine. He gets out and I follow him to the back of the Range Rover, where he pulls out the present we've brought especially for Findlay. He presses the box into my hands.

I turn to stare at the pretty whitewashed house with its pale blue door. There's a wooden trellis attached to the wall from which a well-established climbing rose hangs. The flowers aren't quite open, but there's a splash of yellow at their tips.

Jamie opens the garden gate and stands aside to allow me to pass. I wait for him, and together, we walk up the path. I go up to the door and tap gently.

"Just a minute," a soft voice calls out from within, then the door swings open and Rhona welcomes us with a warm smile.

"I hope we're not intruding," I say.

"Nah. Not at all. 'Tis lovely to see ye both," and she stands aside. "Well, don't just stand there; come on in."

It's like walking back in time. There's a row of quaint little shelves filled with pre-war porcelain and colourful nick-knacks. I spot a couple of Scottie dog bookends and a figurine of a Royal Lothian soldier. There's even a basket-hilted sword, a claymore and a silver dirk hanging on the wall. I brush my fingers across the dirk. Centuries ago, nearly all clansmen carried such weapons. I stare at its hilt; it's cleverly carved with a curious interlaced design.

"It's Celtic," Jamie whispers in my ear, and his warm breath causes me to shiver.

"Yes, I thought as much," I say.

We enter a small parlour. "Please, take a seat," Rhona says. "Make yourselves at home."

There isn't much furniture. The cottage is tiny, just enough room to fit a single chair and a two-seater sofa. Both face the hearth. Rhona gestures for us to take the sofa and she takes the chair. I go to sit down but the sofa is barely big enough for two.

"Och, come sit here, next to me," Jamie says, having already plonked himself down. I hesitate, but he grabs my hand and pulls me down beside him. I feel my cheeks burn at his close proximity and avert my eyes, over to where Rhona's sitting.

Findlay is asleep in a beautiful hand-carved crib by her side. I watch him sleep. His red hair makes the sheet he's lying on look pure white. He stirs and Rhona presses her hand to the crib and rocks him gently. He goes back to sleep and I feel a stab of disappointment.

"Gordy, have ye got that kettle on?" she yells, and I'm surprised to see Findlay doesn't stir.

"Aye, I'm just doing it now, dear," a voice bellows from an open doorway, and there's the clunk of a switch and an array of creaking floorboards before Gordon appears from the galley kitchen to greet us.

Jamie stands and shakes his hand and I go to do the same, but Gordon wraps his arms around me and squeezes me into a bearhug. I'm taken aback and it must show on my face, for both Jamie and Rhona laugh out loud.

"Take it easy, young Gordon," Jamie says. "Ye dinnae want to kill yir visitor just yet."

Gordon chortles and releases me. I take a gulp of air. He's definitely not the kind of guy to pick a fight with. Well over six-foot-tall and just as broad, he has a long ginger beard and mischievous blue eyes.

I turn to offer Rhona the gift we've brought along. "It's just something we bought for Findlay in town today," I tell her.

Rhona's eyes grow wide and she grins. "Oh, ye dinnea have to do that."

"No, really, I...we wanted to buy him a small token."

Rhona's grin broadens. "Well, thank ye for being so thoughtful. Shall I open it now?"

I laugh. "Yes, please. After all, that's the general idea."

She unties the white ribbon and pulls out the sailor suit. Her eyes shine with pure delight.

"Och, it's the cutest thing I've ever seen, and he'll win a few more hearts wearing this." She glances down at Findlay. "You're going to look a wee bonnie bairn, that's for sure," she adds and places the suit, with care, back inside the box. She comes over and kisses us both on the cheek.

"'Tis really kind of ye to bring Findlay a gift. Thank ye both for yir generosity."

She goes and sits back down.

"So, how's yir trip to Scotland been so far?" Gordon inquires, jovially.

"Oh, it's been lovely," I smile, "if a wee bit cold."

"Och, ye think it's cold now. Wait 'til the snow comes."

"The snow…what snow?"

"Haven't ye heard? It's all over the news. It's blowing in straight from Norway."

"No. I had no idea. When?"

"Monday. That's what the met office are saying."

"I hope my husband's back by then."

"Callum's away?"

"Yes, on business."

"You'd best warn him. The last thing you'll want is for him to be stuck in a snowdrift somewhere." Gordon rushes off to the kitchen and then reappears with a tea tray filled with goodies. He places it onto a small table in the centre of the room.

"I hope ye like Dundee cake," he says, and I nod enthusiastically.

"I adore cake of any kind," I say, "especially when it's filled with mixed fruit and topped with almonds."

"I made the apricot jam myself," Rhona says with pride. "And I'll give ye a couple of jars to take home."

I glance at Jamie and he nods. "Aye," he says, "that would be grand."

Rhona busies herself pouring the tea when Findlay starts to grizzle.

"I'll pick him up if you like?" I say, trying not to sound too eager.

"Och, would ye? Thanks," and Rhona sounds relieved. "I cannae have two minutes to myself these days." I jump to my feet and dash over. The baby's face is all red and he's trying to put his fingers into his mouth.

"I think he's hungry," I say, holding him to my chest and rocking him. He smells of baby shampoo and talcum powder, and I breathe in the aroma. I love the smell of babies. His skin is soft, like velvet, and I rub my cheek against his forehead and kiss the top of his head.

"You're probably right, as I've only just changed his nappy," Rhona agrees. "Gordy? Will ye be guid enough to get him a bottle?" but Gordon is already halfway into the kitchen, and within minutes he's back with the baby milk.

"Would ye like to do the honours?" he asks and offers me the bottle. I take it willingly.

"Sit in the chair; it'll be easier to feed him that way," Rhona says. She stops what she's doing to push a bib over Findlay's head. "Be warned: he's a guzzler, so be sure to wind him halfway through the feed," she advises.

I'm thrilled she trusts me. I place Findlay in the crook of my arm, and the second the bottle's in his mouth, he stops crying. He looks up at me and I feel a rush of love.

"He's such a gorgeous wee man," I say, and glance up to smile at Rhona, but catch Jamie's stare, instead, suffering a shudder of unease. I've never seen him look at me that way before. It's so…intense.

"Have ye got any plans for this weekend?" Rhona asks.

I nod. "Yes. Jamie's taking me to a pagan festival."

"Been to one before?"

"No, not here in Camburgh, but I did visit a festival close to Stonehenge once. It's a few years ago now, mind."

Rhona sits a cup and a thick slice of Dundee cake onto a small wooden stool by my feet. "It should be a grand turnout. I've already seen a few young 'uns camping down by the brae."

"I'm excited," I admit. "There's something magical about these ancient traditions, and I love having the chance to embrace nature."

She tips me a wink. "Aye, best makes sure ye get yir wish ready."

My brow furrows. "Sorry, I don't understand what you mean."

She looks at me in surprise. "It's a new moon. Ye have to write yir deepest desires on a bay leaf and give it to the priestess."

"A bay leaf?"

"Aye."

"Whatever for?"

"So she can burn it during the ritual."

"And to what end?"

"To ensure the pagan Gods make yir wish come true, of course."

"You believe in such things?"

"Sure, why not? I've seen many wishes come to fruition."

"You have?"

"Aye; I remember once…"

I can't help it, I catch Jamie's eye. I want him to share our enthusiasm, but he's wearing an expression I can't quite read.

"Och, it's all just fun and nonsense," he eventually interrupts, sounding blasé.

Rhona turns to him, a piece of cake halfway to her lips. "Really, Jamie? Since when did ye become so cynical?"

He stiffens. "Since I lost Claire."

Rhona has the decency to look away.

Findlay lets out a cough and a splutter, and I sit him up, put down the bottle and pat him gently on his back until he stops. He lets out a huge burp. Gordon and Rhona both applaud, as though I've done something amazing.

"Well done, Lassie," Gordon grins; "ye can come here again."

"Do ye want me to hold him so ye can enjoy yir tea?" Rhona asks, stuffing the last of her cake in her mouth. I shake my head vigorously. I'd forfeit all the tea in China to have this beautiful child in my arms for just a little bit longer.

"If you're sure," she says.

"Oh yes, I'm positive," I assure her. "If only you knew how much."

CHAPTER TEN

"Are ye ready yet?" Jamie calls from the front door of the Garden House.

"Yes, just coming," I shout back, and slip the cloak Jamie gave me over my dress—Claire's cloak. It's purple on the outside and black on the inside, and has a hood, the whole garment made from crushed velvet. It's beautiful and I'm honoured Jamie's willing to allow me to wear it.

I move over to the mirror, dab my cheekbones with a light rose-coloured blush and then check my hair. I push a stray curl into place and press down my braids, then go over to a vase filled with fresh flowers and pluck several heads of white baby's breath from the various stems. It's a variety called Million Stars, my fingers quick to interweave the tiny clusters into my hair. I add a few colourful beads and finish off with a string of pale blue feathers, admiring my handiwork before closing the bedroom door and rushing downstairs.

Jamie's standing in the doorway, waiting for me. I brush past, and as I do so, catch his stare.

"Wow, look at ye," he says. "Ye remind me of a true pagan princess."

I laugh and give him a twirl. "That's the general idea. Plus, Claire's cloak is perfect."

His eyes appear warm and soft. "Ye look grand in it. The colour really suits ye."

"Thanks," I grin. "You don't look half bad yourself."

He's wearing black jeans and a thick jersey hoodie. It's green, the colour of moss, and there's a picture in the centre of his chest: a stag, around whose head are numerous Celtic symbols, which, I believe, depict woodland and the earth. A small branch covered with green leaves sits above the animal's antlers, and below its neck hangs a pentangle.

I point to the design. "I've never seen anything like it before. And it's way too cool for you."

Jamie smirks and his fingers trace the outline of the colourful image. "'Twas a gift from Claire," he says. "I dinnae believe in all the mumbo-jumbo stuff. I just enjoyed being with my wife and associating with those who appreciate the more natural things in life."

I link my arm with his.

"And who can blame you? It's good to see you've dressed for the occasion. After all, it's all part of the fun. Come on, let's go and show Claire that you still know how to enjoy yourself."

Jamie pats my hand. "Aye, Claire knew how to have a guid time, all right."

"And you should, too. Let today be all about being truly alive. We should appreciate this wonderful world we live in and give thanks for all it has to offer. Just for once, why not let your hair down, eh?"

Jamie pushes his fingers through his curly locks. "Aye, I suppose I'd better do as ye ask while I still have some left."

I laugh loudly as I open the gate. I hear an engine roar into life, and there's granda, sitting on a tractor in the yard.

"Have a guid time, young 'uns," he shouts over the din. I wave at him and he waves back.

"We promise to do our best," I shout, and Jamie closes the gate behind us.

We set off down a muddy track and I take a deep breath to find the air sweet and refreshing. Even though it's still winter the countryside is ablaze with colour. Dark green leaves from the evergreens are mixed together with luscious reds, yellowish-ambers and the deepest of bronzes. There's a ghostly mist hanging over the mountains and a flock of wild geese fly towards the horizon.

We head through a colourful patchwork of fields and down winding lanes, over fallen logs and around bare, thorny wild rose bushes.

It isn't the least bit cold today. Granda reckoned it's warm because snow is on its way. I have no idea if it's true or not, but just in case it does turn cold later, underneath my dress, I'm wearing thermals, and on my feet, fur lined boots. I've also brought along a small hessian bag, tucked beneath the cloak. There isn't much inside, just my mobile, purse and lip gloss. I've brought a bottle of water, too. Just in case.

We're making our way down a hill when we pass a sign that points the way to the memorial stone, and not long after, we enter a small area of woodland. Soft green moss lies like a rich velvet carpet along the ground, dissolving the dead branches and rotting foliage that have long since fallen, all becoming lost forever beneath its dense soft mass.

I stop and listen, hearing the most magnificent bird songs.

"What are they?" I ask Jamie. "I've truly never heard anything quite so beautiful."

"Ye can hear a mixture of blue, grey and coal tits," he explains. "They all stay together throughout the winter months. It's safer that way."

"They sound so sweet, cheerful even."

"Aye, that'll be because they've plenty to eat for now."

I stare up at the sky through the thin canopy, hoping to catch a glimpse of the birds, but I'm blinded by the dappled light, by the shafts of winter sun that slant down into the exposed gaps between the trunks of the trees. I'm half-expecting a grey wolf to emerge out of the shadows.

"Nae time to dawdle or we'll ne'er get there," Jamie says and sets off at a quick pace, surefooted as ever. I hurry after him. We've decided to walk down to the brae so we can both enjoy a wee dram or two. We've also agreed to meet Rhona and Gordon there. Before long, we climb over a small wooden stile and out into open fields, my excitement rising a notch when I hear loud music and the boom of drums. I start to dance around Jamie in a circle, much to his amusement.

He smiles then laughs. "Och, look at ye; I've ne'er seen ye act daft before."

I let out a peel of laughter, hitch up the hem of my skirt, and twirl around him like an overgrown ballerina. His smile broadens, and he grabs my hand so I can do a complete pirouette.

"I'm letting my inner child out," I say and jump in a puddle to prove it. Mud splashes across the front of my dress, and for a second, I'm fearful it's landed on Claire's cloak.

"Oh, Jamie, I'm so sorry—" but he waves a dismissive hand.

"Och, don't mather. 'Tis only dirt, lass. It'll disappear soon enough when it's dry."

I lift my skirt a little higher to check the mud hasn't splashed across my legs.

"Wow, steady on. I have to say: ye really know how to drive a man insane with desire," Jamie chuckles, pointing to my thermal leggings.

I laugh loudly and quickly lower my skirt.

We keep to the edge of the field and follow a drystone wall. I spot other people in the distance, ambling in the same direction, surprised by the number of tents that have sprung up overnight. There's hundreds dotted across the horizon, stretching as far as the eye can see. There's an array of young people and children milling around them, and I can hear distant laughter.

When we finally enter the festival, it's almost two o'clock in the afternoon and the festivities are in full swing.

"Fancy a beer?" Jamie asks, and I nod. We head inside a small tent that's heaving with revellers, and I stand and wait as Jamie goes off to the bar. The atmosphere is warm and friendly, he soon comes back with two plastic glasses.

"Where do ye wannae go first?" he asks.

I shrug. "I have no idea. Shall we walk around? See what's on offer?"

142

"Sounds guid to me," Jamie says, and we head out of the tent and into the heart of the festival. There are people everywhere. Some are dressed in outfits that must have cost a small fortune, dripping in sequins and heavy with countless folds of material, whilst other, more vivacious women, wear flowery skirts, tie-dye blouses, and bright coloured scarves around their necks. What I also notice are the Disney fans, those dressed in bright yellow ballgowns and who look to have stepped off the set of Beauty and the Beast.

A man walks by wearing a horned mask with a sharp pointed beak. He reminds me of a cockerel. Plumes of red and black feathers sprout from his head and I sense a dark side to his presence. I look down at my own clothes, at an outfit that could be classed as medieval, as I've certainly gone more for the Maid Marion style. I consider the beauty of paganism is to dress simply as oneself, to show who one truly is.

The festival is chilled and oozes with tranquillity. There's a small band of people sitting in a circle with a guitar, singing joyful pagan songs. I don't know the words, but I stop to listen and clap along with the beat, trying not to spill my beer.

Jamie taps me on the shoulder and then points into the crowd. It takes me a second or two to make out the figures heading towards us. I soon realise it's Gordon and Rhona. She spots me and waves, I laugh out loud. She's dressed like a fairy, has lavender and heather in her hair and is adorned with a set of pink nylon wings. The flowers look pretty, and as she comes closer, I smell fresh Rosemary. I grin when I see what Gordon's wearing. He's dressed in a long brown robe, which isn't the least bit flattering. It fits like a sack, as though he's just cut out the arm holes and pushed his head through a gap in the seam. As he, too, draws nearer, I notice he has a henna tattoo of a pentangle on his left cheek. He reminds me more of a clansman, what with his rugged good looks and thick ginger beard, one better suited to a battlefield re-enactment against the English than trying to look the part of a pagan.

"Ye look amazing," Rhona cries as she gives me a hug, and Jamie shakes Gordon's hand.

"I adore the wings," I say. "What a fabulous idea."

She links her arm in mine as we wander towards a stand selling homemade leather belts. There's every colour imaginable, even multicoloured, like a rainbow. Jamie and Gordon trail behind as we browse each table in turn. There's woven coloured bags and tee shirts, wooden coasters and pieces of bespoke jewellery.

"How much for the silver thistle brooch?" Rhona asks a vendor with the longest dreadlocks I've ever seen.

He lifts his thumb and forefinger to his chin and gives it a light tap as he appraises her.

"For you, sweet lady, fifty pounds."

"I'll give ye forty and not a penny more," Rhona tells him, but then a young bohemian-looking girl, large yellow beads strapped across her forehead, steps out from behind the makeshift counter.

"You have a deal," she says. "Forty's fine," and Rhona lets out a shriek of pure delight.

"I have the cash right here," she says, pulling a wad of money from out of her bra. I try not to gasp and quickly close my mouth. Rhona tips me a wink. "I saw them last year but dinnae have enough money on me at the time."

A man dressed like a druid comes up to me, a drinking horn in his hand.

"Here, have a drink," he says. I shake my head and take a step back, but Jamie shoves money into his hand and takes the horn. He lifts it to his lips and throws back his head, takes a large swig and then offers it to me.

"It's sweet wine. Try it; it's guid," he says, and hesitantly, I take the horn which is still brimming with a pale golden liquid. I sip it, to find it's tasty, but it goes straight to my head. I giggle and pass it to Rhona. The druid then wipes my wrist with a fluorescent pen.

"It means ye can drink from any watering horn," Jamie explains, reading my confused expression.

"Is that safe?" I ask with a frown. "I mean, you've heard of people spiking drinks."

"They won't, not if they want to enjoy midsummer here," and Jamie gives me a knowing smile.

"Oh, yes. I hadn't thought of that."

I can hear more drumming, and the noise of the wind in the trees is now pumping through my bloodstream, along with the wine. Older children shriek as they jump between the tents and tables, playing hide and seek. Younger children sit at camping tables, learning how to make wands, or cute animal ornaments out of salt dough.

A delicious aroma sweeps along on the air and my stomach rumbles.

"I'm starved. Shall we go grab something to eat?"

"I thought you'd ne'er ask," says Gordon, and he points to where a thin-faced man wearing thick black eyeliner is busy cooking curried lamb. As we approach, the meat sizzles loudly inside a ginormous frying pan. The aromatic smell of caramelised onions mixed with curry paste tantalises my taste buds. My mouth waters as the man offers me a plate of marinated lamb. Hungry, I devour the delicious curry within a matter of minutes, and as I'm wiping my mouth with a cheap serviette, I hear the tinkle of a bell.

"It's time to go and listen to the shaman," I say, excitedly.

"Not for us," Rhona replies, throwing her empty paper plate into the nearest bin. "We're off to join the Magik workshop. It's all about the power of the mind."

"Enjoy," I say, "and we'll catch up with you both later."

"In 'We', does that mean I have to go, too," Jamie groans.

"Yes, if you don't mind," I say. "It's fascinating how someone has access to, and influence in, the world of good and evil spirits."

I link his arm with mine and drag him to where a woman is shaking a pair of maracas and chanting. She sits, crossed-legged, on the ground, an older lady dressed in a black robe in attendance, who, as we approach, beckons us to join her. She greets us by offering us a small brown carrier bag, but I can't help but stare at her: she has a distinct resemblance to Professor McGonagall from Harry Potter.

"Inside the bag, you'll find essential items needed for casting a circle," she explains. "There's no charge, but a donation to the local donkey sanctuary would be much appreciated." I nod as she ushers us forward. I take a peek inside the bag to find there's a carton of salt, four tealights, a stick of incense, and a small bottle of water. There's also a clear, see-through bag filled with dirt and a piece of card on which is printed a ritual.

I point to a vacant spot close to the shaman and we both go and sit beside her.

"Good afternoon and welcome," she says to those gathered around her, placing the musical instruments down by her feet. "I'm pleased to see you all here today, and I thought I would start the workshop by teaching you how to cast a circle. Now, before we begin, may I say that you don't have to be in a group to create a circle, and in the future, you may wish to do this on your own."

Tiny pinpricks of excitement stab the back of my neck and I'm pleased there's only eight of us in the entire group. The shaman gestures for us to rise.

"The purpose of casting a circle is to create a barrier between you and the rest of the world. Inside the circle, you can raise your energies and protect yourself from negativity or any harmful entities.

"Now I'm going to show everyone how to cast their own circle. You can do it in pairs if you wish,

146

and I will attend each circle in turn and help you with your ritual."

"Shall we do our circle together?" I ask Jamie.

"Aye, why not? That way anyone watching will think you're the crazy person."

"What? You really think people don't know you're loony?"

"Nah, they'll just think I'm yir support worker."

I let out a chuckle. "But you *are* my support worker...of sorts."

"Then I guess you'd better get on with it before someone feels sorry for me and lets me escape."

I narrow my eyes. "It's a good job I'm not a witch or I'd put an evil spell on you right now."

"Who say's ye havenae done so already," Jamie mutters, just loud enough for me to hear.

I give him a sharp dig in the ribs.

"Is everyone ready with their salt?" calls out the shaman, and I grab the carton from out of the carrier bag.

"Excellent. Now draw a circle along the ground and make sure it's big enough for you to be able to walk around without bumping into the other people in the group."

I let the salt spill onto the earth.

The shaman watches me and nods. "That's it, and once complete, I'd like you to place the tealights onto the circle, creating compass points of north, south, east, and west."

I pass the paper bag to Jamie and allow him to do the honours.

The healer claps her hands. "That's wonderful. I'll come to each one of you in turn with a lighted candle, so we can light the incense. Once it's lit, please push it firmly into the ground."

We follow the shaman's instructions until we're all ready for the actual casting of the circle.

"Let's all read the words off the card," says our host.

"May the guardians of this element guide and guard me as I welcome and honour their presence and power," we all say together.

The shaman shows the couple beside us the next steps and Jamie follows suit, offering me the bottle of water. I open it and then walk around the circle, flicking droplets into the air. I then tear open the plastic bag and sprinkle the dirt along the ground.

"That's it," says the shaman. "Now, face one another and close your eyes. Use this moment to heal yourself with the river of forgiveness. Let go of any negativity and heartbreak which may cause you harm."

I take several deep breaths as I close my eyes and prepare to relax my mind, then I feel Jamie's fingers brush against mine. I reach out to hold his hand, and when our fingers entwine, I feel a connection between us as the wind blows softly against my skin. I open my eyes and lift my chin to stare directly into his eyes, at which his mouth twitches and his grip tightens. A shiver creeps down my spine.

"You're shaking, Sassenach," he whispers, and I nod, unable to let him go.

"And now we must close the circle," says the healer. I turn towards her, a little confused. It's as though, for just a second, Jamie and I were the only two people on the entire planet, but we break away from one another and go on to complete the ritual.

In the background, the musicians play on, their music wild and eerie, and before long, we say goodbye to the shaman and thank her for sharing her experiences with us.

As dusk falls, a bonfire is lit the darkening sky becomes ablaze with orange and gold flames. Close by, the memorial stone shines like a glowing beacon as the light from those same flames flicker along its surface.

Jamie murmurs in my ear, "Let's make our way down to the water. It's almost time for the new moon ritual to begin."

I follow him and spot Rhona and Gordon sitting on the grass, just a few feet away from the stone. We're lucky to have found them, for the entire brae is filled with all walks of life. We hurry over and join them.

Another druid walks by with a watering horn and I hold up my hand and give him a wave, and he comes and sits beside me. I take a long drink of sweet wine. It slides, smooth like honey, down my throat. When I take another, in seconds I feel lightheaded and giddy again.

I hear music, panpipes, and they're accompanied by a single drum, a Bodhran. It's a haunting melody which catches my attention. I close my eyes and lose myself in its rhythm, until the music stops abruptly, and I snap my eyes open.

The priestess appears from behind the stone, a thrum of excitement rippling through the crowd as she moves towards a makeshift altar. She's wearing a light orange robe, a loose-fitting hood hiding her face, and in her hands she carries a silver bowl and a lighted candle, both of which she places onto the altar, side by side. Alongside her are five beautiful handmaidens, all in floating dresses and with flowers in their hair, each holding a flickering flame in one hand and something small, concealed, in the other. The beat of the drum begins again, and when it stops, the handmaidens blow out their flames and drop to the ground.

Although the priestess takes off her hood, I can only see the back of her head, but it all looks rather theatrical, her hair as black as night and coiled, like silken thread, on top of her head. Somehow, though, I sense she must be beautiful.

Jamie nudges me and I turn to look at him. He presses something that feels brittle into the palm of my hand, and when I unfurl my fingers, there's a bay leaf resting there. I smile; I really thought Rhona might have been kidding me.

"Make yir wish," Jamie whispers, and I glance over at Rhona who offers me a pen. I write my deepest desire in tiny letters on the surface of the leaf and close my hand, so no one else can catch sight of what I've written. There's an odd sensation in the pit of my stomach, like a hundred butterflies flapping their wings, at which I let out a breath and clutch the bay leaf closer to my chest.

The priestess's voice cuts through the hanging silence, and I look up to see her face the crowd, her tone now as smooth as silk, the flickering light of the bonfire dancing shadows across her face, lending her an air of mystery. Yet somehow, her voice seems oddly familiar.

"May my guides, angels, higher self, and good spirits assist me in this ritual," she declares, before addressing each handmaiden in turn, standing before her in a line. The first bows and puts something into the priestess's hand, at which the priestess turns back towards the altar.

"May these coffee grounds ensure all minds are clear and receptive."

She turns back towards the second handmaiden and again, accepts a small offering.

"What is she doing, exactly?" I whisper at Jamie.

"She's taking a specific herb or ingredient needed for the ritual from each one."

I watch closely as the priestess sprinkles each offering over the altar's candleflame, and as she speaks, I absorb her every word.

"Oregano: may you always find joy and energy in your life. Cloves: may wealth come easily to you. Fennel: may you allow healing and find strength. Poppy seeds: may you always be aware of that which is around you." She grinds the last of the ingredients between her fingers and over the flame before turning back towards the crowd and raising her arms.

"Please, everyone, come forward with your wishes."

Jamie pulls me to my feet. "Best get in line, lass, with the other hopefuls," he says as his eyes dance with amusement.

"You're not taking this seriously," I say.

Jamie shakes his head. "Nah, I'm just waitin' for my cake and ale." He laughs and I feel a stab a disappointment. I don't know why, but I want him to take this part of the ceremony to heart. I want his wish to come true as much as I do my own.

Rhona grabs me. "Hurry up," she says, "you don't want to be at the back of the queue," and she dashes over the grass, dragging me along with her. We're laughing now, and I feel Jamie's hand in the small of my back. I like it there; it makes me feel safe.

A drum strikes out, quickly settling to its mesmeric beat. A piper joins in and yet another tune fills the air, and soon the awaiting crowd are singing the *Skye Boat Song*. I watch in awe as some of the young women dance in small groups. Their arms twist gracefully towards the heavens, their toes pointing towards the earth. They link arms then twirl around, their clothes floating like chiffon. I'm fascinated by the fluidity of their movements and find I can't tear my eyes away.

Rhona lets go of my hand and then I see her, standing in front of the priestess, to whom she lifts the bay leaf, and which the woman then takes and burns over the flame. She bows to Rhona and says: "With harm to none, may these wishes come to those who write them. To the power of three so may it be."

Rhona thanks the priestess, then walks away to where Gordon waits for her under a nearby tree.

It's my turn. I step forward and offer up my leaf, now staring into two beautiful dark eyes, ones that take me aback. I'd recognise those hazel eyes anywhere.

"Bridget?"

She smiles. "Hello, Maddie. What a wonderful surprise. I do hope you've recovered from your fall?"

I'm stunned at seeing her again. "Oh, yes; totally, thanks," I mumble.

"Are you okay, only I can tell by your expression I'm not who you expected."

"Uh-huh, you got that right. I'd never have guessed in a thousand years you were a priestess."

Bridget laughs lightly. "Well, I don't wear a sign around my neck if that's what you mean?"

I laugh back. "No, of course not, only I thought you were just a passing tourist."

"I am."

"Not quite."

"Perhaps not. However, let's get together before I leave."

I nod. "I'd like that."

"Great; it's settled. Meet me by the stone in roughly an hour's time, and we'll swap phone numbers."

"Great, it's a date," but then an irritated cough comes from someone standing in line behind me, and Bridget focuses her attention back onto my hand. "Do you have your wish for me?"

Now that I realise Bridget is the priestess, I'm not keen for her to see my wish. I waiver, but she gently cups my hand in her own and my fingers automatically open. She lifts the bay leaf from my palm and reads the inscription. When she looks up, her eyes bore into mine for a moment before she gives me a knowing smile, the leaf soon burnt over the flame. It ignites in a second and Bridget drops it into the silver bowl, repeating the enchantment as she this time holds onto my hands. "Is this your husband?" she asks, and before I can reply, she reaches past me and plucks the bay leaf from Jamie's fingers.

"Hey, ye cannae do that," says Jamie, but it's too late, Bridget's already read what was written there. She stares at him for the longest time.

"Ah, so you're not her husband," she says thoughtfully, and turns and sets fire to the leaf. She stares at him then bows her head. "You have my blessing and the Gods will favour you," she says.

152

She bows once again, at which Jamie grabs my hand and pulls me away.

"What on Earth's the matter?" I ask, seeing how his brows are knitted together and his lips are puckered.

"How do ye know that woman?" he says.

"That's Bridget: the lady who came to my rescue the day I slipped, here, on the brae."

"Ye ne'er actually told me ye needed rescuing."

"No, I didn't. She was just there at the time. She said she was a writer."

"Aye, she writes books on paganism."

"Well, that explains a lot. But what's wrong; you seem rather disgruntled?"

"Aye, I am. She read my wish in front of ye. She shouldnae of done that."

"Don't be silly. I don't know what it said. And besides, you told me you didn't take this kind of thing seriously."

Jamie shrugs. "Ne'er mind. 'Tis done now," but just then, Rhona hurries over.

"Come on, ye two, the next ritual is about to start," she enthuses.

"Oh, wait; I need to pee," I say. "I'll just nip to the loo and then I'll catch you up."

Rhona nods and heads off in the opposite direction, but Jamie hesitates.

"It's okay," I tell him. "You go ahead and I'll meet you there."

"Ye sure?" he asks.

"Yes, positive."

We part company and I hurry past a huddle of makeshift tents, behind which stands a row of Portaloos. I make a dash for one, but as I pass one of the tents, a hand shoots out and grabs my arm, jolting my head back as I'm stopped dead in my tracks. I yank my arm free, pulling my assailant out of the shadows, then catch my breath.

"What the—"

"Fancy finding you here."

"What do you want, Ally?"

"Interesting question, and one I'm pleased you've asked."

I find I'm losing my patience. "Quit playing games. If you've something on your mind, best spit it out."

"My, you are a spirited one. I can see why Callum fell for you. You're quite fiery."

"No. I just don't have time to waste whilst you do your best to intimidate me. If you have something to say, then get on with it."

Ally heaves a sigh. "It's not that simple."

"It never is," I snort. "But if it's Callum you're after, I'll not give him up without a fight."

"I'd expect nothing less."

"Good, then why are you here?"

"Because it's time he came back to where he belongs, to where we *both* belong."

"He's not yours to have. Not now, not ever."

"That's where you're wrong. He's always been mine. It was simply circumstances that tore us apart."

"So, now you're going to try and win him back, even though we're married?"

"I don't need to try. Once he learns about your affair with Jamie, he'll come running back to me with open arms. Besides, I hear getting a divorce is easy these days."

"What a ludicrous thing to say. You must be grasping at straws if you think he'd ever believe I'm having an affair with his brother."

"I've seen the way you two are around each other. And I saw you earlier, casting a circle and staring into each other's eyes like a couple of lovebirds. No, when Callum returns, he's going to learn the truth about you two."

"That's it; I've heard enough," I hiss. "You can lie, but it won't get you anywhere. Callum's over you. In fact, he's never mentioned you once in all the years we've been together—that's how important you are to him."

She flinches and takes a step back. "Sticks and stone," she says, but then there's a rustle behind me and someone grabs my shoulder. I let out a scream.

"Maddie, are ye all right, lass?" and I turn and stare into the face of Jamie.

"What are you doing creeping up on people," I cry out, relieved to see it isn't one of what I imagined as Ally's henchmen.

"Sorry, it's just ye were taking ages, so I came to see what was holdin' ye up."

I turn to point in Ally's direction, but she's gone.

"Ally was standing right there," I tell him. "She told me she's going to get Callum back."

"Och, that'll ne'er happen," Jamie insists. "He made his choice when he left, all those years ago."

"Clearly, she doesn't seem to think so herself."

"That's because she's found out he's visiting and because she still holds a torch for him."

"She also said something else."

"Oh, yeah; like what?"

"That she's going to tell Callum we're having an affair."

He takes a sharp intake of breath. "She actually said that?"

I nod and Jamie pushes me to arm's length, and I stare deep into his eyes.

"Her accusations are unfounded and he'll ne'er take her seriously. And, more importantly, he loves *ye*, not Ally."

"Then what am I going to do?"

"You're not to let that woman's poison affect ye, that's what you'll do."

I feel my eyes prick with tears. "I can't believe she told me to my face that's she's going to take him from me."

Jamie puts his arm around me and guides me away from the tents.

"She can try, but Callum would die for ye, so dinnae think for one moment he would ever leave ye. Now, forget her and let's go and eat cake and enjoy the rest of the evening."

I pull away from him. "No. I can't."

Jamie shrugs. "Why ever not? Ye said ye loved cake."

"Yes, I do, but I still need to pee."

Jamie shakes his head. "Aye, all right. I'll stand guard outside the door in case Ally decides to show her face again."

"Thanks, I appreciate the offer."

We retrace our steps and hurry over to the Portaloos, where I rush inside a vacant one, but the moment the door closes, I'm scrabbling inside my bag for my mobile. I need to speak to Callum, to tell him what's happened. I push a few items aside and find my phone at the bottom of my bag, swipe the screen and then press his number. When I hear his voice, I breathe a sigh of relief, but then realise I've reached his answer phone.

"Hi, this is Callum McKinley. Please leave your message after the beep." I hesitate, then force my voice to sound light and airy.

"Hi, it's me. Nothing's wrong; I'm just checking in," and I end the call with a sigh, not wishing to upset him or cause him alarm. But I need to talk to him and put my mind at ease. I tell myself he's sure to ring me back as soon as he gets my message, but then again, the signal's pretty lousy up here. Resignedly, I shove my phone back inside my bag, use the toilet then wash my hands. When I open the door, Jamie's waiting for me.

"Are ye okay?" he asks as I approach, and I read concern in his eyes.

I nod and push the corners of my mouth into a smile. "Yes, I'm fine. It's just that I don't know how to handle Ally," I confess. "I've never been in this kind of situation before."

He offers me his hand and I take it, his calloused fingers grasping mine.

"I've told ye already: you've nothing to worry about. She's just making waves, and what she doesnae realise is that she'll be the one to drown by them."

I squeeze his fingers, grateful for his reassurance, but there's something else, too. It's as though a veil has been lifted from my eyes. I no longer see him as Callum's identical twin. Instead, there are certain traits and qualities held within him that I now recognise are so unlike Callum. There's no trace of arrogance or superiority. In front of me stands a man who's kind and gentle. He pulls me close and holds my gaze, his eyes soft and sincere.

There's a cry and then a shout, and Jamie lets go, swinging around to a drunk who's just spilt ale all down his arm and the side of his jeans. "Can ye not see where you're going?" Jamie curses under his breath.

"Be cool, man," says a guy who's the spitting image of Bob Marley, and at whom Jamie only glares. The Rastafarian staggers to a halt, his arms swaying like suckered tentacles, and I swear he's about to fall over. I take a step forward, my hand outstretched to steady him when he swiftly turns tail and hurries away into the darkness.

"Complete imbecile," Jamie mutters, shaking off the last droplets of beer from his clothes.

"Oh, don't be too hard on him," I say with a smirk. "After all, it *was* an accident."

Jamie shakes his head, but his anger has already melted away. "Come on, then; I think it's time we went and found the others," and he grabs my hand and pulls me into the crowd of revellers and leads me back to the safe bosom of my new friends.

The atmosphere is heavy with winter cloud, but this doesn't dampen my spirits. We join in with a small band of gypsies who are enjoying a good old sing-song. The music is soulful and I clap my hands to the beat. I spot Rhona and Gordon dancing together. They make a fine couple, and Rhona seems quite merry. Her cheeks are flushed and she's giggling. Gordon's happy to hold her steady, to have his arms wrapped around her waist.

"'Tis a guid job Malcolm's staying the night to look after Findlay," Jamie shouts over the din. I laugh, because he's right. No doubt, by tomorrow morning, they'll both suffer from stinking hangovers.

"On that note, do you fancy a special brewed ale?" I say.

Jamie chuckles. "I've ne'er been one to turn down a free drink."

"Then stay put and I'll be right back."

I head over to a stall selling wine and beer. There's plenty on offer, a table littered with an assortment of ales, most of which I've never heard of. I ponder over the different varieties and buy two bottles of Old Speckled Hen. On the way back, a woman, waving her hands, catches my eye. I realise it's Bridget and she's pointing to the memorial stone. I nod and lift the bottles of ale and point them in Jamie's general direction. Bridget holds up five fingers. I nod again and she gives me a thumbs up, at which I hurry over to where Jamie's watching a young girl dance to a fiddle, offering him the ale.

"Slàinte mhath," he says as he **makes a toast.**

"Good health to you, too," I say, "only I've just seen Bridget and I'm going to meet her down by the stone."

Jamie halts, the beer to his lips. "What? You're going now?"

I nod. "Yes. I said I'd be there in five."

"Do ye want me to come with ye, in case ye bump into Ally again?"

"No, I'll be fine, thanks. Besides, I won't be long."

I make my way down to the water's edge. There's barely a sliver of moonlight but I can hear the water gurgling downstream. It tinkles along over and between the stones, the sound giving me a moment of pure serenity. A biting wind is heading down from the mountains and I pull my cloak a little closer, taking a swig of beer as I stare out into the darkness, my imagination sweeping me away. I'm now waiting for a huge barrage of men to break through a veil of creeping mist, seeing the clansman, their faces covered in mud and deadly weapons in their hands.

A firework whizzes through the air, drawing my gaze. It explodes with a whistle and a bang, then silver stars and a colourful rainbow fall from the heavens, a trail of grey smoke lingering in the air. When my gaze lowers, I notice the crowds are starting to disperse. A lot of the children have gone to their beds, and there, sitting on the ground, a few die-hards cover themselves with tartan blankets and waterproofs to help keep the cold at bay. Many others have moved closer to the bonfire, still burning, still crackling and popping with life. I sense no one really wants to go home. There's a real sense of belonging here.

I search out Bridget and spot her, sitting on a camping chair, a glass of something resembling red wine in her hand. I stand still and rest my gaze upon her. There's something rather charismatic about her. She's all the things I'd like to be: confident and self-assured, the kind of person people are drawn to like a magnet. She's alluring and poised, and tonight, sitting there by the fire, her silhouette has a golden aura to it. She reminds me of a beautiful but as yet to be discovered orchid, her form oozing a unique mixture of delicacy, sensuality and intoxicating beauty. I'm in awe of her, and as though she senses me watching, she turns around and waves. I'm soon beside her, and she points to a blanket upon the ground, where I sit, cross-legged, by her feet.

When she points to a drink under her chair, I shake my head and lift my bottle of beer.

"I'm good," I say, and we both turn and stare towards the stone.

"I think it's simple but effective," Bridget says. "And it always amazes me how the stone brings all walks of life together."

I nod and take a sip of my drink. "I find it a little eerie," I confess. "You know, how the stone draws everyone to it. And this place, the people, it's as though I've known every person here forever."

"That'll be the beer talking," Bridget chuckles into her glass.

I smile. "Perhaps. But I certainly feel like we've met before."

"Maybe we have; in another life."

"Do you believe in such things?"

"Oh, yes, and in so much more." She places the glass down by her feet and lets out a deep sigh. "Can I ask you something?"

I sense a shift in the conversation and turn to face her. "Sure; what is it?"

Her eyes pierce through mine and her mouth gains a seriousness. "The man you're with; do you love him?"

She's caught me off guard and I let out a cough and a splutter.

"Are you, all right?" she asks and pats me firmly on the back. I regain my composure and wipe the tears from my eyes, but I also avert my gaze.

"Erm…maybe I'd better not drink any more of this stuff," and I pour the rest of my beer over the ground.

Bridget slides to the edge of her seat. "Maddie, look at me."

I feel myself stiffen.

"I sense you do; love him, I mean." I stare up at her, the light from the flames flickering across her face, and I see a seriousness about her.

I shake my head vigorously. "No. You're mistaken. I'm married to Jamie's brother, Callum. They're identical twins. Perhaps you got them mixed up?"

Bridget sits back in her chair. "But he loves you."

"Who, Jamie?" She nods and I burst out laughing. "Seriously, I understand how you dabble in love rituals and stuff, but you're way off the mark this time."

She taps the side of her nose. "I think you're wrong, because I know something you don't."

"Oh, yeah, like what? After all, he's my husband's double, so there's bound to be some chemistry between us."

"No. That's not it."

"It isn't? So, tell me."

Bridget leans closer, her face just inches from mine. "Because of what Jamie wr—"

"Och, there ye are. I've been looking for ye everywhere."

I'm startled by the intrusion and look up to see Jamie standing there.

"Oh, hi. What are you doing here?"

"Looking for ye. Rhona and Gordon are ready to go home."

I jump to my feet. "Oh, right," and I stare apologetically at Bridget. "Sorry, I'd best go."

Bridget nods and slides her fingers inside an invisible pocket. I turn to leave but she calls "Wait" and jumps to her feet, takes a step towards me and presses a small piece of paper into the palm of my hand. "It's my number; ring me. I'm here until the end of next month."

I pull a frown. "I'll be leaving in a few days."

She smiles. "Best be quick, then."

"Okay, I will."

Bridget walks toward one of the makeshift tents. "I'll be waiting," she calls out without a backward glance.

I push the piece of paper inside my bag and then we head towards the music. Jamie leads the way.

"Ye seem to be getting rather pally with Bridget," he says.

"Yes, she's nice. I like her."

"'Tis guid to see ye making friends."

"Yes, I'm even surprising myself this time."

"What do ye mean?"

"Well, I don't make friends easily. I never have."

Jamie turns to me as a bright fragment of moonlight shines across the side of his face. His brows furrow.

"Och, why is that, then?"

I shrug. "Oh, I don't know. I guess I'm a bit of a loner. I tend not to let people in."

Jamie lets out a grunt. "Oh, I would ne'er have guessed."

I tug at his hand and he stops dead in his tracks. "Before you say anything, I simply can't help it," I tell him. "You learn to protect yourself from the outside world when you're raised in foster care. People often pretend to be your friend when they're only out to hurt you."

"What happened to you?"

I feel my muscles tense. "You don't really want to know."

He presses his hand against my arm. "Maddie, that's where you're wrong. I do."

I take a deep breath. "When I was in care, particularly foster homes, the families treated me like I was something disgusting they found off the streets. They would invite me into their homes, but many did it just for the money. The men were usually the worst culprits. They would segregate me from their children and their wives. Leave me home alone whilst they went on day trips to the zoo or on family picnics. From an early age, I suffered seclusion and a life without love. I was never kissed goodnight or hugged, and if I ever fell and grazed my knee, they would ask my permission to touch me."

"But surely that's nae all foster families?"

"Perhaps not, but I was never lucky enough to meet the others. Instead, I grew up believing I was a freak. I made my way through society unloved and unwanted, building a wall so I could protect myself."

"But not everyone's yir enemy."

"I know, Jamie, but I've been burned too many times to dare to reach out and touch the flame."

"Is that how ye see me?"

My jaw drops. "No, of course not."

"Then why won't ye let me in?"

"Jamie, it's nothing personal. After what I've been through, especially with men, I…I just can't."

There's a peel of laughter and I swing around. Through the last of the stragglers I see Rhona and Gordon heading our way.

I breathe a sigh of relief and dash towards them.

"Och, we're ready for our beds. Are ye ready too?" Rhona asks, pulling me into a drunken embrace.

"Actually, yes, I am," I say as she hugs me to her bosom.

"What about Jamie?"

He nods. "Aye, we all may as well call it a night."

Rhona links her arm inside mine. "Come on, let's get out of here. It'll take us at least another hour to walk home." She pulls me close and whispers in my ear: "I hope ye wish comes true."

"How do you know what I wished for?" I ask.

She shakes her head and lets out a sigh. "Ye dinnae need the brains of an archbishop to work that one out," she says, and I laugh because it's true.

Rhona and I wander along the track, laughing and dancing and hugging one another, as though we were born sisters. The men are close behind, but we're surrounded by darkness. The only light illuminating our way is the new moon's bright silvery crescent. We're halfway through singing *The Bonnie Banks o' Loch Lomond* when Rhona stops and says: "This is where we have to bid ye a fond farewell." She hugs me tight. "It's been a memorable day and one I'll cherish," she slurs. Gordon comes over and hugs me too and then slaps Jamie on the back. We both wave goodbye as Gordon throws his arm around his wife. They stagger, somewhat drunkenly, onto a track that will lead them to a spot where they'll be picked up by a close family member.

Jamie and I carry on the last leg of our journey. He walks beside me and I laugh as he keeps bumping into me.

"You're drunk," I say.

"Aye, and so are ye," and he gives me a sharp nudge in the ribs with his elbow. I giggle and grab his arm, allowing my fingers to slide towards his hand, which he locks in his own. He pulls me close and we walk together in silence, contented in one another's company. I stare ahead to see the dark silhouettes of the approaching barn and outbuildings. The wind rustles through the trees and a security light flashes on as we approach the farm gate. Jamie lifts the latch and we push our way through, then head down the path to the Garden House.

Like teenagers we stand outside the cottage, facing one another. The last of the dark cloud has lifted enough to allow the moonlight to shine down onto Jamie's face once again.

"I've had the most amazing day," I say.

Jamie shrugs. "It was a pleasure. We'll have to do it again sometime."

I nod. "I'd like that a lot."

"Aye, so would I."

I can't help but look up into his eyes. They're soft and meaningful yet hypnotising, all at the same time.

"Would you like to come in for coffee?"

"Maddie, I dinnae think that would be a guid idea."

"Why ever not?"

He heaves a sigh. "I think ye ken why."

I drop my gaze, and even in the darkness, I feel my cheeks burn. I try to make light of his rejection, laughing lightly, but it sounds false, even to me.

I turn away from him. "Goodnight, Jamie. Sleep tight," but I don't wait for his reply. Instead, I hurry inside the cottage and shut the door behind me, where I chide myself over and over. After all, I've just set myself up for a fall.

I drag my tired feet, one by one, up the wooden stairs. Once I reach my bedroom, I take off my boots and drop, exhausted, onto the bed. I close my eyes, and behind their lids, an array of dancers move along the ground in bare feet. A wind blows through their hair, their heads covered in a halo of wild roses, cyclamen and pretty snowdrops.

Letting out a sigh, I open my eyes. My head is still buzzing and I need to unwind. I get up and place Claire's cloak on a hook behind the bedroom door, along with the hessian bag, then take out my mobile phone and place it on the bedside table. At the dressing table, I take the feathers and beads out of my hair, unzip my dress and allow it to fall to the floor. Once I've stripped off my thermals, I stand there, in front of the mirror, in just my underwear. I stare at my reflection. Although I'm tired, I can see there's a healthy glow to my skin and the fresh air has done wonders for my complexion. I un-braid my hair and force my fingers through the tight waves. It falls softly down my back and I stroke a stray curl away from my face.

I slide my hand down to my stomach and wonder what it must be like to conceive a baby naturally, then I feel for the thumping heartbeat, the ten tiny fingers and the ten tiny toes. I close my eyes and pretend I know. The bond, though, between mother and baby does not swell. There is no umbilical cord, just an empty womb which will never hold love. A lone tear spills down my cheek and once again I stare at my own reflection. The face that stares back is lonely and sad.

In the bathroom, I switch on the shower and wait until white steam covers the glass before I climb inside the cubicle. Hot water splashes against my skin and the sensation sends shivers down my spine. As I wash away the grime and dirt of the day, Ally pushes her way into my thoughts. Flashbacks of what she said to me at the festival leave me cold: "*It's time he came back to where he belongs, to where we both belong*". Head down, I press my hands against the shower wall. I can still hear Ally scream "*He's always been mine*", and I let out a choking sob, afraid I'm about to lose my husband. "*It was simple circumstances that tore us apart,*" she now yells inside my head.

I switch off the shower and snatch a towel from the rail. As I rub myself dry, Ally's sneering face is all the while in the forefront of my mind. When I finish, I throw the towel onto the floor and put on a set of warm pyjamas, then get into bed and switch off the light. I snuggle down and close my eyes. It's like the night sky but without the stars. I refuse, though, to let Ally stay inside my head, but just as I'm dozing off, I hear a faint buzz and reach for my phone. One eye open, I press the button which lights up the screen. It's a text message from Callum: "*I tried to ring you, but it went straight to voicemail. I'll try again in the morning*".

I place the phone back onto the bedside table. It's too late to call him back now. I pull the covers over my head and turn over, my hand gliding across the spot where Callum should be.

CHAPTER ELEVEN

"Maddie, for Christ sake, will ye get up. Granda's taken a turn for the worse and I need ye."

I sit bolt upright, my eyes still heavy with sleep, but there's no one in my bedroom, so I hurry to the window, pull the net curtain aside and look out. Jamie's there, gesturing for me to go to him, and so I scurry to the end of the bed and snatch my jeans. I dive to the wardrobe, grabbing the first things to hand: a thin blouse and a padded jacket. I tear off my nightclothes and push my arms through the sleeves, press my feet into the fur lined boots I wore the day before, and I'm down the stairs and out onto the drive.

"What's happened?" I ask, pulling the jacket closer when the wind tries to tear if from my body.

"I dinnae know for sure. 'Twas my turn to get up with the fold this morning, and when I returned, granda was in the kitchen, sitting in his chair, clutching his chest."

"Have you phoned for an ambulance?"

"Aye, but they said it could be over half an hour before they get here."

"Then we have to take him ourselves. If he's having chest pains, we can't wait that long for them to arrive."

We dash over to the farmhouse and into the kitchen.

A knot of fear twists in the pit of my stomach when I see granda slumped in one of the fireside chairs. His face is deathly pale and his lips are turning blue. I rush over and crouch down beside him.

"Oh, dear God. Granda, are you okay?" He mumbles something, but I can't quite hear him, so I move a little closer and a wheeze escapes his lips.

"We need to loosen his shirt and trousers," I say, reaching over him.

"Do ye know what to do," Jamie asks, and I glance up to read his expression. He's scared, just as I am.

"No, not really," I confess. "But I did live with a foster family once who had an elderly grandmother with a history of heart problems."

"I'm not dead yet," granda finally rasps.

"I'm glad to hear it," I say, unfastening his shirt buttons and pulling open the collar. "And, I'd like you to stay that way if you don't mind."

He tries to laugh but breaks out into a coughing fit. I unclip the belt on his trousers.

"Calm yourself and take a deep breath," I say. "Tell me: did the doctor say you suffered from Angina?" to which he nods.

"Och, why didn't ye tell me?" Jamie roars. "Ye shouldnae have kept something so serious to yourself."

I give him a hard stare. "Not now, Jamie. Just go and fetch a glass of water, please," and I turn back to face the old man as Jamie heads over to the sink, from where I hear the gurgle of running water.

I squeeze Alasdair's hand. "Think. Did the doctor give you a spray or something to help overcome these attacks?"

Again, granda nods, and I instinctively thrust my hand inside his trouser pockets. My fingers fight through curled up pieces of twine and round sticky objects that make me squirm. I search thoroughly, but there's no spray.

I try to quell the panic that's rising in the pit of my stomach by taking a deep breath.

"Where did you put it?" I ask.

"Maybe it's by my bed?" he rasps.

"Jamie!" I say, and he rushes over, thrusts a glass of water into my hand and dashes out through the kitchen door. I hear his boots on the stairs as I offer Alasdair the water, which he guzzles down, but it feels like an eternity before Jamie returns.

He slaps a red and white bottle into the palm of my hand and I quickly read the instructions, then rip off the cap. Alasdair opens his mouth and I press two squirts under his tongue.

Alasdair lets out a long sigh.

"Does that feel better?" I ask, but when he shakes his head, my eyes fix firmly on Jamie. "I think we may need aspirin. Do you have any?"

Jamie nods. "Aye, somewhere."

"Then find it!"

He doesn't hesitate and rushes over to the kitchen cupboards, opening and banging shut several doors in his search of the tablets.

"Here," he eventually says and throws a small glass bottle towards me. I catch it and unscrew the cap, taking out a white tablet.

"The spray should have worked by now," I explain. "I'll have to give him the aspirin, but then we must get him straight to hospital."

When I look back at Alasdair, I can see by the colour of his skin that he's deteriorating. "Go and bring the car around to the door," I say, "we need to get him there immediately."

Jamie dives out of the kitchen. My attention remains with Alasdair. "Please, take the aspirin," I urge, and I wait for him to open his mouth again. I press the tablet onto his tongue and he sips the last of the water.

"Don't go to sleep," I urge. "Jamie will be back with the car at any moment."

There's a rustle of noise and Jamie bursts into the room.

"The car's outside," he tells me.

"Good. Come on, granda, let's get you out of this chair," and I place a hand under his arm, to support him, but in a flash, Jamie gently pushes me aside and lifts granda into his arms, as though he weighs little more than a feather.

"Get the car door open," he says, and I nod and dash outside and pull open the back door, Jamie close behind. He gently lays Alasdair onto the back seat and I slam the door once I've checked he's comfortable, then run around to the other side and climb in next to him. There's a tartan blanket on the floor, which I quickly unfold and place across his knees and up to his chest. Once I've fastened my seat belt I glance across to see granda's closed his eyes. He lets out a sigh.

"Alasdair, wake up," I say, giving him a gentle shake. "Please, don't go to sleep."

Jamie hits the accelerator and the car lurches forward. He spins the vehicle around and speeds off down the drive.

"Oh, my God. I think he's unconscious," I rasp, and Jamie presses the accelerator even harder.

"Is he still breathing?" he asks as we hit the main road. I stare at him through the rear-view mirror. His eyes are round with fear. I lick my lips, nervously.

"Maddie, are ye listening to me?"

I unfasten my seat belt and slide closer to Alasdair. Stroking his silver hair aside, I put my ear close to his lips, but then shake my head. "It's no use. I can't tell over the noise of the engine," I cry out.

"Then take his pulse," Jamie urges.

I lift his hand out from beneath the blanket. His wrist is limp and his pulse is weak when I find it, then a sob escapes my lips. "I think we're going to lose him," I cry.

"No, not if I've anything to do with it," Jamie affirms. "The hospital isnae far. It's just a few minutes away."

He takes a sharp left and zig-zags around several parked cars, the hospital gates looming up ahead and the sign for A&E. He drives over the speedbumps, the exhaust scraping across their humps, hits the brakes, snaps on the handbrake, and jumps out of the car. He heads straight for Alasdair as I get out and dash around the car to help him.

There's an ambulance sitting empty in a nearby bay, the driver just climbing inside, and Jamie shouts, "Can someone help us, please?" The man slams the door and rushes over.

"'Tis my granda," Jamie tells him, "he needs urgent medical attention."

The driver checks Alasdair's pulse, looks into his eyes, and then puts his ear to his mouth. When he looks up, the seriousness of granda's situation is written all over his face.

"Quick; lie him down on the floor," and the second Alasdair's body is on the ground, the paramedic begins administering CPR. I put a hand over my mouth to stifle a scream as the stranger presses his hands onto the centre of granda's chest.

"Go inside and get help," the driver yells, and Jamie hurtles himself through the double doors.

In seconds a trolley is pushed out towards us and I hear someone shout "CRASH TEAM", then there's a flurry of activity as a stream of doctors and nurses dash to granda's aid.

"Take him straight to resus," a young Asian doctor says once granda's secure, and he takes over the CPR as they rush the old man inside the building.

I can't believe what's happening as I rush in after them, tears flowing like a river down my face. I don't know what to do, there are so many people around granda. I just stand, frozen to the spot, as the A&E department try to save Alasdair's life. Then the trolley's snatched from Jamie's grasp and I watch it disappear down the corridor as the doctor shouts out vital lifesaving instructions.

"Wait," Jamie cries, chasing after them, but a male nurse grabs him by the arm and pulls him back. "Please, try and stay calm," he says. "Right now, he's in the best possible hands."

A set of double doors further down the corridor burst open and a nurse grabs the bottom of the trolley and pulls it inside. I glimpse an array of monitors and medical equipment, and I let out a sob. Then the doors close behind the trolley and I flick my gaze towards Jamie as he draws his hand to his mouth. He bites down on his fist, and for a second, I fear he'll draw blood. I throw myself at him and grab his hand, and he turns to me and his face crumples. I fling my arms around his neck and pull him close.

"They'll save him," I insist, "they have to." He slips his arms around my waist and pulls me closer still.

"I cannae lose him," he whispers against my neck. "He's all I have left."

"You still have me," I croak, and his grip tightens.

Someone coughs and my reaction is to pull away

"Excuse me, but if you wouldn't mind helping us with the patient's details?"

I wipe the stream of tears away from my cheeks by using the sleeve of my blouse and stare at the nurse: a man with dark hair, in his early twenties. He points to a couple of empty plastic chairs in the waiting area.

"If you wouldn't mind," he says, gently, and once we sit down, he goes over to the reception desk and returns with a pile of forms to fill in. I take Jamie's hand in mine. He's shaking from head to toe, and I tighten my grip and give him my best impression of a reassuring smile.

"I'll have to call Callum," I say, once the nurse finishes gathering Alasdair's details.

Jamie nods. "Aye, you'd best do it right away."

"I'll nip outside and do it now."

He nods. "Sure, and while you're doing that, I'll go find a coffee machine."

We both get up together and go our separate ways. I head outside and drag my mobile from the back pocket of my jeans to see I've three missed calls from Callum.

I hit his number.

"Hey, Maddie, where have you been? I've been trying to call you for the last hour."

"Er, sorry, Callum. Something serious has happened."

"What do you mean? Are you okay?"

I take a deep breath. "No, not really. I'm outside the local hospital. It's granda. I think he's suffered a heart attack."

"He's what?"

"It all happened so fast. He's with the crash team now."

"Is he going to be okay?"

I fight back my tears. "I honestly don't know. He looked pretty sick when they took him inside."

"Where's Jamie?"

"He's here. He was the one who found him slumped in his chair."

I hear Callum suck in his breath. "Christ. Okay. I'm on my way. Just ring me if you hear something—anything."

"Yes, I will," and there's a moment's silence. "I love you," I say, but he's already gone.

I try and pull myself together as I go back inside. Jamie's returned with the coffee.

"White, nae sugar," he says as I approach. He offers me a paper cup and I take it from him.

"Has anyone been out to see you yet?" I ask.

Jamie shakes his head. "Nah, nae one."

I go over to the receptionist to see if she can put our minds at rest.

"I'm sure someone will be out to see you as soon as they can," she reassures me, then a nurse taps me on the shoulder and I almost jump out of my skin.

"Mrs McKinley?"

I nod profusely.

"If you would like to follow me, please."

***

I find the small relatives' room a little claustrophobic. There's no window or natural light and the air is stale and lifeless. I leave the door ajar as I step out into the corridor. From where I'm standing, I can see around the ward and along to where Alasdair now lies in an induced coma. I'm so grateful he's alive, but terrified he's going to die. I can't bear to see him lying there, so still and lifeless. He's always been so robust, so hardworking and strongminded. To see him like this, helpless, weak and feeble, is more than I can stomach.

Long curtains hang around each of the beds. Some are pulled closed whilst others are used to separate each patient and give them a little privacy. Medical staff surround Alasdair's bed, but no one has been able to give us any real answers. "He's stable" the nurse had said when he came out of resus. "I hear he's lucky to be alive," the porter in the lift had said.

A flurry of movement catches my eye as the medical team begin to file away from his bed. The consultant is in deep discussions with two of his associates. I stare at the doctor who accompanied me and Jamie to the ward, but he simply walks on by. My gaze follows him, willing him to turn around and retrace his steps, but he carries on going, oblivious to our distress. When he disappears around a corner, I let out a disappointed sigh.

"Mr and Mrs McKinley?"

"Oh, no, I'm not—"

"Listen. You should both go home and try and get some rest."

There's the scrape of a chair along the floor and then Jamie's voice fills the corridor.

"Can ye tell us how he's doing?" he says. "Only no one's given us any updates."

I look at Jamie, but then flick my gaze towards the ITU nurse. Her mouth droops a little at one corner.

"I think the doctor explained to you why Mr McKinley, your grandfather, has been given a paralytic drug," she tells him.

We both shake our heads simultaneously. "No, actually; no one did," I say.

She lifts an eyebrow and glances down to study the paperwork in her hands.

"Well, basically, your grandfather suffered a cardiac arrest. The drug has been administered

174

because the consultant wants his body to rest. He's also been placed on a ventilator and the drugs will help stop any discomfort. Due to the arrest, his brain needs to recover, and so we're doing everything we can to reduce the risk of brain damage."

"Does that mean he may be a vegetable?" I ask.

The nurse squeezes the top of my shoulder.

"I have to be honest; there's always a risk, but so far he's responded well to treatment, and as long as his vital signs remain stable, we'll be weaning him off the ventilator tomorrow morning."

An alarm sounds. It's one of the machines attached to another patient, and a red light flashes at the nurses' station. The nurse spins around to check someone is dealing with it. A tall woman, wearing sensible black shoes, hurries down the corridor and over to the bed. She checks the patient's vital signs and then calmly switches off the alarm.

The staff nurse turns her attention back to us.

"Go home," she says. "We'll call you if there's any change."

I look at Jamie for guidance and he nods. "Okay, we'll be back in the morning."

The nurse smiles, and for the first time I realise she's not as old as I at first thought. "I think that's best," she says. "Your grandfather needs lots of rest if he's to recover."

"Can we just sit with him for a moment?" Jamie asks. The nurse's frown reappears, but she stands aside to allow us to pass.

"Just a few minutes," she says. "Then it's home for both of you."

She leads us to granda's bedside. The blinds are pulled down and bright streams of sunlight seep onto the bedclothes. Alasdair's surrounded by lifesaving equipment and he's hooked up to a multitude of grey wires and long plastic tubes. His eyes are closed and I've never seen him look so pale. There's dark-grey smudges around his eye sockets and thin blue lines across his lids. His skin is chalk white.

The ventilator makes a shushing sound as it pushes oxygen into Alasdair's body, and he's surrounded by temperature gauges and tall silver poles with hooks that can hold bags of either saline or blood. My eyes trail to the hospital gown Alasdair's wearing. It seems wrong to see him dressed in something clinical. I'm used to his old battered cardigan and corduroy trousers, and I struggle not to fall apart.

There's a small upright unit by his bed where his clothes are kept. I can see his shirt hanging inside, and his shoes are placed side by side on a shelf.

I take Jamie's hand, surprised to find his fingers are stone cold.

He lets out a heavy sigh. "It's hard to believe granda's fighting for his life," he says. "He's always been there for me. I just cannae imagine life without him."

"Don't talk like that," I chide. "He's a fighter, and the nurse says everything looks promising. We must stay positive."

He spares just a millisecond to nod at me and then moves closer to granda and gently strokes the back of his hand.

"When Claire died, I couldnae eat or sleep. I was so confused, and angry with the world. It was as though I was stuck in limbo, where nothing made sense and I couldnae differentiate between reality and my own imagination. Granda saved me from myself. He was the one who held me together and stopped the grief from destroying me."

He turns to me then, and tears are flowing silently down his cheeks.

Once again, I fling my arms around his neck and he pulls me tight as I hug him close. I don't ever want to let him go. Words are not appropriate. Only my actions can help him now. I crush his body to mine and hope it's enough.

I hear someone approach, but this time I don't release Jamie. I hold onto him until his grip loosens. I feel my own tears slide down my face, and when

Jamie finally pulls away, his eyes are red and swollen.

"Come back in the morning," says a nurse with kind eyes. "We'll know more by then."

My boots squeak against the linoleum as I walk away, Jamie right behind me. We head past the nurses' station and into the hospital lift. We don't say a word to one another. There is no need.

When we push open the main doors, I embrace the cold that blows into my face. It feels refreshing against my skin. I stare over at the car, still parked at the front of the main building, and let out a sigh of relief.

"I had a horrible feeling the car may have been clamped by security in our absence," I say.

"Or worse, towed away," Jamie says with a sigh.

"Yes, that too."

Jamie checks the windscreen. "Aye, and there's no penalty notice, either." He pulls the car keys from his jeans pocket and unlocks the door and climbs into the driver's seat as I head over to the passenger side.

"Are you okay to drive?" I ask.

He starts the engine. "I'm fine," and he shoves the gearstick from neutral and into first.

He drives slowly through the hospital grounds as I stare out of the window, searching along the side of the building for Alasdair's room. Part of me doesn't want to leave him behind.

"If he survives, it's thanks to ye," Jamie says as we hit the main road.

I turn towards him and shake my head. "No, Jamie, we both did our best to save him. Please don't beat yourself up or take the blame; this was nobody's fault."

Jamie takes a deep breath and grabs the wheel tighter, his knuckles turning white. "But he suffers from Angina and he ne'er told me."

"Again, that's not your fault. He's a proud man and clearly didn't want to tell anyone."

Jamie strikes the wheel with his fist, taking me by surprise.

"But I should've known," he declares. "I should've seen the signs."

"Pull over."

"What?"

"You heard me. I said, pull over."

Jamie steers the car onto the grass verge.

"Get out," I say, and he looks at me as though I've gone stark raving mad. I open my door and clamber out onto the bank. It's freezing, the temperature having dropped dramatically, and I pull my jacket closer to block out the icy wind.

Jamie walks around the car and stands in front of me.

"Let's get one thing clear," I say. "What happened to granda isn't anyone's fault. He's a stubborn old mule, and blaming yourself is only going to make matters worse."

"I cannae help it," he says, shoving his hands into his jeans pockets. "We live together twenty-four-seven and yet I ne'er knew anything about his condition."

I lean my arm against the car. "So, in future you keep an eye on him. Check he's taking his medication."

Jamie rests his back on the car door and stares out across the surrounding countryside. It's bleak, and I can tell, by the tightening of Jamie's jaw, that he still blames himself. He lets out a heavy sigh. "It's times like this I wish I smoked," he jokes, and for the first time the corners of my mouth lift into a smile.

"Yeah, me too," I agree, and the tension between us melts away.

"We should be getting back," he says. "There's work to do and animals to feed."

I reach out and touch the back of his hand. He places his fingers on top of mine and I suffer a delicious sexual shiver down my spine; his touch is electric.

"Jamie, why am I drawn to you? It's like…you're a drug I simply can't get enough of."

His fingers tighten around mine. "Please…don't say another word."

"I can't help it," I whisper.

"But it would only end by us hurtin' the one person we both love."

I drop my gaze and he lets go of my hand then climbs back into the car, and I go back to my side and get in. In silence, Jamie drives us home, and the moment we arrive outside the farmhouse, my mobile goes off.

"I'll grab some outdoor gear from one of the sheds and catch ye later," Jamie says.

I nod, step out of the car and press the phone to my ear.

"Hey, Keira, how lovely to hear from you."

"Maddie, I've had a call from Callum. I'm so sorry to hear about granda."

I switch the phone to my other ear and wait until Jamie heads off in the opposite direction.

"It's been a nightmare," I confess. "Alasdair suffered a cardiac arrest and is on a ventilator."

I hear Keira take a sharp intake of breath. "Oh, no, how awful. Is he going to be okay?"

"We don't know for sure. The nurses couldn't tell us much, but they did say he's in a stable condition for now."

"At least that sounds positive. Callum sounded in a panic when he phoned. He asked if I was willing to hold the fort a little longer. As if he needed to ask."

I head over to the farmhouse and open the front door. "He'd have wanted to put my mind at rest. But I know you're always there for us."

"That goes without saying. And the shop should be the least of your worries."

"It is," I admit. "I need to focus on supporting my family the best I can right now."

"Exactly. It's going to be a rough ride for everyone."

"I know, and I pray he makes it through."

"He will. He's made of stern stuff."

"For once, I hope you're right."

I hear the distinct tinkle of the shop bell in the background.

"I have to go, there's a customer waiting," Keira says. "Ring me, as soon as you have an update."

"I will," I promise, and Keira ends the call.

I look around the empty kitchen. The fire has gone out and all the warmth of the house seems to have disappeared along with Alasdair. I realise, perhaps not for the first time, how important granda is to the farm, to all of us.

I pick up an old wicker basket and go outside to where a pile of firewood is stacked high against the wall. I shiver and stare up at the sky. It's overcast and leaden. My gaze follows a single snowflake as it lazily falls to the ground. I'm surprised when it doesn't melt away. It's followed by another, this one too drifting idly along on the breeze before it lands by my feet. I gather the logs into the rattan basket as a multitude of snowflakes now fall from the sky, and I'm soon back inside, closing the door against them with a shiver.

I busy myself at the hearth, lighting a fire, enjoying watching the kitchen come back to life, then I wash my hands and go over to the fridge. I take out two slices of Gammon and a couple of fresh eggs. I'm hunting around for a frying pan when I hear the front door open.

"Perfect timing," I say, bending down to open a cupboard door and pushing a pile of old pots to one side, trying to locate the elusive pan. "I'm just about to make us something to eat."

"Great, I've been on the road all day. I'm famished."

I jump to my feet in surprise. "Callum, is that you?" and I accidently bang my elbow on the handle of the oven door. "Ouch, that hurts," I cry out.

"Sorry? Are you okay? I didn't mean to startle you."

I rub my arm and smile. "I'm sure I'll live. How did you manage to get back so soon?"

"I put my foot down and thankfully the traffic wasn't too bad. Is there any news on granda?"

I hurry over and plant a warm kiss on his lips. "The nurse says he's stable. If he's the same in the morning, they'll wean him off the ventilator."

"That sounds promising. But I need to see him for myself."

"I'm sure they wouldn't mind you popping in under the circumstances. They'd understand. It's just the nurse said he needs as much rest as possible."

Callum's shoulders appear to sag, and I read the disappointment written all over his face.

I put my arms around him and give him a hug. "Why don't you go to the hospital and put your mind at ease?"

"I want to. I'm scared he might die."

I stroke the back of his hair, as though comforting a child, and then let him go. "And you're worried that you never got the chance to say goodbye?"

He drops his gaze and I give him yet another hug.

"I understand. But have something to eat before you leave." I go back to the fridge and pull out another slice of gammon, then reach inside a cupboard and pull out an extra tea cup.

"Where's Jamie?" Callum asks.

I fill the kettle, put it onto the stove and switch on the gas. "I think he went to feed the horses."

"No, I doubt that, not now snow's falling. He'll be bringing the fold closer to the farm."

"Oh, I didn't realise."

Callum takes a step towards the hallway. "There's an area of sheltered land closer to home, where the snow doesn't drift. I should go and help him."

"What about granda?"

"I'll go once the fold has been brought to lower ground."

I nod and switch off the gas. "Sure. Shall I come with you?"

He shakes his head. "No, there's no need. The snow's coming down hard. Stay indoors and keep warm."

I smile at his thoughtfulness. "Okay, and I'll cook as soon as you both get back."

Callum's phone goes off in his pocket. I can tell by the sound it's a text message. He delves inside and pulls out his Smartphone and glances down at the screen.

"Work stuff?" I ask.

He nods and thrusts the mobile back inside his pocket. "It's nothing that won't wait," and he leaves the house.

I switch on the radio and busy myself by peeling potatoes and chopping green beans and carrots. My occasional glance outside the kitchen window confirming the snow is falling thick and fast. But then I see a dark silhouetted face within the glass, one that's not mine, but Ally's. I desperately want to talk to Callum about her, to put this unexpected episode to bed, but granda's our main priority right now and so it must wait.

I put the potatoes and vegetables into saucepans and leave them sitting on the stove, then go over to one of the fireside chairs and sit and wait for the men to return, but I simply can't get Ally out of my head.

Jumping to my feet, I head over to the front door, find a pair of boots with a thick sole and put them on. I grab my coat, hat and gloves and head outside, shocked to see the trees laden with snow. I head down to the stables. At least if I get the horses fed it'll be one less job for Jamie and Callum to worry about.

The wind has dropped, the world out here now seeming calm and peaceful, and I smile to myself. I'm almost at the stable block when the wind whips up from nowhere and carries a sound—voices. I stop to listen.

"That's impossible."

"I knew you wouldn't believe me, but I'm telling you it's true."

I creep behind the stable block and closer to the main farm buildings. Turning a corner, my heart skips a beat.

Callum is standing by one of the corrugated sheds, talking to someone I can't quite see, his body blocking my view. I take a step closer, snow crunching underfoot. Their voices rise; they're arguing. Callum's back is towards me and I watch his arms fly up into the air. I'm terrified of what I may overhear yet still I put one foot in front of the other. Slowly, I make my way towards him, and when I'm roughly six feet away, my stomach heaves as Callum's white breath rises into the once more still air.

"I'm telling you, she isn't having an affair with Jamie."

He moves slightly to one side and my heart lurches in my chest—he's with Ally.

"But I've seen the way they are together," she says.

"I don't care what you think you've seen; I know you're just looking for an excuse to make me leave her."

Ally shoves her hands deeper into her coat pockets and lets out a sigh.

"Either way, it's time Maddie learned the truth."

"Don't make me do this," Callum says.

"You don't have a choice. You have to tell her."

"You know I can't. It will kill her."

"But you can't keep living a lie," to which Callum lets out a deep sigh.

"I hear what you're saying, but if she finds out what's happened between us, it'll destroy her."

I look down at my hands, jittering of their own accord, and clench my fingers into fists to try and make them stop. I clear my throat but the wind whips away the sound. "Callum," I then say, "what are you doing here with Ally?"

His shoulders arch, as though a cat-o-nine tails had just sliced through the skin on his back, then he seems to recover and spins around to face me. His eyes are wide, and his mouth drops open at the sight of me.

"Maddie. What are you doing here?"

I back away, no longer wishing to hear anything he has to say, but Ally takes a bold step forward and points a gloved finger in my direction.

"Callum, you need to explain everything—now."

"I'm going back to the house," I say, my terror rising a notch.

"Jesus, Ally," Callum hisses. "This is not how she should learn the truth."

"I don't want to know," I cry, shaking my head, hearing my own panic rising in my voice and hardly able to breathe.

He rushes towards me, but I hold my hands out to make him stop.

"Stay away from me," I plead. "Just don't touch me."

"I'm so sorry, Maddie. I never meant to hurt you."

"You're having an affair?" I say, astonished. "How? When?" then I turn away from him, ready to run, but he lunges and grabs my arm. He pulls me so hard I whizz around to face him.

"No, it's not like that. I'm not having an affair," he cries.

I stare at him as though he's told a big fat lie, but then I feel my brows furrow, and for a brief moment, a sense of relief washes over me. "But...I...don't..."

"Tell her, and get it all out into the open," Ally interjects, and Callum's hands slide up to my shoulders.

"I'm sorry, Maddie, there's no easy way to say it, so I'm just going to come straight out with it."

I nod, like one of those dippers that can be won at the fair.

"Okay, I'm listening," I finally whimper.

Callum takes a deep breath. "Six years ago, before we got together, I was in a long-term relationship with Ally." His eyes shoot towards the vet and then back at me.

"As you've probably guessed, it didn't work out and we went our separate ways. Ally found herself a job in Chelmsford and I relocated. We stayed in contact because we both wanted to remain friends."

"Yet...you never told me about her. Why?"

Callum shrugs. "No reason other than I didn't wish to mix the past with the present."

I lick my lips. "So, what changed? Why is Ally adamant she wants you back? Do you want to be with her? Is that it?"

He lets go of me then and glances down at his feet and shakes his head, but then he looks me straight in the eye. "It's far more complicated than that. I received a call from Ally a few weeks after you and I hooked up together. She said she needed to see me." For a moment he hesitates, takes another deep breath.

"I lied to you. I said I had to go away on business, but the truth was...I was meeting Ally. That's when she dropped the bombshell."

I stare at him for the longest time. I don't want to ask the obvious question, but my lips move without my consent.

"What bombshell?" I croak.

Callum gives me a pleading look and presses his hands to the back of his neck. "God, Maddie, I never meant any of this to happen."

"TELL ME. WHAT BOMBSHELL?"

"That...that...Ally was pregnant with my child when we split up."

His words hit me so hard it's as though I've taken a physical blow. My eyelids flutter as I take in their full impact, feeling like I've just stepped off the waltzers. Everything's spinning.

"But that's impossible," I rasp. "We both know you can't…"

"Have kids? Yes. That's true, but the irony is that I caught mumps *after* she fell pregnant."

"And before you met me?"

He nods and my knees buckle, but Callum catches hold of me, stopping me from falling.

"I didn't know what to do," he tells me, his eyes beseeching. "We'd moved in together by the time the baby arrived and you and I had just found out we couldn't have a child of our own. How could I admit I'd already fathered a child? Not when I was so aware of the devastating impact it would have on you."

I'm unable to hide the desperation in my voice. "How long have you been seeing Ally behind my back?"

"Maddie, I—"

"How long, Cal?"

"On and off since she was six months pregnant."

The muscles in my chest tighten and I swear my heart stops beating for a moment.

"So, you've lied to me the whole time we've been married?" I say in a small voice.

He nods. "I'm so sorry. I never meant to hurt you."

"And this child…"

"A boy."

"You have a son?" My chest tightens. "Does he look like you?"

"Please, don't do this," Callum begs.

"Does he have your eyes, your hair colour?"

Callum doesn't reply. He looks down at the ground and remains tight-lipped.

I clutch my stomach and a pitiful cry escapes my lips. "How could you do this to me? And all this time you've made me believe you couldn't have children—*we* couldn't have children." I take a breath. "You said you loved me, and I believed you."

Callum looks up and his grip tightens.

"I do love you, and it's been torture for me, too. I wanted to share my happiness, to shout out and tell the world I had a son, but the guilt's been tearing me apart."

I seriously can't believe what I'm hearing. "You mean…you're actually blaming me for the fact you kept your child a secret?" I stare at the man who has become a stranger to me. "Our whole life together was built on a lie," and although the words are mine, they seem to have come from someone else.

"Surely, we can work something out," Callum whispers.

I stare at him as if he's gone stark raving mad. "You mean carry on as we are? You want Ally and I to share you? Is that it?" Anger is now rising from the pit of my stomach. I clench my fist, draw back my arm and punch Callum straight in the face. Pain shoots down my hand and along to my elbow when my knuckles connect with his jaw. His expression is one of shocked surprise, a trickle of red already oozing from the side of his mouth.

Ally lets out a wail and jumps to his aid. "Get the fuck away from him," she screams, and dabs his lip with a scrunched-up tissue she hurriedly extracts from her pocket.

Tears pour down my cheeks seeing them together: Callum with his fingers curled around hers, Ally all over him like a rash. It leaves a sour taste in my mouth, and I just shake my head, unable to digest the bond they clearly share, no longer able to bear to breathe the same air.

I turn and run.

All I can think about is Callum's child, a boy running in the snow, with cute dimpled skin and a bright dazzling smile. A head of rich auburn curls bounces about his head, and when he turns to me, I see a pair of sparkling sea-green eyes. I clutch my chest at the overwhelming image, my pain leaving me breathless.

His child will never be mine.

I head back towards the farmhouse, the snow hitting my face, sharp like slivers of ice, then I'm past the garden house, my feet refusing to stop. I don't want to go inside, not where the air is warm and the familiar rooms cosy. I no longer feel safe there and so turn on my heels. I need to be alone.

It's growing dark. There are no birds in the sky, and even the chickens have fallen quiet. All I hear is the crunch of the snow under my boots as I make my way towards the gate that leads to the brae.

One of the farm dogs barks as I lift the latch.

"Maddie? Where are you?" Callum calls through the darkening and white-flecked swirling air, but I ignore him, a notch of fear rising within me at the thought of him chasing after me. I glance down. The frozen earth is white now, my tracks easy for him to follow, but I push on into the faster falling snow, seeing almost nothing before me but streaks of white against the deepening blackness. I'm running now, fast in my flight, until my foot jars and I stumble over a hidden stone. I lose my balance and fall to the ground, a sharp pain shooting through my knee. I peer down to see I've grazed it, and I cover my mouth to smother a hiss of pain. Then I force myself back onto my feet, wipe a stream of snowflakes from my eyes and hurry down a path I vaguely recognise. Everything's covered in a blanket of white and the bitter cold is seeping through to my bones.

I head for a row of trees that I know will take me to the woodland. Covered in snow, they look majestic, reminding me of a picture I once saw on a Christmas card; all that's missing is a light dusting of glitter. It feels warmer here, protected by the trees, but still I stumble over invisible clods of earth and decaying branches.

Leaning back against a thick tree trunk I catch my breath, recognising nothing around me. The trees appear the same in all directions.

A gust of wind knocks snow off one of the branches, but there's other movement between the trees and my heart lurches in my chest. I catch sight of a figure in the distance and hold my breath, unsure whether it's Callum or a deer. With my breath back in me, I dash off in the opposite direction, hastening between light snow drifts and frozen undergrowth, and finally I manage to get away. Out of breath once more, I slump down near a large boulder and gulp in the freezing air, sharp within my throat. Something's above my head and I fend it off with my hand, touching nothing more than a frost encrusted low-lying branch. I'm cold, and sit as still as the night, listening to the sounds of the woodland.

A twig snaps and I take off again, like a startled deer, away from the sound, deeper into the darkness, no longer able to see where I'm going. Panicking at another sharp sound behind, I flay my arms out in front of me and let out a scream as I glance back over my shoulder.

The ground underfoot dips unexpectedly beneath my feet, and I turn sharply, only to suffer an almighty thwack against my forehead. Glittering silver stars fill my vision as I feel myself go light for a moment, before I thud painfully into the deepening snow, finally lying there, dazed. As I shakily reach up and touch my head, the stars fizzle ever brighter and more densely before my sight, until I sink through them into the depths of an utter darkness.

CHAPTER TWELVE

*J*amie

The snow's made moving the herd difficult. It's falling so fast I've had to move quickly. I could have left them there. There's plenty of dead grass and forbs sticking up from the ground that they can nose away with their muzzles and eat, but I can't afford to take the risk.

I guide them from the glen on foot, as I always have. The bad weather makes my vision blurred, but the fold moves easily from the high ground to where they will be much safer in the lower field. I check the water trough hasn't frozen over before I leave. Satisfied they're safe, I bolt the gate and head off down the track to one of the sheds that holds the hay.

I'm busy stacking the bales when Callum comes rushing in.

"Hey, bro," I say, "I'm glad you're back." I hurry over and slap his shoulder. "'Tis guid to see ye. Did Maddie tell ye granda's stable and the staff seem hopeful he'll recover?"

I notice Callum's hands are pushed deep inside his pockets and his mood is subdued.

"Hey, dinnae worry yir head. Ye can visit him anytime ye like."

Callum opens his mouth just as Ally rushes in behind him. "I can't find her any— Oh, Jamie. I didn't realise you were back."

My shoulders tense at the sight of her. "What are ye doing here?" I hiss.

"Ease off, bro," Callum says, standing there with his hands now outstretched in a gesture of supplication. "Let's calm down and I'll explain."

I pick up a pitchfork and head back towards the hay. "I'm not interested in anything ye have to say if it involves Ally."

I hear Callum let out a sigh. "Jamie, I need you to listen to me. Maddie's missing."

I spin around and glare at him. "What are ye talkin' about?"

Callum licks his lips.

"Maddie overheard me and Ally talking things over earlier and everything got out of hand."

I feel my eyes narrow.

"What kind of things?"

I watch Callum closely as he struggles to swallow. "I don't have time to explain, but I need you to know that Maddie found out that Ally and I…that we…"

I turn away, to stab the pitchfork into a bale of hay, little strands of gold falling to the floor.

"That you're having an affair?" and my anger rises.

"No, well, not exactly."

I throw the pitchfork to the floor and swing around to face him. "What then?"

Ally pushes her way towards me, her eyes wide, defiant.

"It's time you also knew the truth. We have a child together, a son."

I let out a bark of laughter. "Nice try. Quit foolin' around."

"It's no joke," she snaps, turning towards Callum. "Go on; tell him."

I stare at my brother, a slight smirk resting upon my lips.

"She's right," he says, his eyes dark with shame. "Ally fell pregnant just months before I became infertile."

My smile slides off my face. "And ye ne'er told Maddie any of this?"

He shakes his head. "No. How could I tell her something that would break her heart?"

I struggle to find the right words. "You're an arsehole," I eventually hiss. "All that talk about nae willing to adopt for Maddie's sake. Aye, now I ken why."

"I'm sorry I deceived you," Callum whispers. "I wouldn't have done it if I'd realised Ally was going to force my hand."

"What are ye saying?"

Ally links her arm through Callum's.

"I told him it's time he came home to his son," Ally states, flatly. "Isaac needs him more than Maddie does."

Anger bubbles in my throat. "I see. So ye got yourself a job here, close to his family, and just waited for the right moment to destroy his marriage?"

"Don't make me out to be the bad guy. I just want my child to grow up knowing his father."

"Does Maddie know about Isaac?"

Callum nods. "Yes, she does now, and as soon as she found out, she ran off. We've looked everywhere, but she's vanished."

"Everywhere?"

"Pretty much. We've searched the whole farm, and most of the outbuildings, but there's no sign of her. When she left, I tried to chase after her, but she seemed to disappear into thin air. I rushed to the main house, thinking she'd be there, then, when she wasn't, I went back and tried to follow her tracks. But the snow's falling so fast they're gone in a matter of seconds."

"Aye, well, it's eased off for now."

"That may be true, but that doesn't help us."

"Where were she headin' when ye saw her last?"

"Towards the farmhouse."

"And you're certain she isnae there?"

Callum's stare is one of anguish. "Yes; I checked upstairs and down. And she's not in the garden house, either."

"How long has she been missin'?"

"No more than thirty minutes tops, I'd say."

"Then I think I ken where she's gone." I zip up my coat. "If I'm not back within the hour, get the Search and Rescue team out."

"I'll come with you." Callum says.

I shake my head. "Nah, I move faster on my own, thanks."

I shove a hand inside my coat and pull out a thick woollen hat, then rush out of the shed, leaving Ally and Callum standing there. Once in the farmhouse, I grab a rucksack from behind the door, one filled with medical supplies, a reflective heat blanket, maps, and flares. I delve inside to find a headband with a torch attached to it and put it over my hat, then hurry into the kitchen, where I grab a bowl and fill it with water. I bring it to the boil in the microwave and use some of it to fill a hot water bottle, making coffee for a metal flask with the rest.

Once outside, a security light flashes on, illuminating my way as I dash over to the gate, the pack already on my back. When I switch on the torch, the ground opens up in front of me and I jog down the track, scanning for any signs of movement. Inside, I'm afraid. It's freezing out here and Maddie won't last long, not if I don't find her soon. But Callum was right: the blowing snow has certainly filled in her tracks.

I keep going until I reach the woodland, where the trees seem to bend together as though they're whispering terrible secrets to one another. The wind blows gently through the trees, and as my head-light shines ahead, I see two small globes of white. For a split second I think I've found Maddie, but a back arches like a cat and the thing jerks its head, tearing at something small with its teeth. There's blood on its muzzle, dripping onto the ground.

"Shoo," I cry at the red fox. It glares at me for my unexpected intrusion, let's out a high rasping bark and scurries away into the darkness. With my torch's pool of light on the blood-stained snow, I make my way over. There, I find what's left of the carcass of a baby rabbit, and a sigh escapes me as I continue my search.

"Maddie, where are ye, lassie?" I cry out, but only the fox's solitary bark is returned.

I hunt for any obvious signs Maddie may have passed this way, like broken twigs or a tatter of her clothing, something she may have dropped or been caught on a sharp branch, but my despair grows with every step I take. No matter how hard I scour the ground and the foliage, it all appears undisturbed.

But then I hear a noise, a moan in the bushes, and I quickly dive further into the trees.

"Maddie, I've heard what's happened. Come home and we'll talk about it more there," and now I'm creeping through the darkness, careful where I tread. I'm off the beaten track, but I know every inch of woodland for miles around, so when I come across a strange bulge in the ground, I'm quick to investigate. It's covered in a light smattering of snow, but I can see blond hair there, streaked with dried blood.

"Maddie!" I cry in horror and dive onto my knees, snow flicking into my face. I wipe it away with a gloved hand before reaching out and gently turning her over, her face revealed in the light of the torch. I catch my breath. There's a cut across her forehead, but I'm damned if I can tell how bad it is.

I press my ear to her lips, around which her skin is like blue glass, but am relieved to hear her breathing. Taking off and ripping open the bag, I take out the thermal blanket and quickly wrap it around her, pressing the hot water bottle in between her coat and thin blouse.

"Maddie, wake up," I beg, shaking her roughly. There's a noise from her, a low groan, and she slowly opens her eyes.

"Jamie," she whispers. "Am I dead?"

"Nah. Not today, lassie. Not on my watch."

She lifts her fingers to my face and gently strokes my cheek. A single tear trickles down her pale face.

"Did he tell you he has a child with Ally?" she rasps.

"Aye, that he did, and I also told him what I thought of him."

Her hand drops, then she gives a weak smile. "I knew I could count on you."

Once again, I reach inside the rucksack, but this time I take out the coffee.

"Here, sit up and drink this," I urge, and Maddie coughs and splutters when the hot liquid hits the back of her throat.

"Are ye able to stand?" I ask, and Maddie nods.

"Yes, I think so."

"Guid. Now we need to get ye checked over at the hospital."

"No. Take me back to the house."

"Nah, I cannae do that. Ye need medical attention."

"I'm fine; just take me home, please."

I'm torn, but it's her call. She's coherent and I can see the colour coming back to her cheeks.

"All right, but if I see any signs of hypothermia or frost bite, you're going straight to A&E."

I help her to her feet and she clutches the blanket closer. All I want is to keep her safe. I guide her through the trees: a slow process, the torch not giving much light for two.

"How did ye end up off the trail?" I ask.

"I thought Callum was chasing me so I tried to hide. What about you?"

"I saw something moving in the shadows, probably a deer, but I wasnae takin' any chances."

We eventually reach the path and she stumbles. I grab her tighter.

"You're weak from yir ordeal," I say, and when she lets out a whimper, I bend slightly and sweep her off her feet and into my arms.

"Thanks for saving me from myself," she whispers into my ear.

I pull her closer. "Perhaps I was saving ye for myself."

She snuggles into my chest as I head back to the farm. Maddie's as light as a feather and easy to carry, the snow my only hinderance, but she's shivering from the cold. The farm soon looms ahead in the darkness, and when the security light flashes on, Callum comes rushing out and towards us. I'm relieved to see Ally is nowhere in sight.

Callum opens the gate. "Thank God you've found her," he says. "Is she okay?"

"What do you think?" I snap and head straight for the main house, pushing the front door wide open with the tip of my boot and hurrying through to the kitchen. There's a small fire now burning in the hearth and I place her gently in one of the fireside chairs. Callum's swift to follow.

"Run her a bath, not too hot, and then find her some warm clothes," I instruct.

"Anything in particular?"

"Aye, woolly socks and anything thermal."

Callum nods then heads upstairs as I take off Maddie's boots and pull off her socks. I hear the abrupt gush of water coming from the bathroom as I feel Maddie's feet; they're as cold as ice. Then, when I'm filling the washing up bowl from the sink with lukewarm water, the sound of the bath filling stops and Callum's boots clatter down the stairs. The front door bangs shut as he dashes off to find suitable clothes from the cottage.

She's staring right at me when I come to place her feet inside the bowl. She closes her eyes and sighs as my fingers massage life back into her toes and the soles of her feet.

"You don't have to do all this," she says, "but it sure feels good." I get up and put the kettle on, soon making two mugs of steaming hot tea before grabbing a bar of chocolate from the fridge.

"Eat this; it'll give ye energy," I say.

She opens her eyes and reaches out for the Galaxy bar. "I'd have to be dead to ever turn down chocolate," she says with a smile.

I'm relieved to find her in such good spirits. There's no serious signs of hypothermia and her shivering has ceased. A few more minutes lying unconscious in such extreme conditions and it could have been a different story. I next clean the blood from the wound on her forehead to find it's superficial. I shake my head in amazement, she's one lucky lady.

The front door opens and Callum enters the kitchen.

"I've brought what I could find," he says as he lays the clothes neatly onto the kitchen table. "There's a set of thick PJ's and a dressing gown. And I've brought a pair of hiking socks that are double-knit."

I glance at Maddie who's now wearing a grave expression.

Callum goes over and places a hand on her shoulder.

"Don't touch me," she hisses and shrugs his hand away.

Callum looks startled. "Maddie, please. I understand you're upset."

"Just leave me alone," and she stares into the fire. "What you've done is unforgivable."

"Please, don't say anything rash. Let's talk this through."

Slowly, she turns in the chair, her eyes dark and serious. "There's nothing to say. You're five years too late."

Callum grimaces, his chin dipping towards the floor.

"I tried, really I did," he whispers.

Maddie shakes her head. "Don't stand there and lie. You had ample opportunity to tell me about your son. If you'd just told me from the very beginning, it wouldn't have been a big deal. But no; you didn't want your perfect life to have a blemish, did you? I bet you didn't even want him until you realised Isaac would be the only child you'd ever father."

A flush creeps across Callum's cheeks, and Maddie looks away. "You should be ashamed of yourself. You've betrayed us all."

I stare at my brother, his eyes now shining like glass. His Adam's apple bobs up and down as he tries to speak. "I'll go and pack the rest of my things, then," he finally manages. "There's a hotel just down the road. I'll stay there for the time being."

Maddie continues to stare into the flames. "Why? Isn't Ally accommodating you anymore?"

The silence that follows is deafening. Only the fire crackles with life as Callum turns and walks away.

The front door bangs shut and Maddie bursts into tears.

I reach out to comfort her, my arms pulling her close, and she wraps her own around my neck.

"It'll be okay," I sooth, and as she lifts her head, I wipe the tears from her cheek. I stare into her eyes. Even upset she's still beautiful. My breath catches in my throat, then a desperate need wells up in my chest, threatening to overwhelm me. This woman is all I want, right down to the bones of my soul.

I hold her gaze as her dark lashes flicker, and to my surprise, she leans forwards and her mouth crushes against mine. I shudder with delight when I feel her cool lips upon mine, a sudden and intimate gesture that sparks a jolt of desire. I can't help myself; I pull her closer and we both rise. The ferocity of her kiss is overwhelming; hard, passionate, yet controlled. I lift her up into my arms, crushing her body against mine and the blanket falls away. I carry her up the stairs and into the bathroom. The room is hot and steamy, and I place her feet gently onto the floor, but then she's taking off my jacket and unbuttoning my shirt.

I grab her hand and hold it tight. "Are ye sure ye wannae do this?" I barely breathe.

She looks up into my eyes and sweeps her finger across my brow then down my cheek.

"Yes. I am," she whispers.

CHAPTER THIRTEEN

*M*addie

"Guid mornin', beautiful," Jamie whispers into my hair and I look up and smile lightly at him.

"Hey," I say, huskily. "I hope you slept well."

He props himself up on one elbow and gently pushes me onto my back, then he lowers his face and his lips glide silkily across mine.

"Hmm," he murmurs. "It took a wee while, but after ye had ye wicked way with me *for the third time*, I slept like a log," and he chuckles.

"I guess I wore you out," I say.

Jamie lets out a snort of laughter. "Aye, lass, that ye did, at no mistake."

"Any regrets?"

He slides closer and his eyes search out mine. "Nae, lass. Although, if I'm honest, I wish I'd allowed this thing between us to happen sooner."

"Me too. And there's no going back."

"But what about Callum?"

I squirm under the sheets. "We're over. I'm asking for a divorce."

"Are ye sure it's what ye want? After all, it's so final."

I nod and wrap my legs around him. "Yes. I'll not be his doormat for a moment longer. I guess I saw the train wreck heading my way. Of course, I didn't think it would be because he'd had a child with someone else," and then I swallow.

"It must have ripped ye heart out to learn such a thing after what ye went through."

I push a blond curl behind an ear and let out a sigh. "If it had been anything else, I could have probably forgiven him. But not after such lies and deceit. No. He must be made accountable for such a deception."

I turn onto my side and lie in the crook of his arm, taking a deep breath. He smells masculine, musky and woody with a hint of Hugo Boss. I kiss his neck and his skin tastes sweet, like honey. He drops his chin and I kiss him again. His stubble tickles my cheek as I sweep my tongue towards his ear.

"I'm crazy about ye," he whispers.

"You don't know that much about me."

"I ken enough," he tells me, brushing his thumb gently across my mouth, and my stomach lurches. There's passion in his eyes and I lose myself within them.

An alarm goes off and Jamie reaches over to the bedside table. He picks up his phone and lets out a deep groan.

"Oh, no; have ye seen the time? I should've been up hours ago, and we need to go and see granda, too." He pushes back the covers and dives out of bed. I enjoy watching his naked form clamber into a pair of jeans, my eyes devouring every part of his body, from his rippling torso to his strong muscular legs. There's so much I've yet to figure out, and yet…we're as one when we're alone together. My head's reeling with possibilities. Already, I've learned he's clever, smart and fiercely passionate.

"You're only a little late and I can help feed the cattle," I say, punching a pillow and resting my head into it.

He stops and gives me a smile. It's the way his top lip curls slightly at the edge that makes my heart skip a beat.

"Then get yir gorgeous arse out of bed."

There's a noise from downstairs, then a door bangs and footsteps come up the stairs.

I sit bolt upright and grab the covers, clutching them to my chest. Jamie quickly zips up his flies and then rushes to the bedroom door, but he's too late. Callum comes barging in.

"Hey, bro. Have you seen Maddie? Only her bed hasn't been—"

Callum stops dead in the doorway. His eyes switch from his brother, to stare at the me, lying in his bed.

"What the—"

My heart pounds at the sight of him, but Jamie tries to push him out of the room. Callum, though, pushes back.

"You've got to be fucking kidding me!" he cries.

"Get out," I scream, lifting the bedsheet to hide my face. Although I'm angry with him, I'm also ashamed at being caught in Jamie's bed.

"You've got no room to talk," says Jamie, "not after what ye done."

Callum's jaw drops. "You conniving sonofabitch."

The sheet's ripped from my clutches and I scream as I try to claw it back. Callum pounces on Jamie, his arm drawn back. He throws a punch, but Jamie ducks and Callum hits the door, instead.

"Argh!" he cries, shaking his fist, and Jamie lifts his hands in surrender.

"We dinnae have to do this," he says, breathlessly. "Just do the right thing and leave."

Callum's mouth twists with spite. "Oh, you think you can just take my wife without a fight, eh?"

"I'm not taking anyone," Jamie says, his eyes angry. "Just do us all a favour and get out before things turn ugly."

Callum lets out an unexpected peel of laughter. "Oh, you think you can get rid of me that easily? Well, I've got news for you."

I take a deep breath. "Don't make this any harder than it needs to be," I say, and his head snaps back towards me. I suffer a shiver of unease, for Callum's eyes are bulging and it scares me. He points an accusing finger in Jamie's direction.

"So, you think he's sweet and innocent, do you? Well, let me tell you—"

Jamie's taken a sharp intake of breath. "That's enough," he yells. "Now, get out!"

Callum shakes his head as a dark cloud crosses his face. "No. Not until Maddie learns the truth of what you did to her."

"I dinnae do anything," Jamie says and turns to me, his eyes now pleading.

"Lies. All lies," Callum shouts, and my gaze switches to Jamie.

"No," he says, shaking his head. "Please, Callum; dinnae do this."

"What's he talking about?" I whimper.

Callum stands tall, his eyes wide, triumphant.

"We had a pact, Jamie and I."

"A pact? What do you mean?"

Jamie moves closer to the bed and kneels beside me. "Dinnae listen to him," he begs, "he just wants to tear us apart."

My eyes flick back to Callum, standing there all smug.

"Go on," I say.

"It was the night of the pub quiz. We made sure you had a few drinks too many. We planned on getting you drunk."

I feel my brows furrow. "Why would you want to do that?"

Jamie's hand creeps up and tries to take mine, but I pull away.

"Please, ye have to believe me: I dinnae go through with it."

I focus my attention back on Callum.

"What did he do?" I ask, a chill creeping up my spine.

Callum takes a step closer to the bed.

"I asked him to sleep with you, if he'd be willing to take my place, and he agreed."

I pull the covers closer, suddenly feeling violated. Bile is rising in my throat and I find it impossible to swallow.

"Why the hell would you do such a thing?" I rasp.

"Because I knew you were desperate to have a child. I could think of no other way for us. Jamie's the perfect candidate. If you fell pregnant, you would never have known the difference, and the child could easily have passed for mine."

Tears sting my eyes as I turn to look at Jamie. "Is this true?"

Jamie hangs his head. "He asked me and I agreed, but when it came to the crunch, I couldnae go through with it. I wanted ye so badly, but if it was to ever happen, I wanted it for the right reasons."

I start to shake. I can't believe what he's telling me.

"You were willing to take advantage of me?" I cry.

"No. That's just it: I wasnae," and he lifts his head and pushes his fingers through his red hair. "I'd ne'er do such a terrible thing," he cries, and now he's staring straight at me. "Aye, I admit I thought seriously about it. Stood at the end of yir bed and almost went through with it. But at the last second my heart stopped me. I've wanted ye for so long that it killed me to contemplate doing something so despicable to ye. I guess I just wanted ye to love me."

I pull away from him, wrapping the sheet around me as I do. As I climb off the bed, he stands back, and I scurry past, relieved that neither Callum nor Jamie try to stop me leaving. I hear the bedroom door bang shut as I hurry away, my feet silent on the stairs. I open the front door but then hear a loud crash and hesitate, looking back over my shoulder, a sob escaping my throat when Jamie staggers into view, Callum's fingers tight around his throat.

"Stop it, both of you," I cry, and Callum spins towards me, his face white, ashen. He lowers his hands and stares at me, and a shiver creeps down my spine. His chest heaves, his eyes round and wild. When I flick my gaze to Jamie, his arms have fallen to his side, his head bowed low. I turn away, pull the front door towards me and fill my lungs with the day's cold air, then I step out into the freezing snow, the shock on my bare feet making my teeth chatter. I follow the path to the garden house, rush upstairs and throw off the sheet as soon as I'm in my bedroom. I'm trembling now and draw a shaky breath, scurrying naked into the bathroom. I hit the shower, its burst of hot water erupting against my skin as I run a hand over my wet hair and allow a river of salty tears to pour down my face.

I simply can't believe what Callum is capable of, to see how far he will go. To ask his own brother to sleep with me, to *switch places*, for God's sake. My night with Jamie comes rushing back like a tidal wave, an intense swell that having sex with him evokes, the one that's swept me out beyond the breakers. My body now floats in an eternal sea of ecstasy. He's kind and considerate, totally unlike Callum, but then I think back to the night of the pub quiz. Callum came to bed late, and our lovemaking was the best it had ever been, but it *was* Callum. No matter how drunk I may have seemed that night, I was not drunk enough not to know my own husband.

I dry myself, grab my spare pair of jeans and a warm arran jumper, then clean my teeth and scoop my honey-blond hair up into a top-knot. I go back into the bedroom and hunt down my phone, relieved to see it's switched off by my bed. I turn it on and scroll through my contacts, hitting a number which then rings three times.

"Hey, Maddie. Finally. I thought you might have left without saying goodbye."

I try to hold back the tears and my voice crackles with the effort.

"Can we meet up?" I ask.

"Sure; like when?" Bridget replies.

"Like now?"

There's a pause.

"Maddie, is everything okay?"

"No, and I need to talk to you…please."

"Of course. Where would you like to meet?"

"Somewhere local. How about in town?"

"Too public, and I sense you need a little privacy. How about coming over to my place? We won't be disturbed here."

"That would be perfect. Are you sure you don't mind?"

"No, not at all. Does your car have satnav?"

"Yes, it does."

"Good, then write down my postcode and make your way over as soon as you're ready."

I hurry down the stairs and into the living room in search of a pen and paper. I'm turning over a pile of old magazines and newspapers littering a dark oak coffee table when I spot a small writing pad and pen by the Trill telephone Jamie insists will be worth a small fortune someday.

"Okay, I'm ready," I say, and scribble down the directions.

"Just head straight for Allanfearn and keep the Moray Firth to your left and you'll not go far wrong," Bridget advises.

"That's great," I say. "I'm on my way."

I grab my handbag and search inside and am soon clutching the spare set of car keys. Hurrying down the stairs, I lift my coat from off the peg, shoving my feet inside the first pair of boots that fit.

Outside, I head straight for the red hatchback and climb into the driver's seat, and am just spinning the car around when Jamie and Callum come out of the farmhouse. I press my foot to the accelerator that little bit harder when Jamie makes a dash towards me. His hand hits the roof of the car as he tries to stop it, but I refuse to slow down, my mind now focused on where I need to be.

***

I drive carefully, slowly, and watch Balinriach Farm disappear in my rear-view mirror. I switch my eyes back to the road ahead and reach a T-junction, indicate, and turn left onto the A96. The sky above me is grey and miserable and I wonder if more snow is on its way.

Switching on the radio, I try to find an upbeat song, something to take my mind off what's happened at home. *Home*, what a joke. I glance out of the window, to see a large fold of Highland cattle grazing in a field, the farmer busy dropping off bundles of hay. He's thickset, stocky, and wearing a flat cap. He reminds me of Alasdair and a wave of guilt washes over me. I should be making my way to the hospital not searching for a shoulder to cry on, but there's no turning back now. I need to speak to Bridget, to tell her everything.

I find a local station playing the latest top ten hits, but the sound is jarring to my ears, just noise, and I can't stand such an assault right now. I switch the radio off, grateful for the sudden peace and quiet.

The satnav breaks through the silence to tell me to take the next right. I slide the wheel through my fingers and ease off the accelerator, now heading inland, towards open countryside. A patchwork of dark earth and fallen snow wraps itself around me. In the distance, slate blue water sits peacefully along the horizon.

I drive down the country lanes much more slowly. The snow hasn't been cleared here, being off the beaten track, and I feel the ABS kick in when I hit a patch of black ice. I suffer a shudder of unease, and for the first time, I wish Bridget didn't live in such a remote area.

The wind blows wildly as I turn onto a narrow dirt track, a signpost up ahead welcoming me to Achnamara cottage. The moment I draw up outside, I'm in awe of the place. It has large eco-friendly windows everywhere, even in the roof. I step out of the car and the front door opens. Bridget waves and I hurry over.

"Did you find me easily enough?" she calls, and as soon as I reach the doorstep, she hugs me tight.

"Yes, the satnav brought me straight to your door, although the weather could be a little kinder."

"If it was kinder, it wouldn't be Scotland," she laughs. Bridget stands aside to let me pass then closes the door and pulls a thick tartan curtain across the doorframe.

"I've already put the kettle on," she says, turning to face me. "Unless you'd care for something a little stronger?"

I smile. "No, tea's fine. Thanks."

She gestures for me to follow her into an open plan kitchen. The cottage is like nothing I expected. I thought it would be log fires and antlers on the wall, but I couldn't be more wrong. It's modern and minimalistic, and the far wall has been replaced with a full sheet of glass. I'm drawn towards it like a magnet and am instantly surrounded by panoramic views of the loch, of mist-peaked mountains and snowy glens. The wind is blowing through the trees and I find myself waiting for William Wallace to appear on one of the hills, riding a black horse, his face painted blue and white in readiness for war.

"It's beyond breath-taking," I sigh. "No wonder you love staying here."

"Yes, it's my little piece of heaven. There's nowhere else in the world like it."

"I can see why you'd think that."

"Milk and sugar?"

"Hmm, just milk please," and Bridget soon offers me a lime green mug.

"Biscuit?"

"No, the tea will do nicely, thanks."

"Let's go into the sitting room. It's cosy there, and then you can tell me what's on your mind."

I take a gulp of hot tea as we enter another room that has two fireside chairs covered in a pale grey tartan. We sit down and my eyes are drawn towards a brightly coloured mural painted on the wall. It's of deep purple mountains surrounded by a skyline of pale blue.

"Wow, that's stunning," I say. "Did you paint it yourself?"

She smiles. "Yes; I got the owner's permission, of course."

"You must be good friends," I say, lifting the mug to my lips again.

"Kind of. He's my ex-husband."

I almost choke. "Oh, I didn't realise you'd been married."

She waves her hand, as if to pooh-pooh the situation. "It was a long time ago, and we've gone our separate ways." She places her vivid orange mug down onto a glass coffee table. "Still, we're not here to talk about me, are we?" and I let out a sigh.

"I don't know where to start. I'm so confused."

"I find the beginning can be useful."

"My life's a complete mess," I tell her, and the first tears prick my eyes. "Callum, my husband, has been lying to me since the first day I met him. In fact, our whole marriage was built on a lie."

I stare into Bridget's eyes and can see the concern that's written there.

"So, what's he done?"

I take a deep breath. "Callum's been having an affair."

"Is it with Ally?" she asks softly.

I suck in my breath. "How did you know?"

She shrugs. "I have eyes. I may live in the middle of nowhere, but that doesn't mean I'm blind. I've been coming here for many years now and know a lot about the locals. I was aware Ally and Callum had a thing going at one time."

"Then you know she has a son."

A shadow flits across her face and she looks away.

"Did you also know that Callum's the father?" I ask.

"I guessed," she says, reaching for her tea. "To be honest, it wasn't exactly hard."

My gut tightens as I place my own mug onto the coffee table.

"You've seen him? The boy, I mean?"

She shrugs again. "Once or twice."

I let out a sob and her jaw drops.

"You mean you've never met him?"

I shake my head. "No, and until yesterday, I wasn't even aware he existed?"

I lower my lashes as the tears start to flow.

"Christ, Maddie, how could Callum do something so wicked? I'm sorry, but I've got to be honest, I'm finding this hard to take in. I am genuinely shocked," and she jumps to her feet. "I'm a firm believer that in times of crisis a stiff drink is in order," and she heads off back into the kitchen, returning with two crystal tumblers filled with whisky.

"Here; drink this," she orders. "It'll make you feel better."

I shake my head. "I can't; I'm driving."

She frowns. "Then stay. There's a spare room, and you can leave whenever you're ready."

I wipe away my tears with the back of my hand as Bridget places the tumbler onto the table, next to my mug. She reaches for a box of paper tissues from a shelf behind her and offers them to me.

I take a Kleenex and blow my nose.

"Thanks for the offer, but I'll have to go soon. Alasdair's in hospital, you see, and I need to see him."

"Why, what's the matter with him?"

"He suffered a cardiac arrest."

"How awful for you all. Is he going to be okay?"

"We don't know for sure, but we're trying to stay positive."

Bridget sits back in her chair and takes a large gulp of whisky.

"You really are going through the wringer."

I try to laugh, but a hysterical noise leaves my throat, instead.

"Yes, and if that wasn't bad enough, I've suffered yet another revelation."

Bridget halts, the glass to her lips. "How can anything be as bad as finding out your husband has been lying to you about a child you never knew he had?"

"It gets much worse. What you don't know is that Callum caught mumps soon after Ally got pregnant, which made him infertile."

"You mean…Callum can no longer have kids?"

"That's pretty much the crux of the story. We found out after months of trying for a baby. We used all our savings on IVF, but nothing worked. I craved a child so badly, I even said I was willing to adopt, but Callum wouldn't hear of it."

Bridget looks down into her whisky. "Yes, I'll bet."

"I learned this morning that, out of desperation, Callum tried to convince Jamie to sleep with me."

Bridget lifts a hand to her throat. "You can't be serious."

I pick up my tea. "Oh, never more so."

"But why would he do such a thing?"

"Because Callum thought that if Jamie was able to get me pregnant everything would be all right between us."

"You mean he asked his brother to switch places?"

I stare into my cup, unable to look her in the eye. "Yes."

"What? Without your consent?"

I force myself to look at her. Her face is pale, her eyes wide.

"It was the night we visited the Scran and Sleekit. I got a little drunk and…Jamie, well, he was supposed to sleep with me that night."

"And did he?" Bridget asks, arching a pencilled brow.

"No. I may have been drunk, but I wasn't *that* drunk."

"Are you sure? I mean, they are identical."

"Of course I am. I sensed someone in the bedroom not long after I went to bed. I thought it was Callum, but when he never got into bed, my subconscious woke me."

"So, do you think that's when it came to the crunch? Jamie couldn't go through with it?"

"All I know is that he didn't sleep with me that night. But I just wish he'd told me what Callum had planned."

Bridget shakes her head fiercely.

"Are you kidding me? He's never going to admit that to you, or to anyone. Put the shoe on the other foot; would you?"

My shoulders sag as I stare down at the pale-yellow carpet.

Bridget comes over and kneels in front of me, placing her hands on the tops of my arms.

"Jamie loves you," she insists. "I've known ever since the day of the festival. And why I refuse to believe he would ever deliberately hurt you."

A single tear slides down my face. "How can you be so sure?"

"Because of what he wrote on his bay leaf."

My brows furrow. "What does that have to do with anything?"

"Everything."

I take a steadying breath. "Okay, so tell me: what did it say?"

She lifts my chin with her forefinger and stares deep into my eyes.

"Jamie wrote: '*Maddie, my heart and life is forever yours*'."

I try to hold back the tears. "He actually wrote that to me?"

Bridget nods. "He's the one you should be with, not Callum. I've sensed this all along. Whatever mistakes Jamie's made, they were all for you; because he loves you."

"But couldn't you say the same for Callum?"

"I guess it depends on how you look at it. Were his actions truly because he loved you or because he was riddled with guilt over having a child with someone else? But whichever way you choose, at the end of the day, it's your call."

My mobile goes off just as Bridget rises. I reach inside my handbag and learn I have missed calls from both Jamie and Callum.

There's a text message, too, from Jamie.

I open it and read the few words.

"I need to go," I say. "Jamie says it's granda."

"Do you want me to drive?"

I shake my head. "No, you can't, you've had a drink. Even I'm aware there's zero tolerance to alcohol in Scotland."

"Damn my foolishness," and Bridget's eyes fill with regret.

"Don't worry; I'll be fine. And thanks for the tea…for everything."

I squeeze her hand and she reaches out and hugs me once again.

"I'll always be here for you, whenever you need me," she whispers in my ear, and when she breaks away, I smile at her.

"I'm so glad I fell on my arse that day at the brae."

"Me too," and her voice has filled with laughter. "It was the funniest thing I'd seen in ages!"

CHAPTER FOURTEEN

The drive to the hospital takes forever and all I can think about is granda lying there, helpless. The guilt of not going to see him earlier this morning plays on my mind as I press my foot down a little harder on the accelerator. The roads are busier than when I left, and I curse and swear for other drivers to move out of the way.

The dark clouds shift to reveal a thin trickle of sunlight. A bitter wind still blows, and I turn up the heating—just a notch. I can't get there fast enough, and I arrive at the hospital within half an hour of receiving Jamie's text. I head for the visitor's carpark and grab a ticket, flinging it carelessly into my handbag, then hurry through the automatic doors and head straight for the lift. The hospital is buzzing with everyday dramas. The infirm and the elderly are being pushed around in wheelchairs and porters scurry about with empty lunch trolley's.

I press the button that will take me to the second floor, my heart pounding like a drum, convinced they'll have me attached to a heart monitor the second I enter ITU. Then the doors open and I hurry along the corridor, my eyes searching for a member of staff who can help me. I head for the nurses' station and am relieved to see the ward manager sitting at the desk, filling in paperwork.

She glances up and gives me a hesitant smile when our eyes meet.

"Oh, Mrs McKinley; please go on through. Your husband's already at your grandfather's bedside." The pressure in my chest tightens. It all now feels so real, as if I've fallen from one of those high-limbed apple trees I've seen growing close to the farm. I can't bring myself to ask the question that's perched on the edge of my tongue, too busy fighting the bile that's rising into my throat, and so I hurry on past.

The curtains around Alasdair's bed are closed, and I stop dead in my tracks, rooted to the spot as the room takes a slow, sickening spin. I cannot move and my vision blurs.

Then there's the swoosh of curtains being flung back and I see Jamie, not Callum, standing there. My eyes flit from his face to granda's, and I let out a heart-wrenching cry and run over to the bed. Alasdair is sitting up, sipping water from a beaker.

"You're all right," I cry, astounded, and reach out for his hand. His calloused fingers are warm to the touch and there's colour in his cheeks. "You had us all worried," I chastise, and his fingers tighten around mine.

"Aye, lassie. Well, I'm a bit weak after my ordeal, but I'm not ready to meet my maker just yet."

I glance over at Jamie, but he won't look at me. "Could I have a word with you, please? Alone," and Jamie finally turns towards me and I can see the hurt, the fear, that flickers behind his eyes.

"Aye, but you'd best be quick. I've got to get back. I've work to do."

I bend over and peck Alasdair on the cheek. "Don't go anywhere. I'll be back in five," I promise.

Jamie and I both head over to the relatives' room and I go and stand by the small sliver of glass they call a window, peering in. The place is empty, so I pull at the door handle and make my way inside.

"Close the door behind you," I say as Jamie enters, my back still to him.

I hear the click of the latch, and when I turn, Jamie's only inches from me. His shoulders are hunched and the light in his eyes has diminished.

"What you did was wrong," I say.

He looks up at me then, his eyes wide with alarm.

"How many times do I have to tell ye? I dinnae do anything," he protests before letting out a deep sigh and dropping into one of the plastic chairs. "Callum kept on and on at me, begging and pleading, until I lost my resolve. I could see how much a bairn meant to ye, and after what ye told me, and seeing ye with Findlay, I couldnae deny ye a chance to be a mother."

"But the implications… If you'd gone through with it, it would have been classed as ra—"

"Aye, I realise that now, but I dinnae at the time. All I wanted was to help ye."

"What? By pretending to be my husband? By taking advantage of me and having sex without my knowledge?"

Jamie's voice starts to rise. "You're making it sound sordid. What I was willing to do was out of love for ye both, not through some depravity on my part."

"And I'm supposed to thank you for trying to deceive me?"

Jamie jumps to his feet and takes a bold step closer, his face now inches away from my own.

"I told ye I couldnae go through with it. Seeing ye lying there, ye looked beautiful and seductive, yet I wanted more. I wanted ye desperately, Maddie, but I also needed ye to give yourself to me willingly."

"So, you think I should just swoon at your feet and forget the whole thing because you had my best interest at heart? Is that it?"

"Nah, of course not. But what I am asking for is yir forgiveness. I'm sorry, Maddie; truly. I ne'er meant to hurt ye. I know how much ye want a family and I thought maybe, just maybe, I could give ye what ye desired."

I bite my lip.

"And giving me a child was your sole driving force, the only reason you were willing to go ahead with Callum's ridiculous plan?"

"Aye, I somehow got sucked in. I guess losing Claire and having no family of my own made me realise what it's like to live a half-life. To just exist."

I stare into his eyes. They're open and honest and I can't be angry with him a moment longer. My fury deflates and Bridget's voice rings loudly in my ears: *"Whatever mistakes Jamie's made, they were all for you. Because he loves you"*.

I take a deep breath. "All right, I forgive you," I whisper, and he lets out a cry and sweeps me into his arms. His lips crush down on mine and his body presses ever closer. I sense his hunger and suffer a moment of longing, wanting to be devoured by him.

"I love ye, Maddie," he breathes in my ear, and a delicious tingle fills the pit of my stomach.

"And I you," I say, and he smiles for the first time. His mouth searches out mine once again and my body relaxes, wrapped securely in his arms. When he pulls away, his eyes are smouldering with passion.

"I think we should stop before we get carried away," he whispers. "Perhaps we can continue tonight, when ye come home."

I nod and touch my swollen lips with my fingertips.

"Yes," I say, "we've lots of catching up to do, but let's get back to reality for a while. I'm just so relieved granda's alive and well."

Jamie nods. "Aye, the nurse said he's out of immediate danger, but that it'll take a fair wee while for him to fully recover."

"I'm not going anywhere until he's permanently back on his feet," I announce, and Jamie breaks into a grin, then grabs my hand and kisses my fingers.

"Ye dinnae ken how happy that makes me to hear ye say so," he says.

I smile as he lets go of my hand, and as he opens the door, I realise a new chapter in my life is about to begin.

"I'll walk to the main doors with you," I say to him as he waits just beyond the door, but as I go out into the corridor, I see the ward manager. "I'll be right back in a few minutes," I say to her, and she smiles, then Jamie grabs my hand once again, squeezing my fingers.

We're just approaching the lift when its doors start to open, then I jerk back when Callum steps out. I'm riveted to the spot and automatically let go of Jamie's hand. But there's someone standing behind Callum, and to my horror, Ally steps out, a smartly dressed little boy at her side, and my legs start to shake.

"What are ye doing bringing *her* here?" Jamie roars, his voice filled with disgust. "Granda isnae fit for any shocks just yet. His heart cannae take it."

Callum switches his gaze from Jamie to me, then back to his brother, his eyes hard, like pieces of flint, his mouth drawn to a tight thin line.

"Don't worry yourselves," he says, "my family will wait in the relatives' room," at which my heart contracts, and for a second I fear I'm going to be physically sick. I stare down at the beautiful child holding tightly to his mother's hand. He's just as I imagined. Those luscious thick curls and big sea-green eyes make him Callum's double.

When I realise I'm becoming light-headed, I take a deep breath. "I think I need some air," I tell Jamie.

"Then let's go," he says, and slips his arm around my waist, guiding me into the lift.

"That man looks just like daddy," Isaac says as we walk past.

"Hmm, that's your Uncle James," Ally tells the boy.

"And who's the pretty lady?" Isaac goes on to ask, pulling at her hand.

Ally turns to face me just as the lift doors start to close. "She's no one important, sweetie," and her lips spread into a triumphant smile.

I wait in the car until Callum leaves. I still want to see granda, and Jamie's had to go, to get back to work. I let out a sigh. The thought of being in the same room as Callum, or breathing the same air as him, turns my stomach. I've heard about men like Callum, leading double lives, but I never thought it possible. Yet not a million miles away is a man who proved me wrong.

I glance at the clock, then stare out of the windscreen to spot Callum and Ally walking out of the main entrance. My gut tightens and I feel a vein throb in my temple. Isaac's in Callum's arms and they're both laughing, clearly enjoying father-and-son time together. The little boy wriggles in Callum's embrace and there's a light step to his walk, almost on tiptoes. Their laughter is carried to me by the wind and I can see the bond they share, a closeness I can only dream of.

A stab of jealousy pierces through my heart, sharper than any blade. I try to keep a tight lid on my emotions as I watch Callum have the life he once promised me. My eyes switch to Ally. Her hair is loose, her fingers entwined with his. They look every inch the happy couple and I close my eyes and push the tears away.

Did I truly love him? I wonder. Yes, for a while, I guess.

They all get into Ally's white 4 x 4 and I slide down my seat as they head for the exit.

I wait a few minutes, check my rear-view mirror to ensure they've left, and then head back inside to see granda.

As I step out of the lift and into the corridor, I put on a painted smile. I nod to the nurse at the nurses' station, realising it's no longer the ward manager, then hurry over to granda's bed. His eyes are closed and I fear he's sleeping, but when I turn to leave, to creep away, his dulcet tone stops me.

"If ye think ye were only gone five minutes, ye need to buy a new watch," he says, sarcastically.

I spin on my heels, a genuine grin spread across my lips.

"Sorry, Alasdair; I got slightly waylaid."

"Ye dinnae say, lass. What's going on between ye and Callum? He came here with a face like a smacked arse."

I find it hard to swallow as I move closer to the bed and pull up a chair and sit down. "What do you mean?"

Granda lets out a deep sigh. "I maybe old, lass, but I'm not senile. Things havenae been right between ye two since ye got here. I can always tell when people are unhappy together."

"Listen. You're not to worry about us," I say, picking up the beaker from the table and holding it to his lips. "Here, drink some of this."

He gently pushes my hand away. "Have ye two reached the point of nae return?"

I lower my gaze, placing the beaker back onto its resting place, struggling to find the right words. "Kind of…I guess."

He draws a long breath. "I cannae say I'm surprised. He was ne'er the right man for ye, in my opinion. He's always been too self-centred."

I blink several times, unable to digest what Alasdair has just said. "Granda! Why would you say such a thing?"

"Because it's the truth, hen."

"Then I may as well tell you he's moving in with Ally."

"The vet?" He shakes his head and tuts. "That dinnae take long."

"I didn't want to say anything, not with you being so ill."

He shakes his head again and his veined blue fingers reach out to pat my hand. "I don't need sheltering from his seedy escapades, and besides, I had a hunch he was up to no guid long before today."

I stare into his watery grey eyes. "You were not to know he's been seeing someone else."

He pulls his lips into a grimace. "Although it saddens me to say it: best let him go, lass."

"How do you know it's the right thing to do?"

His fingers tighten around mine. "Because my màthair always told me: ne'er settle for second best. If ye do, you'll ne'er find yir true soulmate."

Footsteps come from behind me and I glance over my shoulder to see a staff nurse approaching.

"It's time Mr McKinley got some rest," she says. "I'm afraid visiting time is over."

I automatically let go of Alasdair's hand, stand up and go to plant a kiss on his cheek. His arms reach out and he wraps them around me, pulling me close.

"Just be happy," he says in my ear, and when I pull away, he grabs my hand. "Ye only have one wee life, lassie, so live it to the full."

***

I arrive back at the farm as darkness is descending, get out of the car and head towards the farmhouse. The downstairs lights are on and there's a golden glow illuminating the frost covered windows.

I pause outside the front door, aware there's a man inside who truly loves me. I smile to myself, happy and contented for the first time in a long time. Jamie is all the man I need. I think about that gleam in his eye and the way his arm curls around my waist and pulls me close, his warm breath on my cheek.

I loved Callum, truly I did. We had such hopes and dreams together; the flower shop, his great job, the hope of a better life for our children. But I chose to ignore the warning signs, to overlook his mood swings and his nights away, believing I simply wasn't enough for him. Never for one second did I think it was something in his past.

My fingers tighten around the handle and I push the door wide. As I step inside, I breathe in deeply, inhaling the delicious aroma of pie, and my lips spread into a grin. Hetty's clearly been here while I was away and brought the weekly supplies.

I take off my coat and hang it on the hook next to Jamie's, and my fingers touch one of the sleeves. It's the same coat he wore when he came to my rescue. I take off my boots and drop them noisily to the floor.

"What took ye so long?" Jamie calls out, and I follow his voice towards the kitchen. Pushing the door ajar, I see there are candles on the table, along with a small vase of red and white roses adorning its centre.

"What's all this?" I ask in surprise.

Jamie's standing by the stove, a pair of tatty old mitts in his hands.

"I thought I'd cook for ye," and he opens the oven door and pulls out a brown pot covered with shortcrust pastry.

"What? You've made it yourself?" and I try to mask my amazement.

He hurries over to the table, placing the pie on a large serving mat.

"Aye, and dinnae look astounded. Hetty's not the only one who can produce a meal from scratch." He dashes back to the stove and takes out two more dishes, this time filled with roast potatoes, broccoli and buttered carrots.

"Best wash yir hands quickly, so this lot doesnae get cold," he urges.

I hurry over to the stone sink and wash and dry my hands on a small threadbare towel. Placing it back on the rail, I turn to see that Jamie's already seated at the table, pouring white wine.

I walk over and take a seat.

"The food looks scrumptious," I say, placing a napkin across my knee. Jamie's sitting next to me, and he picks up his wine glass and makes a toast.

"To new beginnings," he says, and I lift my glass to his.

"To new beginnings, and to us," I rejoin, and our glasses chink together. I take a sip then place my glass down onto the table. Jamie offers up a piece of venison pie.

"Help yourself to the vegetables," he says, and pushes the dishes towards me.

I smile. Being with Jamie feels so natural. Any shyness I may have felt vanished long ago. I'm relaxed for the first time in years and stare at him, as though seeing him for the first time. Twisting flames from the fire send flickers of bright orange light to dance upon his skin, his angular jaw now less prominent in the candlelight. He looks devilishly handsome sitting there in his open neck shirt. I stare at his throat and then towards his plump moist lips, at which I start to tingle all over. I lick my own lips, no longer tempted by the food.

"Jamie…"

His eyes catch mine and they widen as he reads the message written there. He leans forward, takes my hand and presses butterfly kisses to the tips of my fingers.

A slow burn ignites in the pit of my stomach and I look back at him with the same intensity. He rises and gently pulls me towards him, his hands then sliding across my shoulders and up behind my neck. And as his fingers entwine in my hair, I close my eyes.

His body shifts closer to mine and my heart flutters, my mind spinning when his lips touch mine. His tongue slips into my mouth and he tastes so good, like sherbet lemon mixed with wine. When he pulls away, my eyes shoot open and he guides me closer to the fire.

"I want ye so badly, my balls ache," he says, huskily, and I giggle, not too sure whether I should be flattered or insulted.

The flickering flames warm our bodies as we stare at each other for an age. I don't move, and neither does he, both lost to one another, and it's sublimely divine. Jamie's hands snake under my jumper and I feel his fingers slide against my skin. He bows his head and his kisses are no longer tender but filled with longing. I let out a low moan as my own passion mounts, and he lifts the jumper over my head, unhooking my bra.

Urgently, I unbutton his shirt and he throws it to the floor, quickly taking off his trousers as I unzip my jeans and pull my bare legs free. I lie naked on the rug as the sound of the fire snaps and crackles around us, then Jamie kneels and his arms stretch out beside me. With such tenderness, he leans forward and gently lies on top of me. As the flamelight flit across his face, I trace my fingers along his shoulders, sending ghostly shadows dancing across the walls. He has become my sun, my moon and stars—my everything.

Stroking my hair, Jamie rasps "Maddie," my name magic on his lips.

"Yes," I whisper, "what is it?"

"Are ye willin' to have my bairns?"

"Bairns? That's plural?" I gasp between hot kisses.

"Aye, well, I want at least four."

My breath quickens as he angles himself over me, his body resting on mine, the pressure too delicious to bear.

"I'll have as many as you're willing to give me," I say with tenderness, and he kisses me again as we move together as one, the heat from his body seeping into me, and I let out yet another low moan.

"I love you," I say softly.

"And I, ye," he breathes, lifting his hand so I can take it. "I'll ne'er let ye go," he whispers in my ear, and I pull him closer, wrapping my legs around him, contented he's mine forever.

He lets out a groan and his body shudders then relaxes, his back now covered in sweat, and presently he looks down at me, his eyes soft, and I kiss him warmly and smile.

"Our first child will be a boy," I say. "And we'll name him Alasdair James McKinley."

Mia's life is spiralling out of control.
The only person who can help save her
is a man who's already dead.

Cracks in the Glass

Lynette Creswell

Mia Stevens is a young girl on the verge of womanhood. Her mother is about to remarry, but her fiancé comes with serious baggage. His two sons are notorious for being troublemakers, the eldest, Jacob, wanting what he can't have—Mia and his freedom.

Everything rides on the wedding, but Mia refuses to attend. Jacob sees his chance of a new start slipping away, and to frighten her into being cooperative, threatens her. Terrified he'll do it again, she runs away to London, where she meets and falls in love with Ethan, a student.

When circumstances force her to attend her mother's big day, her past comes back to haunt her. Attacked and left unconscious, Mia's life spirals out of control. A new baby, a lost love and a life entwined with deceit and lies is only the beginning. Dark, suppressed secrets begin to unravel, and the only person who can help save her is a man who's already dead.

'A dramatic tale of love and heartbreak, this story gives you an emotional punch. It's haunting, magical and full of surprises.'

Available Via Amazon.co.uk And Amazon.com

Follow Lynette on Twitter: @Creswelllyn
Website: Lynetteecreswell@wordpress.com
Facebook: Lynette Creswell - Author

Lightning Source UK Ltd.
Milton Keynes UK
UKHW03f0127270318
320093UK00001B/17/P